There's something about Greece

BOOKS BY SUE ROBERTS

My Big Greek Summer

My Very Italian Holiday

You, Me and Italy

A Very French Affair

As Greek as It Gets

Some Like It Greek

Going Greek

Greece Actually

What Happens in Greece

Take a Chance on Greece

Christmas at Red Robin Cottage

SUE ROBERTS

There's Something about Greece

Bookouture

Published by Bookouture in 2023

An imprint of Storyfire Ltd.
Carmelite House
50 Victoria Embankment
London EC4Y 0DZ

www.bookouture.com

ISBN: 978-1-83790-540-9
eBook ISBN: 978-1-83790-539-3

For lovers of Greek islands. And four-legged friends.

PROLOGUE

TWELVE MONTHS EARLIER

There is just something about the air out here that fills the soul with joy. The pine-scented freshness in the mountains, the salty sea air further towards the beach, and the feel of the burning sunshine caressing my arms and legs as I walk.

I've popped out for a walk on my own, having exercised the dogs at the rescue earlier. The little café at the side of a dusty road, where I now sit outside enjoying a frappe, looks down towards the sea, taking in the forest dotted with white houses that cling to the hillside. A church bell rings somewhere in the distance as I sip my cooling drink and take in the view.

A wooden cart is parked up nearby selling huge watermelons and bunches of fat purple grapes. A donkey strolls lazily by carrying baskets loaded with aubergines and figs and the old man wearing a cap and walking alongside it wishes me a *kalimera* as they pass.

I love it here. The days are long and sultry, the sun easing away thoughts of a life back home that has been in the doldrums for long enough.

I finish my drink and take the ten-minute walk back to the

animal sanctuary that my aunt runs, and where I have spent the last few weeks getting over a broken heart. It's time to go home. Back to everyday life. But I know it's a place I will return to again and again.

ONE

It's a bright sunny morning as I head out of my beautiful canalside apartment in Parbold village, and set off for a walk. Slightly up ahead on the canal footpath is my neighbour Kerry, so I call out to her and we fall into step.

'I'm surprised you're not jogging along here, rather than taking a gentle stroll,' I comment, as she is usually haring along the village footpaths like Usain Bolt.

'Normally I would be, Tania, but I pulled a tendon in my calf last week so I'm just taking things easy. I have a half marathon coming up next month,' she explains.

'Which charity are you running for this time?' I ask Kerry, knowing that she usually raises a fair amount of money.

'For a local hospice. Sadly, the smaller charities often struggle to raise money,' she tells me as we walk along the canal, passing a blue-and-red painted barge. An older man sitting on deck, wearing a flat cap, wishes us a good morning and we return the greeting.

'I never really thought about that,' I admit. 'Although, actually, my aunt has to do a lot of fundraising for her animal sanctuary in Greece. So many places rely on the generosity of the public.'

'It's true, unfortunately. Not that the larger charities don't need the support, of course they do, but smaller ones are even more in need of donations. They can't afford the huge advertising campaigns,' she explains.

Strolling on, we pass more barges, with some residents sitting out on deck drinking tea, others watering colourful blooms displayed in a variety of pretty pots. Passing under a bridge, we encounter cyclists and dog walkers, all out enjoying the bright sunshine in early June. I feel a little stab to the heart when a golden Labrador that looks exactly like my Bruno did walks towards us with its owner and runs over to me, its tail wagging, hoping to be petted.

'Hey there, boy,' I say as the dog jumps up at me. Kerry, clearly not a dog lover, has already walked on ahead.

'Sorry,' the owner apologises for her dog's over-enthusiasm, pulling it gently towards her on its lead.

'Oh, please, don't worry, it's fine.' I have to fight back tears as I pet this gorgeous, friendly dog.

'His name's Leo,' she says.

'Well, he's adorable,' I say, before having to practically jog to catch up with Kerry.

'I take it you're not much of a dog person then?'

'Hmm, not really. I don't dislike them exactly, just a bit wary, and I must admit I prefer cats,' she says as we walk on.

We walk along the picturesque section of the canal for just over an hour, chatting about Kerry's upcoming half marathon and this and that, stopping to watch a family of gorgeous ducks glide by on sun-dappled water, until we arrive back at my favourite local café.

'I really enjoyed that,' says Kerry, glancing at her watch.

'Me, too. Do you fancy a drink?' I ask, nodding towards the café.

'I'd love to, but I'm afraid I'm a bit pushed for time.' She glances at her watch again. 'I'm taking Mum out to lunch shortly. She's getting on a bit now and doesn't get out much since my dad died.'

'I'm sure she'll love that.' I smile. 'Enjoy yourself. And thanks for the walk.'

As it's a bright day, the chairs and tables outside the café are all occupied so I buy myself a vanilla ice-cream cone and take the short walk back to my ground-floor flat.

Once home, I enjoy my ice cream on the patio area that has a square patch of grass and bamboo fencing. It's a peaceful space that gives a view of an old windmill in the background that backs onto the canal. As I sit, I think about Kerry's comments about her mum being alone since her dad passed away.

My parents are both in good health thankfully and living their best life in Spain. They've asked me several times to go and join them. 'As you don't have much going on at the moment, a change might just do you good,' Mum said during our last conversation, as if I needed reminding that my life here is going nowhere. My grasp of Spanish just about extends to asking for a beer in a bar or inquiring where the toilets are. I reminded Dad of this fact, asking him what exactly I would do for a job out there and he muttered something about opening a little bar, as if I have the finances or the expertise to do such a thing. But, at times, I feel guilty for feeling so restless here. Maybe I should head over to visit them for a little while.

I know I'm lucky to live in a great village that has several restaurants, a row of shops and a train station for easy access to nearby towns and cities. I have a couple of close friends, but they are all married so Saturday night drinks with them are usually out, although I do occasionally tag along. I have an okay job as a doctor's receptionist at the local surgery, and until recently I had the company of my beloved golden Labrador,

Bruno, who sadly passed away a few months ago and I miss him every single day. He'd been a family dog, and my parents made the decision to leave him with me when they moved abroad, which I think we were both thrilled about – me and Bruno, that is. I was the one who took him for walks most days after all, and he slept in a dog basket in my bedroom.

It was lovely having his company, especially as I've been single for almost a year now. My boyfriend of just over two years decided he wasn't ready to settle down yet – two years wasn't settling down? I met him on a beach in Spain during a visit to see my parents, and it turned out he lived a half-hour drive away from here, in Manchester.

A small village isn't exactly the best place to meet a boyfriend. Most of the young men who were born here have upped sticks and moved away; the remaining ones I've known since I was a kid and attended the local schools with, and see them all as brothers. Money has become a little tight since my boyfriend bailed, especially as I'm trying to save for a deposit on a small house, which is virtually an impossible task with the increase in house prices as well as everything else. Even though my ex never actually moved in with me, he often stayed over and would buy food, or pay for nights out and so on, which are things I now have to fork out for on my own.

As the sun filters through the leaves of a tree beyond the garden wall, I turn my face to catch the rays and feel the warmth wash over my face. Ten minutes later, though, the sun has been obscured by a cloud and refuses to come out again. As it has turned a little overcast, I head inside.

TWO

Sitting reading a book in the lounge, my mind flits to this time last year, when I spent two weeks at my aunt's dog rescue centre, high in the hills in Crete. I recall the long, sunny days looking after the dogs and several worn-out donkeys who live in an adjoining pen. The easy evenings, sat chatting to the volunteers, sipping drinks and eating food at a long wooden table shaded by olive trees are memories I will treasure forever. They certainly got me over my broken heart. I'd have loved to have stayed for even longer, but I had work commitments which called me home. Many of the volunteers had no such commitments, spending a whole six weeks there, which is the minimum requirement from my aunt for volunteers. During the summer months, the group mainly consists of students on summer holidays or taking gap years and travelling. Others have saved up and decided to just forget about their life and get away from it all, for various reasons. I love learning what brought each of them out to the shelter.

With the sun refusing to come out again, my thoughts stay on Greece, enjoying the imagined warmth. But my thoughts are interrupted, when out of the blue my aunt calls.

'Hi, Judith. Gosh, that's so strange as I was just thinking about Greece,' I tell her.

'It's funny when that happens, isn't it? So, how are you?'

I can picture my aunt, her long grey hair in a bun, wearing something long and floaty and with a smile as wide as a river.

'Not too bad, thanks. How are things with you? I bet the sun is shining brightly there.'

'Oh, it is. And I'm okay, thanks, Tania, although I won't lie, I'll be glad when this bloomin' knee of mine has been replaced. I never seem to get around to having it done, as things are so busy here. Silly, I know.'

'You shouldn't put it off for too long, the damage will get worse. Although I don't suppose you need a lecture from me. Just promise me you will book it in soon.'

'I promise.'

'Good. So how is Eric doing?'

Eric is my absolute favourite donkey. The old boy had arrived exhausted after a lifetime of overwork, trudging visitors up mountains to monasteries. He's a funny character who took an immediate shine to me on my last visit. Apparently, he ignored most people, but would always saunter over to me and nudge my arm with his head for an affectionate stroke, before disappearing again. Any interaction with Eric, I quickly learned, is strictly on his terms.

'Still going strong. Living his best life out here. Still a moody old bugger.' She laughs.

'It's good to know that some things never change.'

Judith tells me she is enjoying an iced tea in the shade, and I have a pang of envy as I picture my aunt sat beneath a huge olive tree, sipping her cooling drink.

'We're actually having a bit of a heatwave here,' she informs me. 'Some of the volunteers are struggling with it a bit, to be honest. Even the dogs aren't too bothered about being taken out for walks, preferring to snooze in their cool pens until it's slightly cooler in the evening.'

'Maybe you should have a siesta too?' I suggest.

'I might just do that. Most of the staff have headed down to the beach to catch the cool sea breeze and enjoy a late afternoon swim.'

'That sounds wonderful. So, you are doing alright then, apart from the heatwave?'

'Oh, I'm fine. As I said, my right knee has been playing up a lot these past few weeks so I'm not getting about quite as quickly as I would like to.'

'Which is why you have the volunteers,' I remind her.

Judith had spoken of her doctor recommending knee replacement surgery last year, but she'd hesitated, worried about who would take the reins and run the rescue centre during her recovery. Sadly, she became a widow three years ago.

'Maybe it's time for that knee operation sooner rather than later,' I suggest, with a crazy idea bursting in my head. 'Especially if you have a family member over there to help out.'

'What are you saying?' she asks in surprise.

'I'm saying I could come over and stay with you. And maybe for longer than a couple of weeks this time. Perhaps I could stay for the whole of the summer?'

'You're serious?' I'm relieved by the enthusiasm in my aunt's voice.

'I think so. I mean, why not? To be honest, I might be up for a complete change,' I tell her. 'My job here is going nowhere, and truthfully I'm feeling in a bit of a rut. I think a change of environment is exactly what I need. And you know how much I love the dogs.'

'I know you do. But are you talking about handing in your notice at the doctor's surgery?' A note of concern creeps into her voice.

'I am seriously considering it, yes.'

It seems strange when I actually say it out loud to someone. Handing my notice in, giving up my flat and leaving the life I have here behind. It might have come to me on the spur of the moment but I realise it is something I have been quietly considering for some time.

'Well, of course I'd love to have you here! If you're absolutely sure. What about when you get home, though, would it be easy for you to find another job?'

'Probably. There are always job adverts for medical receptionists at a big practice in the nearby town and I have enough experience.'

Even though the thought of returning to the same type of work doesn't exactly fill me with delight, it's what I'm trained for. I don't want to alarm my aunt by telling her I would be willing to do anything, as she would only worry about me.

'Dad said I ought to consider moving over to Spain, but I think there would be even less work opportunities for me there.'

'You could be an English-speaking tour guide. Your mum and dad are not too far from the Alhambra Palace, aren't they?'

'They are, but there are job cutbacks everywhere. I wouldn't be surprised if they only offered audio tours these days, with headphones.'

'Not true I'm sure, people will always want the experience of the tour guide, but I suppose you would need to be fluent in Spanish too, or at least have some grasp of the language.'

'*Exactamente.*'

We chat for a while longer and I can hear a dog's bark in the background and Judith calling out a name. The dogs have huge, cool stone pens to lie in, and are walked regularly by the volunteers. They are fed well and loved by all. If that's a dog's life, then it ain't half bad.

'Come here, Smudge.' I hear her speaking to a dog.

'Is he a new boy?' I ask, as she never mentioned a Smudge

last time we spoke, and Judith talks about all of the dogs like they are her own children.

'Yes, he's a gorgeous red Hungarian Vizsla. With a brown splodge on one leg. I thought the name Smudge sounded nicer than splodge,' she tells me. 'Sadly, his owner died recently and none of the neighbours in the small hamlet where he lived wanted him.'

'Ah, that's a shame.'

'It is, but he's a bit much for some people. Let's just say, he's a little bit excitable. And a bit needy.'

There's a sudden howling sound in the background.

'Gosh, what was that?' I can't help chuckling. 'Is it a full moon?'

'That's Smudge. It's because I've stopped stroking him.' She laughs. 'He likes to be near people constantly, as most of the breed do. They are sometimes referred to as Velcro Vizsla,' she says with a deep chuckle.

'Well, I can't wait to meet him, he sounds adorable. If a little over the top.' I laugh.

'I can't wait for you to meet him either, you'll have a friend for life. Right, that's my break over,' says my aunt. 'I've got a bit of paperwork to do. Let me know when you have an exact date to come out,' she says.

I can hear a low whine, presumably from Smudge. My aunt must have stopped fussing over him again.

'I will do. It's so good to hear from you, Judith. Hopefully I will see you soon.'

We finish the call and I stroll into the lounge and flick on the television. I start watching an episode of a medical drama, where the receptionist is flirting outrageously with the handsome new doctor in the practice, who seems to be lapping it up. If only it were like that in real life, I can't help thinking to myself.

My mind flits to the handsome Greek doctor I had to see

last time I visited Aunt Judith, when I was taken ill with tonsillitis. I recuperated in the glorious sunshine, ice-cold drinks in hand, thinking it a shame he didn't need a receptionist. Ah, Crete, it really is good for the soul. I can almost smell the pine forests and taste the salty feta and delicious Greek salads. It's time to fire up my laptop and check out some flights.

THREE

'Well, I'll be sad to lose you, Tania. Good receptionists are not easy to come by.'

I'm sat opposite Doctor Jackson in the village practice, having just delivered my resignation letter.

'You've been invaluable these past years. We'll all miss you.' His smile is warm and genuine.

'Thanks, I'll miss this place too, and all of you.'

I'm not sure it's true that I'll miss the work exactly. I've had my fill of patients who think I am deliberately out to stop them seeing a doctor, when we are stretched so thin as it is. I will miss the staff here, though, especially my co-worker and friend Angie, who's ten years older than me and makes me laugh every single day. She has a wicked sense of humour and will have me trying hard not to burst into fits of giggles as a patient approaches the counter.

'So, you're going to Greece?'

Angie's mouth has fallen open in surprise as we sit in the staffroom having a break, in between surgeries.

'How long for?'

'I'm not exactly sure,' I tell her truthfully.

'I can't believe it. What will I do without you here? Not everyone appreciates my humour.' She grins. 'And, just as importantly, who is going to provide our weekly sweet treats?'

'I'll give you some recipes, if you like.'

'No, thanks. My one and only experience of baking was at school when my cake burnt to a crisp and set the smoke alarms off.' She chuckles. 'So, when are you going?'

'I was actually hoping to go in two weeks' time, but Doctor Jackson has hinted that it won't be so easy to find a decent replacement, so I might have to work a full month's notice.'

'Ah, I might be able to help with that.' Angie wipes a crumb from her mouth. 'One of my neighbours once worked as a doctor's receptionist. She gave up work several years ago to nurse her husband when he became ill. He has sadly died now, and during our recent conversations she's hinted at going back to work. She'd be great here, and the bonus is, I like her,' she says, winking.

'Sounds like a great solution. You should speak to Doctor Jackson before he starts advertising the position.'

'Will do.'

She leans towards me, wraps me in a hug and squeezes me tightly.

'Do you think I'm doing the right thing?' I say into her shoulder.

'Do *you*?' She throws the question back at me as she lets me go.

'That's not fair, I'm asking you.'

'Ah, but if I give you the wrong advice, I'll be the one to blame,' she says, diving back into her tuna sandwich. 'Although,' she says, chewing thoughtfully, 'if you ask me, I think most people already know the decision they want to make about their life choices, they just want some sort of reassurance. So, for what it's worth, I think you would regret it if you didn't go.

Given all the time you've spent moaning about how bored you are.' She raises an eyebrow.

'Gosh, have I been that bad?'

'Not really, I'm teasing. But anyone can see you are ready for a complete change.'

'It's true, there is no denying that,' I admit. 'Once I've given the flat up, though, I don't know where I'd live if I wanted to return, what with my folks being in Spain.'

'You could stay with me,' says Angie firmly.

'What, really?' I say in surprise.

'Definitely. I've got three large bedrooms, two of them empty. I'm rattling around in that house.'

Angie married at nineteen and is now divorced with two grown-up children, one away at university, the other living with her boyfriend.

'I suppose it's good to know I would have somewhere temporary to stay if I needed to come home. Thanks, Angie, you're a real pal. Would you look after a few bits of furniture too?'

'Not a problem. I admire your spirit. Do what makes you happy, love, follow your dreams in life. There are times I wish I could turn the clock back. I'd have had a few more adventures, that's for sure.'

'Thanks, Angie. And you're right. If I don't leave the surgery now and see what's out there, I'm not sure I ever will.'

'That's my girl.' She smiles, before turning to the cake tin and popping a piece of rocky road into her mouth. 'Now then, don't you want those crisps?' She eyes the unopened packet on the bench.

'Help yourself.' I pass them over to her. 'It's the least I can do.'

. . .

Just over two weeks later, we are gathered at the local pub to have a few drinks to mark the beginning of my new adventure. Doctor Jackson gave a nice little speech and bought us all a round of drinks, before he quietly disappeared, leaving the rest of us to party until quite late into the evening. The staff at the surgery had clubbed together and handed me some euros in a card with lovely messages written inside, and a silver-framed photo of me and Bruno. I choked back tears as I unwrapped it from the tissue paper, admiring the heavy silver frame.

'We thought flowers and wine would be useless, as you're going away tomorrow, so decided to give you some money for spends in Greece instead,' explained Angie.

'That's brilliant, thanks. And that photo was so thoughtful.'

'I thought it was something you can take wherever you go,' said Angie.

FOUR

The next morning, I haul my red suitcase down from the top of my wardrobe and pack all the clothes I have left in the flat. I fling sundresses, vest tops, T-shirts and shorts into it, before adding a pair of trainers and walking shoes. The terrain is quite rocky in places around the forest so sturdy footwear is necessary, as I will be working with the animals. All the same, I pack a couple of pretty dresses, in case we dine at a restaurant in a nearby village, or maybe down at the harbour in Hersonissos on my days off.

Case packed, I head into the kitchen and make myself a coffee. Tomorrow morning, just after eight, I will be catching the train from the village to the airport. I get a little flutter in my stomach as it hits me. This is really happening. I'm really leaving the life I've known behind.

Taking my drink into the lounge, I study the room, which feels empty without my knick-knacks, and feel a tinge of sadness. The flat came fully furnished, so I've just moved my personal items to Angie's place. I did have a few larger items, a lounge unit and two pine bedside tables, that I revamped and modernised. Angie is storing them in her garage for me, saving me having to fork out for storage, for which I am hugely grateful. Upcycling became a little bit of a hobby for me when I had some leftover wallpaper from my newly decorated bedroom and transformed the bedside cabinets, using a découpage method I learned from watching a TV programme.

I pop the photo of Bruno into my case to take with me on my travels. I'll soon be seeing lots of dogs and thinking about that makes me smile. I'm especially looking forward to meeting Smudge the Vizsla.

Before I leave my flat for the last time, I take a tin of coins I've been collecting to Kerry across the road. She opens the door dressed in navy capri pants, a pink top and her long hair loose and silky smooth.

'Morning, Kerry. Would you like this for one of your charities? I'm afraid I didn't have time to change it into notes.' I hand over the tin.

'Tania, thanks, that's really kind of you.' She smiles, taking the tin from me. I told Kerry all about my plans to stay with my aunt over the summer when I called over a week or so ago and she invited me inside for tea.

'There's not that much, about forty quid, I think.'

'Well, it's very generous and every donation helps. Actually, I was going to call over before you go and give you something.'

She beckons me inside and I follow her into the lounge, which is as pristine as Kerry. She opens a drawer in a stylish cabinet, then hands me something wrapped in pink tissue paper. I open it to reveal a beautiful fan.

'I thought you might need it in those temperatures. Especially as you told me Crete is experiencing a bit of a heatwave right now.' She smiles.

'Kerry, its beautiful.' I turn the fan over in my hand; it's made of wood, the fan decorated with shimmering tapestry.

'You're very welcome. I bought it in Thailand years ago and, to be honest, I've never used it. I thought you could make more use of it.'

'I'm sure I will. Bye, Kerry. And thank you.'

'Bye, Tania. And good luck. Keep in touch.'

We hug briefly before I set off across the road back to my flat.

The next morning as I hand over the keys to the flat, it seems strange to think that I lived here, with my boyfriend only staying over at weekends, never fully committing. He clearly liked to keep his options open, which became apparent when he started seeing a receptionist at his local sports centre behind my back. I wonder why I put up with his reluctance to take our relationship to the next level, but maybe deep down, I never thought we were forever. I hope whoever rents this place next gets their happy ever after here, or at least some good times.

I glance around the place that has been my home one last time, before stepping outside and taking the short walk to the station with my huge red suitcase. A fluttering of nerves rises in my stomach. There is no turning back now. My new adventure is about to begin!

FIVE

'Delayed?' I find myself saying out loud.

As I continue reading the departure board, I can't help sighing with dismay – my flight to Crete is going to leave two hours late.

'Bummer.' A guy next to me, around my age and carrying a canvas backpack, is staring at the same board. He smells really good...

'Has your flight been cancelled?' he asks and as he turns towards me I take in his handsome face and bright blue eyes, framed by curly blond hair. He is smiling easily, despite the predicament we find ourselves in.

'No, just delayed.' I sigh.

'Ah well, at least it isn't cancelled. My flight has been delayed too. I'm heading to Crete.'

'Oh, me too. We must be on the same flight then.'

'Which means we have two hours to kill. I don't suppose you fancy joining me for a coffee, do you?' He winks.

'Sure, why not?' I say, thinking it preferable to sit with a charming companion than alone in a corner somewhere, trying to find a charger for my phone.

We head towards a coffee shop that has plenty of seats.

'I'm Euan, by the way,' says my new friend as he dumps his bag on a chair and heads to the counter for our coffees.

'Tania,' I tell him.

A few minutes later, I'm sat with a frothy cappuccino, Euan with a flat white, and we are chatting about our travel plans. He tells me he has taken a sabbatical from his job working for a large IT company. I wouldn't have had him down as an IT guy. I would have put money on him working outdoors, especially as his skin looks so healthy and lightly tanned. Maybe he enjoys outdoor pursuits as an antidote to his time spent in an office.

'My housemate died last year,' he tells me as we chat. 'Thirty-two, just like that.' He snaps his fingers together. 'He had an undiagnosed heart condition apparently.'

'Gosh, that's awful.' I can't imagine how horrible that must have been.

'I won't lie, it was a dark time. We'd been mates since we were teenagers, attending the same school and often going camping and hiking at the weekend.'

So, I was right about his love of the outdoors.

'Anyway.' He takes a sip of his coffee. 'It made me think I should get off and see a bit of the world. The Greek islands, then who knows. Something like that kind of gives you a reminder that tomorrow is promised to no one.'

'You're so right.'

As we chat, I'm surprised to find myself telling Euan all about how my boyfriend cheated on me with the receptionist at his local sports centre. I should have figured it out really, when his visits to see me became less frequent and he developed a sudden desire to constantly play badminton. Maybe he just has a thing for receptionists.

'It wasn't just that, though. My job is a bit samey, and living in a small village, I fancied a complete change,' I explain as I sip my coffee. 'If you don't make changes happen yourself, then no one else is going to do it for you.' I shrug.

'I know what you mean. You're only young once. I'm determined to travel and see the world while I can, especially after what happened to my buddy.'

'So, what are your plans?' I ask.

'I don't strictly have any.' He shrugs. 'I've got a week's work lined up, working for a mate who runs a bar in Stalis, to keep the bank account topped up.' He grins. 'After that? I'm not really sure.' His smile is infectious, along with his apparent lust for life.

I tell him about my aunt's place up in the hills.

'Sounds amazing. I love dogs. I take it you're a dog lover too?'

'I am.'

Once again, I find myself telling my story, and all about losing my beloved Bruno. Spilling my guts to this guy is just a little bit too easy.

Euan is charming, funny company, and the time passes quickly. Another coffee and a sandwich later, we part ways for a little and I head off and do some shopping, purchasing another dress in a sale at one of my favourite shops. Soon enough, the board flashes up details of my flight and I make my way towards the departure gate.

I bump into Euan again in the queue, and we chat until we take our seats on the plane. To my surprise and delight, Euan's seat is next to mine.

'What are the chances of that?' he says, before loading his rucksack into the overhead locker. 'It must be fate.' He winks.

Settling down, I think about what a nice guy he is. In a way, I envy his adventurous spirit as I'm not sure I would have the courage to go off alone without a plan. In fact, I am pretty sure I wouldn't, and I thank my lucky stars I was able to come to Crete and stay with my aunt. So many people are stuck in situations that they can see no way out of. Our knees brush at one point during take-off and Euan turns to me and smiles. This could be a very interesting visit.

The flight goes smoothly, me reading in between chatting to Euan, who watches a movie on his tablet. He kindly offers to share his earphones so I can watch too, but as it isn't really my type of movie, I flick through a magazine instead.

As we approach Heraklion Airport, I glance out of the window to see the lights on the runway and a sky streaked with pink. I take a deep breath and smile. I'm finally here in Crete.

SIX

Having said goodbye to Euan, I wheel my suitcase out to the arrivals area. My aunt looks cool and chic in patterned cotton trousers, a white vest and a straw fedora, and I squeeze her tightly. I'm slightly regretting choosing a denim dress to travel in. It was fine back home, but it's a little heavy in this heat. I can hardly wait to change into something cooler.

'Let's get into the car and get the air con on,' she says, as I retrieve a tissue from my bag, and dab my brow. Crete, it seems, is still experiencing the hottest temperatures in a long time, she tells me as we walk. I guess I should have checked my weather app before I left. My long curly hair is already expanding in the humidity, even though it is tied back.

'It does help that there are lots of trees at the rescue. There's always somewhere shady to cool down,' my aunt reassures me. 'And, of course, there is the pool.'

We step into the car, my aunt taking her time and carefully easing her way into the driver's seat and being very careful with her knee, I can't help noticing.

Pine Forest Rescue is around an hour's drive from the

airport, and soon enough we have left the city roads behind and are heading out along the quieter highway.

'It's so good to see you,' says Judith as we drive along the open roads, with hills and mountains in the background, the old white church with a blue roof perched on top. We drive through a gorge flanked by craggy rocks and ancient trees, seemingly a hangout of local mountain goats. It always makes me smile when I spot one of them stood high on a tree, surveying the roads below.

'So, what have you been up to since we last spoke?' asks Judith.

'Not much.' I shrug. 'Not an awful lot happens in the village. When I found myself embroiled in a conversation in the local shop about one of my neighbours' rose bushes, and how it hadn't bloomed so well this year, I thought it was time to get out,' I tell her. 'The worst part is, I was actually invested and worrying about the old dear's bush.'

My aunt chuckles. 'Do you miss having a boyfriend?' she asks.

'It would be nice to have someone to do things with at the weekend,' I admit. 'My coupled-up friends do ask me to tag along occasionally, but I feel like a spare part. I would rather be on my own, though, than be with the wrong person.'

I think of my ex and his cheating ways, wondering if I will ever trust anyone again.

'Well, that's sensible.' She turns to me and smiles. 'There is no point in being in a relationship because you don't want to be alone.'

'Agreed. And I'm okay with my own company actually, at least most of the time. I did consider having a go at meeting someone online, but I'd kind of like to meet someone organically. Maybe I am just an old romantic at heart.' I shrug.

My aunt smiles. 'You usually meet someone when you least expect it.'

'So they say.'

I suppose it's true, but I'm not sure how that was ever going to happen at home. A doctor's surgery isn't exactly the best place to meet a prospective partner. Or at a women-only yoga class. And even though walking Bruno along the canal always encouraged conversation from other dog walkers, most of them were wearing their wedding rings.

'There's nothing wrong in believing in romance,' says Judith as we climb higher into the hills. The twinkling Mediterranean Sea can be glimpsed in the distance through the trees as the sun continues to drop behind the mountains. 'Don't forget how I met your uncle Ray.'

Judith had met her husband on a train journey from Bordeaux to Paris, where they were both living at the time, when my aunt was working as a nanny. They shared an empty carriage, and during the journey he offered her a glass of Bordeaux, which he produced from a bag along with two glasses. He'd been working as a wine merchant at the time and was on his way home from visiting a vineyard. She often tells me that by the end of the journey, she knew he was the man she was going to marry. They were never blessed with children, but they had a shared passion for dogs and the outdoor life; they had three dogs at their home in England. When Uncle Ray retired, they sold up and came to Crete, spending ten happy years running the dog sanctuary before he succumbed to the cancer he had briefly battled with.

I switch the air conditioning off, and wind the window down, feeling the slightly cooler, but still warm air outside waft over my face. The scent of the pine trees is suddenly mixed with the unmistakeable aroma of food sizzling on a BBQ as we drive past a pale-yellow painted house.

'That's a holiday home,' Judith tells me. 'They're a lovely couple, who come out here regularly. Sometimes they take the dogs out for walks.'

Pine Forest village could be described as a hamlet more than a village, the only facilities being a small shop and a tiny bar at the top of a hill near the church. In the summer months, the bar makes most of its money from tourists, who call in for a cooling beer and a snack after they have climbed the two hundred steps to the church of the Virgin Mary.

There are around ten houses in the immediate vicinity and Judith is part of a WhatsApp group that share local news. It's reassuring to know that she has these contacts, although she is never alone, as the place is filled with volunteers pretty much all year round. Even Christmas time, when there are always at least a couple of people who need to get away for the festivities for whatever reason. I've learned from Judith that sometimes they talk about their reasons for escaping Christmas, sometimes they don't.

We make a slight descent and follow a narrow road, soon pulling up outside the sprawling house and surrounding forest, a tantalising strip of sea just visible. The sound of barking dogs greets our arrival and, stepping out of the car, I take in a lungful of the mountain air. It's good to be here.

After a quick shower and change, I head outside with Judith and take a seat at the long wooden table, the trees above threaded with lights. Some of the volunteers had prepared the evening meal whilst Judith was out collecting me from the airport, and I'm sipping a glass of chilled white wine, facing a table groaning with delicious-looking food.

'Gosh, this looks amazing.'

'We all pitch in with the cooking, as you know. Tonight, Wes and Chloe have done the honours in the kitchen.'

They both say hello.

'And I was chief washer-upper.' An older, deeply tanned

bloke with a Swedish accent, who's about my aunt's age, chimes in. He introduces himself as Lars.

'We also have Liz, who isn't home yet, so may not be joining us this evening,' Judith tells me, glancing at her watch. 'I do hope she gets back at a reasonable hour.'

'Where on earth would she go around here?' I can't help asking.

'Down into Hersonissos. She met some dude there the other day at the beach,' Wes, an American, reveals as he takes a sip of beer from a bottle. 'I imagine she doesn't fancy the drive home on her moped in the dark,' he says.

'There's obviously something she does fancy, though. Or should I say someone.' Chloe raises an eyebrow.

'Well, of course it's up to Liz how she spends her free time,' says my aunt. 'I just prefer it if the volunteers let me know if they are going to stay out overnight. I like to lock everywhere up, as it disturbs the dogs if people arrive home too late. No one wants to be scared half to death by this lot howling in the middle of the night!'

My aunt stands and begins to collect some plates to take into the kitchen, limping slightly, so I give her a hand. I'm surprised that it's almost eleven thirty; the hours seem to have rolled by here, sitting chatting with everyone.

We load a dishwasher in the large kitchen that's simply furnished, with a terracotta tiled floor, solid wooden units, and a long pine table. Several shelves line the walls, displaying jars of every spice and herb known to man. Off the kitchen is a huge utility room that stores dog food and supplies.

When everything is tidy, we head off towards the bedrooms. Most of the volunteers share a dormitory, or at least share a room, with another person, but I'm lucky enough to have a small room of my own that looks out over the forest.

'Goodnight then.' I stretch my arms out and yawn. 'I

imagine it will be an early start tomorrow, I'd better get some sleep.'

'You can bank on it.' Judith smiles. 'The dogs start barking round about the same time as the cock starts crowing.'

Which explains why everyone is ready for bed at a reasonable hour. Before I go to sleep, I can't help thinking about Liz and wondering if she is okay out there. What if she had ridden home after all and had an accident in the woods? I'm not sure she would get a phone signal in the mountains. As no one else seemed to be too concerned, though, I put it out of my mind and settle down to sleep. Tomorrow will be a busy day, and I am looking forward to it already.

SEVEN

I pull open the curtain of my bedroom window, just after six thirty, and gasp at the sight that never fails to take my breath away. The vast forest, in various shades of green, slopes towards the glistening Mediterranean Sea, just as the sun is beginning to rise over the mountains. I push open the door of my tiny balcony and stand and just take it all in for a few minutes, before I head along the narrow corridor for a quick shower in the nearest bathroom. I'd tossed and turned a little in the heat, the ceiling fan doing little to stop the warm air from washing over me as I slept.

Knocking on the bathroom door, I'm surprised when it opens and Wes is stood there with wet hair, freshly showered.

'Good morning.' He beams a bright smile. He's stood in front of me wearing blue shorts, revealing a bare torso. I find myself having to avert my eyes from his undeniably impressive six-pack.

'Sorry, are you done?' I ask brightly.

'Yep. The shower is on a cold setting that you might want to adjust. I like to take a cold shower in the morning.' He beams again. 'It's really good for you.'

'I believe so,' I say, a little unconvinced, as the last thing I feel like doing is risking a heart attack in the morning with a freezing cold shower, having sweltered all night.

'Catch you downstairs,' he says as he saunters off.

After a quick shower – I did need to adjust the temperature, it was freezing! – I dress and head downstairs for my first coffee of the day. There are plates of croissants, bread and fruit, cheeses and meats set out on the large table.

'There's Greek yoghurt and honey in the fridge.'

A girl with cropped black hair and wearing tiny denim shorts and a white T-shirt nods towards the fridge.

'Oh, and my name is Liz.' She gives me the brightest smile.

'Hi, Liz, good to meet you. I'm Tania.'

'Did you arrive last night?' she asks as she munches on a piece of toast.

'I did. Judith's my aunt,' I tell her.

'Oh yes, of course, duh! She said you were arriving yesterday. I think she was pretty miffed with me last night. I arrived home quite late.' She pulls a face. 'Although it wasn't entirely my fault.'

'I'm sure she'll be fine. She doesn't like the dogs being disturbed, I guess.' I echo my aunt's sentiments.

'Oh, I completely get that.' She nods. 'But last night, the traffic coming out of Hersonissos was a real nightmare, as there had been some music festival or other. And then,' she chatters away ten to the dozen, 'one of the roads on the route over here to the forest was inaccessible. A huge tree had come down and was blocking the road. I had to take a detour around the side of the mountain. It's a good job my petrol didn't run out. I sometimes forget the bike runs on petrol.' She giggles.

'You should be careful out there in the dark.' Maybe I was right to be concerned about her riding home alone in the evening.

Gosh, I hope I don't sound like her mother.

'I guess so.' She shrugs. 'Anyway, it's good to meet you, Tania. I'd best get on now, hosing the pens down is the first job but I guess you already know that.' She gulps down a glass of orange juice and heads off. 'Catch you later.' She smiles.

Liz is petite and pretty and seems like good fun. I was also to discover that day that she is a real grafter, working tirelessly before the sun was up, cleaning the dog pens, walking and feeding the dogs and checking in on the donkeys in the adjoining field. The rest of the volunteers worked just as hard, and just after one o'clock we all took a break for lunch.

'It's me and you on dinner duties tonight, I think,' says Liz as we graze on Greek salad and soft, warm olive bread.

'Not off out again, Liz?' enquires Chloe as she sips some iced water.

'No. I might hang around here and go for a swim later. And I'll be staying home this evening,' Liz replies.

'Did this one not work out then?' Chloe runs her finger around the rim of her glass.

'What do you mean "this one"?' Liz frowns slightly.

'Oh sorry, I never meant anything.' Chloe tucks a strand of her blonde hair behind her ears. 'It's just that you always seem to meet blokes down at the beach.' She smiles sweetly.

They stare at each other for a second, and I can't help wondering if something has passed between them.

'That must be down to my sparkling personality.' Liz grins, before turning to chat to me.

She chats away, charming everyone with her engaging, easy-going personality. Soon enough, we are sharing dog tales from back home.

'Honestly, the first time I went away for a weekend with a new bloke, who was also a dog lover, we took our respective dogs,' says Liz as she scoops some hummus into some pitta bread and chews it. 'Anyway, it was a bit of a long drive, and when we checked into the hotel, intending to head straight back out again, one dog took a dump on the hotel floor, and the other jumped on the bed and puked all over it.'

'Oh, my goodness, no!' I clasp my hand over my mouth.

'Yep. My boyfriend had gone to collect the cases from the car, and when he returned, he found me gripping both dogs by their collar, shouting hysterically.' She gives the most infectious laugh. 'Thank goodness I can laugh about it now.'

Everyone else is laughing loudly, apart from Chloe, who gives a weak smile, seemingly not amused by Liz's story.

We finish lunch, and I decide to take Smudge the Vizsla out for a walk, whilst Liz heads off to the pool. My aunt was right about him being an excitable one. Whilst most of the dogs are snoozing, Smudge is still a bundle of energy and has made a beeline for me, probably because I'm the newbie who lavishes him with attention. Annie, a black cockapoo, is apparently his best friend and looks just as eager to have some fun.

'Mind if I join you?' asks Wes as we are about to head off for a walk.

'Sure, why not?' I smile, deciding some company might be rather nice.

'Do you want me to take Smudge?' he offers.

'Thanks, but I think I ought to get used to taking him on the lead. He pulls along a bit in his excitement.'

'Best take some snacks,' says Wes, heading to the food store.

We walk downhill, Smudge pulling at the lead slightly, and Wes instructs me to just stop and then give a little doggie treat.

'It might take a bit of practice, but he will get the message eventually if you stick with it.'

Annie walks obediently on her lead for Wes, sniffing just about everything around her like a bloodhound, excited to be out amongst nature.

It feels so peaceful walking along with the sunlight filtering through the trees making patterns on the road.

'So where are you from?' I ask Wes as we walk. I can glean

that he is from America. 'I mean, America, obviously, but whereabouts?'

'Connecticut. I've been island hopping and, well, to be truthful, I was running out of money,' he tells me. 'When I saw the ad online for dog carers, in exchange for board and lodgings, I hopped on a ferry over here. I was in Santorini at the time, which isn't exactly the cheapest place to stay.'

'Beautiful, though, I've heard.'

'No doubt about it. Although I found it a bit too perfect, if I'm honest.'

'Are you enjoying it here? The rustic forest surroundings couldn't be more different to Santorini, I imagine.'

'Look around you.' He grins. 'Who wouldn't. Anything that keeps me in Greece a bit longer than I can afford is okay with me.'

'So, no plans to head back to Connecticut in the near future then?'

'Not really. I'm just enjoying doing my own thing for a bit, figuring out what I want.' He shrugs.

'Sounds a bit like me,' I reveal.

Suddenly, the sound of a car can be heard approaching the bend we are heading towards, and Wes gently takes my arm and steers me and the dogs to the side of the road, until the car has passed.

Half an hour later, we stop at a clearing with a cooling mountain stream running through, as the sun climbs higher in the sky. Water is cascading over rocks, and we let the dogs off the lead, and they happily dive straight into the rushing waters of the stream, lapping up the cold water and splashing about. Wes climbs a little higher upstream and taking an empty water bottle from his rucksack, fills it.

'Fresh mountain water. It's the best.' He takes a long gulp of his drink. He asks me if I have a bottle, then fills mine too.

'Thanks,' I say gratefully, having tipped out the water in my bottle that was already becoming a little warm.

'So, what about you then?' Wes asks.

We're sat on a large, flat rock, the hot sun caressing our arms and legs. Wes's arms are strong and muscular, I can't help noticing. His brown hair, which is the same colour as his eyes, looks expensively cut. Even wearing shorts and a T-shirt, he looks very well groomed.

'Not a lot to tell, really. Bored at home, single, generally in need of a change, I guess.' I pick up a stone and toss it into the stream. 'Plus, I wanted to come over and give my aunt a chance to have her knee operation.'

Wes is a good listener, appearing interested in everything I have to say.

'The rescue centre is your aunt's place? I guess you're lucky to have somewhere you can visit whenever you like.'

'Oh, I am lucky. Although I have to work just as hard as everyone else,' I remind him.

'I can vouch for that,' he agrees.

We move on and a while later, we reach the bottom of the road, before doing a loop and heading back. There's a fenced-off area of field next to the farmhouse, and Smudge, obviously still keen to exercise, is let off the lead for a run. Even in this heat, he's running about like crazy.

'Right then, mister,' I say to Smudge. 'It's time for you to cool down.'

Back at the rescue, I switch on a hose and give him a good dousing of water. His friend Annie joins him, and the pair have fun, enjoying the shower. Smudge is dancing around, his energy seemingly boundless. I had forgotten how joyful it feels to be around the animals. They really are good for the soul.

EIGHT

After settling the dogs inside, I head off for a swim and Wes says he might come and join me shortly.

The pool is accessed by rough stone steps, in an area surrounded by trees, and enclosed by white painted walls. Bright-pink bougainvillea snakes over the longest wall, and terracotta pots with shrubs and flowers are dotted about, along with several sunbeds. The pool area looks stylish, in contrast to the rest of the rustic forest setting, and makes a relaxing retreat. My uncle and aunt were determined to have a relaxing space to enjoy the Greek sunshine, away from the animals when the working day is done.

Chloe is sprawled out on a sunbed when I arrive, wearing huge sunglasses and a white bikini, a bottle of water at her side.

'Hi,' I say as I place my towel down on a nearby bed. She eases herself up slowly at the sound of my voice.

'Oh, hi, Tania.' She smiles a wide smile. 'What have you been doing?'

'I've just taken the crazy Vizsla out for a walk with Wes. He's so gorgeous.'

'The dog or Wes?' she teases.

'Gosh, maybe I didn't phrase that correctly. I meant the dog.'

'Although Wes is pretty gorgeous too, right?'

'I suppose he is good-looking.' I shrug. For some reason I don't say too much. Despite his good looks, I don't feel any spark of attraction towards him.

'He's a dream.' She sighs. 'Although he seems oblivious to my charms. His loss.' She shrugs, before she settles down on to her sunbed once more.

A few minutes later, Lars appears and dives straight into the pool and swims goodness knows how many laps, before telling us he is off for a bike ride in the hills.

'Where on earth does he get his energy from?' I comment to Chloe after he leaves. 'He must be at least retirement age.'

'He's seventy,' Chloe tells me, as she applies sun cream to her long, tanned legs.

'No way! He puts me to shame when it comes to exercise.'

I realise I don't do an awful lot of exercise, apart from walking, that is. Maybe I can address that here, if I get the time. I'd have a go at lake swimming, if I wasn't so worried about what lurks beneath the water.

'Me too. I think he was an athlete or something in his day,' she tells me vaguely. 'No doubt he will tell you about it soon enough. The rest of us have heard his story, many times.'

She picks up her book, telling me the conversation is over for now, so I climb into the pool and enjoy a long leisurely swim myself. As I push through the water, I wonder what her story is. A very attractive woman, maybe early thirties, out here in the middle of a forest. I imagine her to be more suited to sipping cocktails in a trendy beach resort than working in a kennels up in the hills, although noting her interaction with the animals here, there is no doubting she is a dog lover.

Later that afternoon, Liz and I are in the kitchen preparing the evening meal, which means I've thrown some lamb and a load of herbs into a pot with a ton of fresh tomatoes on a low setting. My own version of a kleftiko but using almost every herb and spice from the shelves in the kitchen.

'Where did you learn to cook?' asks Liz as she prepares a Greek salad and takes some pitta breads from the fridge.

'TikToks and Instagram reels mainly. I've lived on my own for a while, so couldn't always be bothered cooking for one. I did make a few treats for the office, though. It's nice being able to feed other people.'

'It is. Food brings people together, doesn't it? I didn't have a clue about food when I first arrived here,' Liz confesses. 'Judith has taught me a lot these past few weeks and I haven't poisoned anyone so far, so I think it's going okay.' She laughs. 'My mum would never let anyone in the kitchen when she cooked. It was always a mystery to me. I'm mad on food, though.' She pops a slice of cucumber into her mouth as she cuts it up for the salad.

Liz likes her food, but is so slender I wonder where she puts it, but then she does have boundless energy.

'Do you fancy coming down to Hersonissos with me later?' she asks as she slices a giant tomato for the salad. 'We usually eat around seven, after the second dog feed and general cleaning. The night will still be young.'

'Umm, okay, sure, why not?'

I can think of nothing nicer than a cooling sea breeze in the early evening, as the glorious hot weather continues.

'I promise we will be back well before midnight.' She smiles. 'I thought a couple of soft drinks and a wander around the harbour might be nice. There's a night market there this evening too,' she tells me.

'Ooh, yes, that sounds lovely, I love a market. Would you like me to drive? I could borrow Judith's car,' I offer.

'I think it might be more fun if we go on the bike. There's room for two, and it adds to the excitement,' says Liz, who clearly doesn't want to invite anyone else along.

'Actually, yes, it might,' I say, giving a knowing look. Besides, I think it could be fun to enjoy an adventure with my new friend, the wind blowing through our hair as we descend the hills. Why not live a little?

'Great,' she says with a beaming smile, before covering the huge salad bowl in cling film and popping it into the fridge for later.

With the stew simmering away, I head over to the field with the donkeys, and Eric makes a beeline for me.

'Hello there, how have you been?'

He bows his head for me to give him a stroke, and brays contentedly. After a few minutes, he strolls off, ignoring Judith, who has come over too.

'Charming.' She laughs.

'How's the knee today?' I ask, noticing how she was dragging it ever so slightly earlier.

'A bit sore,' she tells me. 'But the good news is that I have a date for my operation. That's what I've come to tell you. I've just been on the phone to the doctor, and it's scheduled for a week on Wednesday.'

'Well, that's great news!'

'Are you sure you can run things whist I recover?' she asks, a hint of uncertainty in her voice.

'Of course I can. I offered to come over and do just that, didn't I?' I reassure her.

'I know you did. And it won't be for long, I'm sure. A day or two in hospital, then a few days' rest here, although I have been advised to get moving as quickly as possible.'

'I'll look after you.' I loop my arm through hers as we head back towards the farmhouse. 'Just like you looked after me when I was little.'

I recall the times I would stay at my aunt's when my parents went on holiday. They favoured strenuous mountain-biking breaks in the mountains of Andalusia, so I was happy to spend time with my aunt who had no children. I used to enjoy playing with her dogs and the little girl who lived next door.

'You're a good girl.' She pats my hand as we walk.

'And you're a good aunt,' I tell her and she smiles warmly. 'Oh, and I'm off out this evening with Liz. Don't worry, though, I'll make sure we're home at a reasonable hour.'

'That sounds nice. Do you want to borrow the car?' she offers.

'To be honest, I did think about that, but Liz seems keen on travelling on the bike. Unless you would like to come with us? Then we can take the car.'

'Oh no, really. I'm pretty tired today, and too much walking will only aggravate my knee further. Thanks, though. You two go off and have some fun.'

'Thanks, Judith, we will.'

'Just be careful, though,' she adds. 'I know Liz is an experienced rider, but some of the bends in the road can be quite sharp.'

'I know. Don't worry, we'll be fine.'

I don't tell her about the tree in the road, as I don't want her worrying.

Judith tells me she has some future volunteer applications to look through, so I head off to make sure all the animals are comfortable before returning to my room for a little siesta, suddenly feeling a little fatigued by the hot weather. I'm really looking forward to spending the evening near the beach with Liz later on, already imagining that cooling sea breeze.

Passing the pool area, I notice Wes and Chloe lying beside each other on the sunloungers. Chloe is throwing her head back and laughing at something Wes has just said. I can't help thinking what an attractive couple they make, despite Chloe telling me that Wes doesn't seem to see her in that way.

I wake from my nap an hour or so later, refreshed, and, after showering, head downstairs to check on the casserole. The huge pot has had a couple of hours on a very low heat in the oven and it's almost there. I lift the lid on the dish and a tantalising smell hits my nostrils. I try a piece of lamb, which is cooked but I want it melt-in-the-mouth tender, so I return it to the oven for another hour.

'That smells amazing.'

Liz comes bounding into the kitchen and grabs a bottle of water from the fridge.

'What time are we eating?' she asks.

'In around an hour, if that's okay?' I glance at my watch that shows almost six.

'I can't wait, I'm starved.'

'Nothing new there then.' I laugh as she picks at some grapes from a fruit bowl.

Outside, after that last hour to finish it off, I place the casserole on the table, whilst Liz brings the huge salad and a mountain of pitta bread. Judith plays mother and ladles the stew into bowls before handing it around. I return to the kitchen for some chilled wine and jugs of iced water.

Everyone compliments me on the casserole, and I feel happy that they have enjoyed it, especially as it was a chuck everything in the pot and hope for the best type of dish. I've really enjoyed cooking for people other than myself this evening.

'This reminds me of a dish back home,' said Lars as he cleans his plate. 'I think it is the rosemary in the sauce. Maybe the hint of cinnamon. Whatever it is, it's delicious. Thank you.'

'I'm glad you enjoyed it,' I say, feeling rather pleased with myself.

'Right. I have ice cream in the freezer if anyone would like some for dessert?' Judith offers as she stands up. The others accept, but I'm saving myself for one later at the harbour, maybe even a chocolate crêpe from one of the little stands in the back-streets.

'No, thanks. I might grab one later,' says Liz, echoing my thoughts. 'Are you ready to hit the road?' she asks me.

'Yep. Let's just get these dishes inside.'

'Off out somewhere?' asks Chloe as she pours herself a second glass of wine.

'Just for a ride down to the harbour. I thought Tania might like it,' says Liz.

'I'm sure she's seen it many times before,' says Chloe, tossing her hair over her shoulder.

'It's true, but never from the back of the bike.' I smile at Chloe. What is her problem with Liz?

We say our goodbyes, as the group chat around the table and Lars heads inside to make coffee. Judith doesn't mind people drinking the cheap local wine at dinner, which they often purchase themselves, but most of the volunteers don't go in for too much alcohol consumption as there isn't the luxury of leisurely lie-ins or hangovers here.

Helmets on, and soon Liz and I are heading downhill towards the harbour. It's true there are many bends in the road, but Liz expertly takes them with ease. I feel the wind blow through the half-style helmet and caress my legs that are clad in knee-length cotton shorts. It feels so free here, and I breathe deeply as we head down lower, the trees and rocks keeping us company along the way.

A short while later, Liz pulls up at a viewing point at the side of the road.

'This is the best place to watch the sunset,' she tells me as we climb off the bike.

Several other people have parked up too, to witness the ball of orange sun slowly begin its descent, casting a magical glow across the sea.

'Oh wow. How gorgeous is that?' I snap away with my camera phone.

'I think you know more about the local beauty spots than I do,' I tell Liz. 'I usually just head out for a walk, or with my aunt to the shops, or a local restaurant in the hills.'

'I like exploring,' Liz explains. 'I've always been that way. When I was a young girl I used to take hours going to the shops, wandering around and finding different ways home. Thinking about it, I was probably a real worry to my parents.'

I can't take my eyes off the setting sun.

'Shall we make a move then?' she asks after I have asked one of the viewers to take a photo of the both of us, the mountains rising into the background, illuminated by lights from the surrounding houses giving a lovely vista.

'Can you send me that picture, please?' She gives me her number and I send the picture to her Messenger inbox.

'Cheers.' She opens her phone and smiles at the image before we fix our helmets on again, and head off.

As we approach the harbour, a boat is returning tourists from an early evening cruise and lights from the bars and restaurants illuminate the streets as the sky darkens even more. A few lively bars have music gently pumping out into the warm night air. Liz secures her bike safely at a parking area and we head off along the front.

'Ah, it's much cooler down here,' I say as we stroll along listening to the sound of the rolling waves. Some of the waiters wish us *kalispera*, and gesture to the menu board outside their restaurants, and I kind of wish we hadn't already eaten. Eventually, we find a trendy-looking bar, with ferns in silver pots outside and stylish black furniture on blonde wooden floors inside. It's almost empty, as it's only early in the evening, but as some of the tables give a tantalising sea view, I suggest we head inside.

'Strictly mocktails, don't worry,' Liz tells me as we approach the bar and order. The young guy behind the bar tells us he will bring our drinks over.

'So how long are you planning on staying in Greece?' I ask as we sip a delicious strawberry and pineapple drink. Liz had told me to go ahead and have a real cocktail, but I don't think that's fair as she's driving.

'I'm not sure,' she tells me. 'I agreed to stay at the dog rescue for six weeks, and I've been here for four weeks already. It's gone so fast.' She sucks her drink through a stripy straw. 'I have a friend who is working as a nanny in London. She said she could get me job, as friends of the family she is staying with are looking for someone, but I'm not sure I fancy it.' She shrugs.

'Did you have a job back home?' I ask, wondering if her story is like mine, in that she just needed a change.

'Kind of. Part-time. It was a lot of fun, but I don't think I can spend my life being a mermaid.'

I almost spit my drink out, wondering if the sun has got to her.

'Sorry, did you say a mermaid?'

'Yep. In a SEA LIFE Centre. We wear full costume, glittery tail and all, and dive down into the water amongst the fish. The kids absolutely love it.' She grins.

'That's amazing! I can imagine the look on the kids' faces.'

'I know. We just wave at them for a few seconds, then disappear, which makes it even more magical. We can only hold our breath for so long, and a snorkel and goggles wouldn't have quite the same effect.' She laughs. 'Actually, you would make an amazing mermaid, with that fabulous hair.'

'I might give it some thought, although it would end up as a tangled mess.' I smile as I touch my long curls. 'Being a mermaid is a lot more interesting than telling someone you're a doctor's receptionist when they ask you what you do for a living, though, that's for sure.'

As we chat I wonder whether I will ever have a child myself to take to aquariums and such places. I don't have siblings, so it's not even as though I have a niece or nephew to take on outings, which is a shame really. Especially as I so wanted to watch the Paddington Bear movies, but would have felt a bit daft going to watch them on my own.

I tell her all about my work back home.

'So, in some ways, I'm a bit like you, in that I haven't got any firm plans,' I tell her.

'Cheers to not having any plans.' Liz smiles and raises her glass and I tap mine against it. I remind myself that is what being young, free and single is all about. All the same, I can't help suddenly feeling a little rudderless. I don't have time to dwell on that, though, as Liz tells me to drink up so we can head to a market stall down a side street that sells the most wonderful bags and silver jewellery.

'Lead the way,' I tell her as we head out into the warm evening air.

NINE

It feels wonderful strolling along, hearing the music from bars and watching groups of people sipping drinks at outside tables, just watching the world go by. One guy, who is sat with two other blokes, taps an empty chair next to him when I catch his eye and gestures us over.

'He's full of himself,' I say with a laugh as we walk along.

'Who?' says Liz, swinging her head around.

'A bloke outside that bar eyeing us up. Keep walking, I'm looking forward to the shopping.'

'Spoilsport,' she says, before adding, 'Only joking,' and laughing.

The market is bustling with stalls selling everything from jewellery to leather goods. We gently push our way through the crowds, where families and couples are out for the evening, the children eating ice creams or gyros from nearby stands. There's a stall selling T-shirts and I can't help remarking on the one Liz is wearing.

'Yours is nice, where did you buy it?' I ask. There is nothing quite as unique on the rails.

'I made it. Well, I bought a white T-shirt and customised it.'

Her white T-shirt is covered in little sewn-on fabric pictures that include flowers, clouds and rainbows.

'Really? It looks amazing.'

'Thanks. I like customising clothes. Most of my clothes started out plain white. I do shoes too.'

She points down at her black canvas pumps, embellished with little jewels.

'Wow,' I say, impressed. 'You really do have talent.'

'Thank you,' she says, a little coyly. 'It's just something I enjoy doing.'

'It's nice to have a creative outlet. I must admit I enjoy taking a paintbrush to old furniture and revamping it.' I tell her a little about some of the things I have restored.

Presently, we arrive at a stall selling beautiful silver jewellery. Necklaces, bracelets and Greek-patterned arm cuffs are all displayed on purple velvet, looking beautiful and at very reasonable prices. My eye falls on a twisted silver pendant and I can't resist buying it. Further on, I spy a stall selling leather shoes and buy myself a pair of tan-coloured flip-flops.

'You'll need to rein me in, or I'll be broke if I carry on,' I tell Liz as we pass a stand selling pancakes that I know I won't be able to resist.

'Oh, come on, say you'll have one too. It's been two hours since dinner,' I plead, but Liz takes little persuading.

'Of course I will,' says Liz, who adds Nutella, banana and a sprinkling of coconut to her order.

A few minutes later we're sat on a wall looking up at the moon against a dark sky and with twinkling lights from the harbour, making appreciative noises as we tuck in. The sound of laughter can be heard from a group of local teenagers who are ending their day with a final dip in the sea.

'Right, what next?' asks Liz, after we've wiped our hands and thrown paper napkins into the bin.

'Maybe a walk. Then I guess we ought to be making tracks,' I say. It's just after ten and the time has flown by.

'I know. I did think about a drive around the racing track at Star Beach, but we might be a bit pushed for that, it closes at ten thirty.' Liz glances at her watch.

'I'd definitely be up for that another time, though, it sounds like fun.'

'You're on.'

Fun is definitely something I could do with a little more of in my life. I think, at my age, there should be more to feel excited by, other than the latest series on Netflix.

We stroll along the harbour, where small speedboats tied up for the evening are rubbing shoulders with medium-sized vessels advertising excursions to secluded beaches and blue lagoons. A man on board is inviting holidaymakers out for the evening to book seats for the following day as they stroll by. Across the water, twinkling lights can be seen from another island, the distant strains of music playing. An impressive-looking yacht has just moored up and an impossibly glamorous couple emerge from inside, along with some equally gorgeous children.

'That's the life, hey? What do you reckon their story is?' I ask Liz as a waiter brings a tray of nibbles and drinks to an outside table where the family are now assembled.

'Oh, I like this game,' says Liz. 'Okay, I think she's an ex-model and he's a Russian oligarch. I reckon he owns a premiership football club.'

'Interesting. Although it could be *her* money. She could be the princess of a little-known principality somewhere. He was a lowly farmer, and love conquered all.'

'So, you're a romantic, hey?'

'Not really. Although deep down, yes, probably,' I admit.

I tell her all about Judith and how she met my uncle Ray. 'So she's kind of set the benchmark for me. Or at least it lets me believe that chance encounters can lead to the real thing.'

'That's amazing. She doesn't talk about her husband much,' Liz tells me. 'What was he like?'

'She does if she's asked. And Uncle Ray was great. Funny and kind. They had a really good marriage.'

'She's lucky,' says Liz. 'So many marriages don't seem to last these days.'

The harbour is bustling now as we walk, with lights and music everywhere.

'I kind of wish I hadn't come down on the bike now,' says Liz, taking it all in.

'Do you find the early mornings a bit restricting?' I ask, pretty much thinking the same thing.

'Not really. I'm an early riser, despite being a bit of a party animal.' She grins.

We grab takeaway iced lattes from a kiosk as we walk.

'I hope you don't mind me asking, but what's the story with you and Chloe?' I ask as we sip our drinks. 'She seems a little bit off with you at times.'

'You've noticed then.' She raises an eyebrow. 'It's probably because she's jealous that Wes and I slept together,' she says casually. 'And as she has a serious crush on him, I don't think it went down too well.' She grins. 'I bet she's wondering why her charms didn't work.'

'You slept together?' Now it's my turn to raise an eyebrow.

'Yes. Although, actually, that's all we did, sleep,' she quickly adds.

'Tell me more.' I'm suddenly all ears.

'A few of us were hanging out one evening and Wes produced a bottle of ouzo and we got chatting, late into the evening,' she explains. 'Anyway, Chloe went to bed in a huff when she realised Wes wasn't paying her any attention. We were laughing quite loudly, so we continued our chat in my room.' She sips her coffee. 'We got drunk and crashed out. That was it. I haven't told Chloe that, though.' She grins wickedly. 'Wes is good company, but he isn't my type,' she reveals.

A muscled, tattooed bloke with his long hair tied back walks past with his friend and smiles over at us.

'Now him, on the other hand.' She smiles back. As the two blokes walk on, the long-haired guy takes a backward glance before they turn a corner.

'Now I really wish we'd taken a taxi down here.' She sighs.

'So what's your story?' I ask as we stroll back towards the car park for the bike.

'You like to ask a lot of questions, don't you?' She's smiling, but I get the impression she's gently telling me to back off a little.

'It's true. I just like knowing about people's lives, everyone has a story to tell. Maybe it's because mine is an open book.' I shrug, thinking of Euan at the airport and how I practically gave him my life story. I wonder how he's getting on.

'I'll tell you sometime.' She smiles before we head to the bike and remove two helmets from the box on the back and fix them on.

The journey home is lovely, the coolness of the evening a welcome respite as we navigate the roads. I've never been afraid to ride pillion as I had an ex-boyfriend with a motorbike once, although the blackness in the hills makes it slightly scary. The viewing point we passed earlier with the glorious sunset now shows a vista of twinkling harbour lights and white stars against a dark sky. I ask Liz to stop so I can take another photo, thinking I might display the contrasting pictures in a frame when I get home.

'It's so gorgeous, isn't it,' says Liz with a sigh as she runs her fingers through her short hair and admires the view. 'I wish I could stay here forever.'

'What, right here? On the top of a mountain road. Might get a bit boring after a while.'

'What are you like?' She pushes me gently on the arm.

The roads are black as we climb higher into the hills, the only light coming from an occasional house in the distance, and I must admit I feel relieved when I see the lights from the dog rescue up ahead. Safely back inside, we head upstairs to bed.

'I enjoyed myself tonight, Liz, thanks. Next time I'll drive if you like,' I offer.

'No chance. Next time we will take a taxi and party the night away,' she says with a smile as she heads off to her room.

TEN

I wake early the next morning, and after doing the usual clean-ups and feeding of the animals, I take myself off for a walk. My tumbling curly hair is expanding in the heat and humidity, so it's firmly tied back and fastened beneath a baseball cap. Smudge is eager to come out with me too, but my aunt tells me a local couple are keen to take him for a walk later, and I can't help wondering if they know what they are letting themselves in for. Other volunteers have arranged to walk the rest of the dogs too, later in the day.

Walking down the road, I take a left turn in a different direction to yesterday. After ten minutes, I approach a bench near the end of a stream, where a man is sat, just staring into space.

'*Kalimera.*'

He looks up, a little surprised by the sound of my voice. '*Kalimera.*'

'Such a beautiful day, isn't it?' I remark.

'It is always a beautiful day in Greece,' he agrees, in his strong accent. 'Although some people would say it is maybe a little too hot right now.'

'A heatwave. As if you need one in Greece,' I say.

'*Kafsonas*,' he tells me.

'Pardon?'

'*Kafsonas*. It means "heatwave" in Greek.' He stares off somewhere into the distance.

'Oh, right. I have learnt another word then. My vocabulary just about extends to "good morning" and "good afternoon".'

'Hmm,' he says, barely making eye contact, so I decide to be on my way.

'We Greeks appreciate it,' he says finally. 'Although almost everyone speaks at least a little English.'

'Your English is very good. I'm Tania, by the way.'

'Nice to meet you,' he says, before looking out across the valley once more.

'See you then.' This guy is clearly not in the mood for a chat.

'Forgive me, I am Nicos,' he introduces himself, and gives a smile that transforms his extremely handsome face. 'Are you here on holiday?' he asks.

'I am staying at the dog rescue with my aunt.'

'Ah, the dog rescue?' He nods. 'So, Judith is your aunt?'

'She is. Do you know her?'

'Not really. I have only recently arrived back in the village, but we have said hello in passing.'

'She works hard. Too hard, really. We could always use some help with the dog walking, if you ever fancy it,' I suggest.

'Maybe I will do just that,' he says, surprising me.

'That would be great. We always need help. There are currently thirty-two dogs, not to mention five donkeys, so it's pretty busy. Some of the dogs are being rehomed tomorrow, though.'

Four dogs are going to live with some ex-pats who are travelling from a nearby village, two English families and a French couple. Hopefully it will be their forever home. It's always a joy as, even though Judith misses them, she knows it's better for the dogs. There's an old boy who has been with the rescue for two years, older dogs sometimes being a little harder to rehome.

Nicos tells me he has just moved into a house across the road from the dog rescue. 'I have inherited the family home after my parents died. I was going to sell it when I realised how much land it has. Far too much for a man on his own,' he reveals.

'I'm sorry to hear about your parents. How long have you been here?' I ask.

'Just over a month. I can't seem to tear myself away from it.' He smiles that gorgeous smile once more.

'Well, it's certainly beautiful around here, that's for sure.' I return his smile.

'The internet can be a little tricky sometimes. If it wasn't, then I suppose it would be perfect. And nothing in life is,' he says, with a faraway look in his eyes. 'Well, it was good to meet you, Tania.' He stands, ready to leave.

'How do you say that in Greek?' I ask.

'*Goitevmenos*. Although that does not exactly mean "pleased to meet you",' he adds. 'At least, not the whole sentence,' he explains. '*Goitevmenos* means "charmed".'

He walks off, and I practise the word repeatedly. *Goitevmenos*. I was charmed by you too, Nicos, I think to myself as I stroll on.

When I arrive back at the rescue, my aunt is in her small office, a desk fan beside her as she works. Each of the bedrooms have ceiling fans that do help a little, but air conditioning throughout would be very expensive to install. Thankfully, there is air con in the large kitchen, though, where we often gather for some respite. And, of course, there is the swimming pool to cool off in, as well as the lakes and Greek sea not too far away.

'Good morning, Tania,' she greets me. 'How are you today?'

'I'm good, thanks. I've just been for an early morning walk. I met your neighbour, Nicos.'

'Nicos, is it? I haven't actually met him yet. At least, not formally, just said hello in passing. I've noticed him once or twice over the years, visiting his parents. I wondered if the place was occupied now. The elderly man passed away a couple of months ago, a year after the death of his wife.'

'Yes, he told me it was his parents' place. He's inherited it.'

'He told you that?' She smiles knowingly. 'It would appear you had quite the chat. He's barely said a handful of words on the odd occasion I have seen him in the village,' she reveals.

'Only for a few minutes. He also told me the Greek word for heatwave. It's *kafsonas*,' I say, feeling proud that I have remembered it.

'No sign of it abating anytime soon either,' she tells me, as she takes a sip of water from a bottle on her desk. 'This is the hottest spell we have had in a long time.'

I don't tell my aunt that as I was walking back I noticed a water helicopter heading off to a fire somewhere, hopefully in the far distance. After googling local news, I saw that the fire was indeed quite a distance away and now under control. Even so, I know the thought of extreme heat and fires would only unsettle Judith.

'So what's he like then?' she asks, getting back to my meeting with Nicos.

'Tall, dark, good-looking. Gosh, he sounds like a cliché, doesn't he? Handsome, brooding even.' I laugh.

'He sounds wonderful. And you certainly seem to have brought him out of his shell. Maybe we should invite him over for supper some time. Does he like dogs?'

'He does, actually. In fact, he even offered to walk them.'

'He did? Well, that's even better. Perfect, in fact. Maybe he could come for Sunday lunch, if you would like to ask him? You could do your delicious casserole again. Everyone raved about it last time,' she says kindly. 'Anyway, back to the present. Tomorrow is the day you shake your tins at the tourists down at the harbour and do some fundraising.'

'Is it, oh right.' I can't disguise the lack of enthusiasm in my voice.

'Oh, come on, Tania. I know it's not your favourite thing to do but the centre runs on charitable donations, remember, and we are running a little low on funds.' She smiles, noting my expression.

I know that a fair chunk of Judith's personal income has been ploughed into the rescue, including some of the payout from Uncle Ray's life insurance. I know that my mum has gently advised Judith in the past that she ought to save enough for her old age and maybe wind the rescue down, but I know that she would never consider doing so. Even so, charitable donations are essential to keep things ticking over.

'I don't mind really.' I smile brightly. Although in truth, I do feel it is a little like begging, without offering people something in return.

'The local restaurant owners are on board now too, so raffle tickets will be sold to win a meal in exchange for a donation,' she tells me, as if reading my thoughts. 'There's also a shopping voucher up for grabs to spend at a local shopping mall, where the stallholders have all chipped in.'

'Really? That's brilliant! I feel much more comfortable selling tickets to raise funds if there is a prize to be won.'

'I know. I never liked to ask the businesspeople to offer support, as times can be hard enough for them as it is, especially out of season, but Vasilis said one free meal is nothing, in return for the business it might drive if they post a favourable review on TripAdvisor.'

'That's a great idea,' I tell her, feeling far more comfort-able flogging raffle tickets rather than just asking for donations. And I can vouch for the food at Vasilis's taverna; it's amazing.

Vasilis and his wife are old in years now, but still proudly run their restaurant on the waterfront, along with their grown-up children. It serves up the most delicious food and I loved eating there when I was here last year.

He has donated a voucher for a family meal for up to six people, which is very generous of Vasilis. I think families will enjoy having the chance to win a free family meal, especially with the beautiful sea views.

'Oh, and the vet will be arriving today to do a check-up and microchip a few of the new dogs, so that will eat into the bank balance. Let's hope people are generous tomorrow.'

Two couples holidaying in the area have just arrived to walk the dogs as we walk out into the sunshine.

'*Kalimera*,' says one of the women, around my age, who is with her partner. They are accompanied by a middle-aged couple, who the chatty younger woman informs me are her parents.

'I know you're English,' she says with a laugh, 'but I want to keep practising Greek, even if it is only "good morning" and "good evening".'

'I know what you mean. It isn't the easiest language to learn. I'm slowly trying to master a little of it too,' I tell her.

The four visitors take two dogs each, making a real fuss of them. Annie and Smudge are desperately bounding around in the hope of joining them.

'Ah, just look at these two,' the young woman says with a smile. 'Can we take them along too?'

'Maybe another time, and I'd suggest just take the two of them as... let's just say, they are both very energetic.'

'Okay. I'll look forward to it.'

She bends down to the dogs and they cover her in kisses, as her smiling husband looks on.

Wes, Lars and Chloe take the rest of the pack, expertly walking several on a leash at once. I decide to take Smudge and Annie, which is quite enough.

'We'll probably be down near the dog park later,' Wes tells me as they head off first.

'Right, see you there.' I top up my water bottle and get the dogs ready. Most of the time, we end up near a river or stream, so that the dogs can have a splash around and cool off. Occasionally, we bundle a few of the more energetic dogs into the old beaten-up truck and drive down to the beach, although it has been known to be quite eventful. It didn't take us long to realise that the dogs need secluded, even remote beaches, after Smudge made off with a family picnic at a beach not far from Malia.

Ten minutes later, I make my way along the leafy lane and turn left towards the handsome pale-pink painted house with the dark wooden window frames that has been inherited by Nicos. The houses dotted about the hamlet are painted in pastel shades and my aunt often refers to them simply as the yellow house, or the green house and so on.

I stop for a second and look at the beautiful home that has a terrace, draped in wildly overgrown pink and white flowers, along with withered plants in terracotta pots that give a clue to it being unoccupied for a while. At the end of the vast gardens, there is what looks like an empty stable block. There is no sign of Nicos, who I thought might be around, and I surprise myself by feeling a little disappointed that he is nowhere to be seen.

The dogs are walking obediently today in the heat. Instead of straining at the lead, they are padding along without trying to leap off into the bushes, which I'm grateful for. For a second, I find myself worrying about the young couple, as my aunt told me that Smudge leapt so high after a butterfly last year that he fell and injured his leg. Despite having insurance, the increase in premiums after such unexpected incidences can be costly.

Before we join the others, we stop at a clearing where I can see the stretch of sea down at Hersonissos. I can just make out a red and white ferry in the distance, taking tourists to another island; people are bobbing up and down swimming, and look like tiny ants as the sun shines on the turquoise sea. My dogs head to a small section of stream and lap the cooling water. The only sound, apart from the gentle rushing of the water, is the sound of birdsong from high in a tree somewhere nearby. I take a deep breath and inhale, connecting with my surroundings. Even though I come from a village back home, it's still a world away from here.

Suddenly, someone emerges from the bushes, and I jump slightly. Smudge stands next to me and gives a low growl. To my surprise it's Nicos.

'Hi, Nicos.' I'm delighted to see him stood in front of me.

'*Kalimera*, Tania. Sorry if I made you jump.' He smiles. 'I was taking a shortcut, away from the main road. I have been to collect some honey from a friend,' he explains, lifting a hessian bag. 'Thyme mountain honey.' He removes his sunglasses and places them on the top of his head.

'Thyme honey? I don't think I've ever tried that.'

'It's quite delicious. Or at least, I think so. And good for the immune system too, apparently,' he informs me.

'I should probably take some of that back to the UK then. It will be cold and flu season when I return home,' I inform him, although where to exactly I'm not entirely sure, but I don't suppose I can stay here forever. And I do have that offer of a room at Angie's place.

'Would you like to try some?' He reaches into his bag and produces a small pot of honey and hands it to me.

'Thank you, that's very kind. Does it actually taste of thyme? It seems like an unusual flavour.'

'Not really. Obviously, the pollen is from thyme, which gives it a strong, distinctive flavour.'

'Did you say your friend keeps bees?'

'Yes. He runs a small honey farm with a shop. It is worth a visit if you like honey. They sell lots of honey beauty products too. He has hundreds of hives dotted around the island.'

'That sounds interesting. Where is it?' I glance around unable to spot a single house in the direction he has just walked from.

'On the main road, towards Koutouloufari.'

'You walked what must be about...' I calculate in my head. 'You walked five miles, in this heat?'

'Six miles, to be precise. I think maybe I need the exercise.' He pats his stomach, which looks perfectly flat to me. I feel reluctant to move on, happy to stand here in front of Nicos, chatting to him, but I have the dogs to think about. Smudge has decided that Nicos isn't the enemy after all, and has already made several attempts to leap up at him.

'He's trying to hug you,' I explain. 'It's just what he does. He's a big softie.'

'Hug me?' Nicos can't help smiling.

'I'm afraid so.' We have tried to dissuade Smudge from doing this, especially to children who could literally be floored with affection.

'If I walk the dogs, I will maybe take this one.' He strokes Annie. 'Would you like that?' he asks and she wags her tail appreciatively, lapping up the attention.

'You can take Scooby-Doo,' he says as he walks off, leaving me with a smile on my face. So, he thinks that we might walk the dogs together? I can hardly wait.

'Actually, before you go,' I call after him. 'My aunt wondered if you might like to come over for Sunday lunch. She's thinking she ought to get to know her neighbours a little more.'

It feels like an age before he answers.

'That sounds good, thank you. What time?'

'Um, I'd say around four? Although maybe arrive for three thirty, for a drink.'

'Sunday it is then. See you soon, Tania.' I like the way he says my name...

I give my head a little shake. What on earth is happening? I've only seen this man twice, but he seems to have got under my skin already. As I head off to meet up with the others, I find myself giving him a lingering backward glance. To my slight disappointment, he doesn't do the same.

ELEVEN

I wander off, a little lost in my thoughts after my encounter with Nicos. It's clear he is a dog lover, and the dogs in turn seemed happy to be close to him. I've learned over the years that dogs can be very good judges of character. I also think of how handsome he looked; even dressed casually in long shorts and a T-shirt, he exudes a charisma I find extremely attractive.

There's an open field in the forest, flanked by hills that we discovered quite by chance. Apparently, someone once purchased the land intending to build on it, but nothing transpired. Years passed, and the land was never claimed, so these days it has become a kind of unofficial park, frequented mainly by dog walkers and their pooches. It's a real suntrap here, and somewhere I always enjoy spending time, especially with its gorgeous view down across the valley towards the sea. Sometimes, hillwalkers pass through the clearing and, over a little chat, they learn about the dog sanctuary, sometimes even offering a small monetary donation. Over time, tyres and wooden structures have been assembled at the site, much to the delight of the local dogs.

'Right, off you go.' I let the dogs off the leash and they go crazy, running around with fallen tree branches. A tiny terrier tries to pick up a huge log and has us all laughing. 'You have to give it to the little guy; he has spirit, hey,' I comment.

'Indeed. On the inside he's a lion,' says Lars, who I have strolled over to and started a conversation with. Chloe and Wes are throwing a ball to one of the dogs to retrieve and it races off after it. I still think they would make an attractive couple and can't help wondering why Wes doesn't seem to notice her.

'Talking of lions, where on earth do you get your energy?' I ask Lars. I'd already noticed him out jogging this morning, from my balcony, as dawn broke.

Lars tells me all about his army years, and his lifelong love of running. He tells me how he travelled the world as a runner, competing in several marathons and vowed to keep himself in shape as the years advanced.

'I've always loved the great outdoors,' he tells me. 'I find it very cathartic. Running up a mountain, with nothing but nature all around, can be very healing,' he reveals, and I can't help wondering what he is healing from.

I find him interesting company and recall Chloe practically rolling her eyes as she told me she had heard his story many times. Well, it's the first time he has told me anything about his life, and only because I asked.

We're chatting easily, when suddenly there's a loud scream. Smudge has leapt on Chloe, and flattened her, after she absent-mindedly picked up his ball. Liz is stood nearby, covering her mouth with her hand, trying to stifle her laughter. Wes helps Chloe to her feet and I notice her white shorts are streaked with soil as she brushes away some leaves.

'That thing is out of control,' she says a little snappily, which is unusual for Chloe as she is usually so patient with the animals. Poor Smudge. Whoever rehomes him will need the patience of a saint or energy to match his.

'Those two are in the wrong bodies,' Lars says with a laugh, pointing to our largest and smallest dogs. 'Smudge still thinks he's a puppy, and the little fella thinks he's a beast.' He nods at the small terrier, who is still wrestling with a log.

When the dogs have had their fill of exercise and the sun begins to burn brighter, we all start heading back to the rescue.

Turning a corner, we pass the pale-pink house once more and I see Nicos walking across the garden, carrying a garden hose. He's bare-chested and wearing denim shorts and sunglasses; his dark hair is stylishly cut and styled. I find myself staring over at him, when suddenly he turns and catches my eye, before waving. I can feel my cheeks tingling and a smile spreading across my face as we pass the front door.

'You should get more sun factor on your cheeks,' Wes teases. 'They seem to have turned a little red.'

Back at the rescue, the two pairs of volunteers tell us they have really enjoyed themselves and would like to arrange another day helping out before they head home. Chloe asks if anyone fancies going for a drink to support the local bar. It's a ten-minute walk, slightly uphill at the foot of the church, but the thought of an ice-cold beer appeals, so Wes and I agree to join her.

Wandering the quiet roads, we hear birds chirping in the trees and the occasional drone of a bike on the mountain roads. Tourists often come up this way on quad bikes to visit, some to the church, others climbing higher to the monastery that reaches towards the sky. Walking a quiet stretch of road, the sun scorches down and I can hear the unmistakeable sound of cicadas chirruping in the trees.

'I don't think I will ever tire of that sound.' I sigh as I walk along, taking in my surroundings.

'I know what you mean. It's so different from the sound of buses and traffic on the main road outside my flat,' says Chloe.

The bar, a simple dark wooden structure with tables and chairs outside, some made from pallets and painted pale blue, is fairly busy with tourists when we arrive, sipping frappes and cold beers.

'*Kalimera.*' The smiling bar owner greets us as we take a seat. The bar offers snacks, and the smell of village sausage and halloumi grilling on the BBQ has Chloe saying she is starved and shall we have some food?

'Not for me,' says Wes. 'I'll save myself for dinner later.'

Chloe orders a grilled haloumi salad and I succumb to a few fries. 'Perhaps I'll walk up to the church after this,' I decide, popping a chip into my mouth.

'All those steps in this heat?' Chloe pulls a face.

'I'll take it slowly.'

After eating, I leave Wes and Chloe chatting below and make my way up the stairs to the church, recalling the view at the top across the valley is really something. At the foot of the steps is an ancient olive remembrance tree that is tied with coloured ribbons in memory of loved ones. Some bright and new, others old and faded, an everlasting memory to a life once lived. Some even have pictures of loved ones and I always find it a very touching sight.

I ascend the steps, stopping every now and then to take in the view below: pine forests stretching out to meet the sea are dotted with terracotta roofed houses. Chloe catches my eye and waves. When I eventually reach the top, I step onto a large stone veranda in front of the traditional white church, and gasp at the view below, which is every bit as breathtaking as I remember.

Green forest gives way to white villages and mountains that seem to soar towards the sky. I spend ten minutes taking it all in, before I enter the tiny, but beautiful, chapel that has several paintings of the Virgin Mary and two rows of dark wooden pews. At the front of the chapel is a small altar that sits in front of a stained-glass window, the sunlight streaming through and flooding the tiny church with colour. I light a candle for my uncle Ray before I make the descent below, to where Chloe and Wes are stood at the foot of the steps ready to leave.

'Did you enjoy that?' asks Chloe.

'Do you know, I really did. The climb is worth it for the view.'

'It is, but I walked up last week so I didn't feel the need today.' Chloe smiles. Wes confesses that he isn't really one for visiting churches, and maybe it's because he was reluctantly dragged to church every Sunday as a child by his parents.

We saunter leisurely back downhill to the rescue and I feel happy to be here with my new friends. Summer days surely don't get any better than this.

TWELVE

'Does anyone fancy a boat trip tomorrow?'

Wes is scrolling through his phone as we are eating breakfast before we head to the harbour to do some fundraising.

'A boat trip? Where too?' I ask Wes with interest, as I love a boat trip. I remember lots of happy times, heading off somewhere and having fun on the water, both here and at home – although the weekend with my ex in the Lake District doesn't evoke such pleasant memories. Mucking about on a canoe on Lake Windermere, I had no idea he was about to end things, when we spent that last weekend holed up in a cosy stone cottage at the edge of the lake.

'A little uninhabited island,' says Wes as he reads. 'Which is probably a deserted beach really, but hey. It leaves from the harbour at Hersonissos.'

'That sounds rather nice. I like the idea of a beach without the tourist crowds,' I say.

'Well, it says here that there is literally nothing there but the sand and the sea. It might be nice to just swim and chill.'

'Are there no facilities at all on the beach?' Chloe looks horrified. 'Not even a toilet?'

'I'm sure there will be a toilet on the boat. If not, you can always top up the water in the sea.' He grins and she tells him not to be disgusting.

'Maybe I'll come along.' She shrugs. 'But it's a shame there won't be a nice beach bar to enjoy a cocktail.'

'I'm in,' I tell Wes. 'It sounds nice to get away from everything for a few hours. We could pack a picnic. Judith, you have cooler bags, don't you?' I ask, turning to my aunt.

'I do indeed. I don't think I'll be joining you, though,' she tells me. 'I think my days of diving off boats into the sea are over,' she says, a little wistfully.

'You don't have to dive off the boat,' says Wes, but I think her mind is made up.

'You don't mind us all going?' I ask Judith, mindful that there are usually a couple of us at the rescue at any one time. 'We will make sure any chores are done first.'

'Of course I don't mind. Nobody works twenty-four hours a day. As long we are on top of things, it's fine.'

'I won't be going either,' says Lars. 'I'll stay here with Judith and keep an eye on things. There's a new restaurant up the hill near the monastery. I might take a walk up later and check it out.'

He glances at Judith, and I get the impression she would jump at the chance of going with him, if they were to take the car. Lars then suggests maybe driving to the mountain restaurant together, and leaving his walk to the monastery for another day and Judith tells him she would like that very much.

'Well, I'm definitely up for that,' says Liz, getting back to the boat trip. 'I love secluded beaches. Then again, I suppose it depends on how many people are on the trip. It won't be that quiet if there's a ton of us descending from the boat onto the beach.'

'True enough. Even so, it might be nice to discover something completely wild and natural,' says Wes. 'A bit like you,' he says cheekily to Liz, who is sat next to him, and she thumps him playfully on the arm, under the watchful eye of Chloe.

'Shall I book us on then?' Wes asks. 'It's a bargain price. And loading a picnic up will save money. Sorry to ask, but can you all transfer me the money? I don't have too much in my account at the moment,' he admits. 'There's an optional mystery excursion when on board for a few more euros too, apparently.'

'Sounds interesting. Okay, count me in,' says Liz.

'I guess I'll come too. I don't want to be hanging around here on my own with the oldies,' whispers Chloe, not before Judith hears her and raises an eyebrow. 'I mean, without you guys.' She smiles sweetly at the rest of us.

'Sorted. We'll have to be up super early that morning to sort the animals first. The boat leaves Heraklion at ten. If that's okay, Judith?' I ask my aunt.

'Of course it is.' She smiles. 'As long as the jobs are done and the animals given their first feed, you young ones go off and enjoy yourselves. As long as you bring plenty of donations home today, that is.' She winks.

'Great, thanks, Judith.'

I wave the pretty fan, the gift from Kerry, in front of my face. Even beneath the trees and sipping ice-cold drinks at this early hour we are almost melting in the heat.

Chloe pulls a face when she holds up the shapeless, bright yellow T-shirts emblazoned with the Pine Forest Recue logo, and a silhouette of a dog in the corner.

'Do we have to wear these?' She pouts.

'It's not a fashion show,' says Liz.

'I know that, but I don't think I've ever worn anything so unflattering.' Chloe pulls a face.

'Well, we will certainly attract attention,' I say positively. 'And it's all about raising funds for the rescue,' I remind everyone, although Liz and Wes don't appear to have any problem wearing the uniform.

The harbour is soon busy with tourists and Wes smiles his most charming of smiles and flogs a load of raffle tickets to a trio of middle-aged women wearing floral dresses and large sunhats. There is an afternoon in a hammam spa up for grabs as well, along with a free beauty treatment.

'Not that you ladies need any beauty treatments,' he says and they look suitably flattered.

Liz puts her fingers down her throat and asks me to pass her the sick bucket, which makes me laugh.

'Oh, and talking of beauty treatments, have any of you helped yourself to my expensive conditioner?' asks Chloe. 'I left it in the bathroom and it's half gone now. It costs twenty pounds a bottle.'

'How much? You must have more money than sense.' Liz shakes her head.

'It was a present, actually. I can't afford to pay those prices. Well, not these days anyway,' she adds.

We all tell Chloe we know nothing about the disappearing conditioner but I'm sure Liz is suppressing a smile.

The sun is beaming down from a cloudless sky, and even at this early hour, it's clear the high temperatures are continuing here in Crete. We're thankful for the gazebo that has been erected, along with a couple of camping chairs on the harbour front to give a little shade.

As well as the beauty treatment and restaurant vouchers up for grabs, there's a tombola on a table, with dozens of toy dogs for prizes. The children are very attracted by these and business is brisk, the children smiling when they pick a winner and select a dog toy. Even the non-winners are given a little pencil and a sticker. Wes takes a bucket and walks along the harbour a little way, rattling it and smiling broadly, which pays dividends, especially with the groups of young women on girls' holidays.

Three hours later, having taken it in turns to take breaks for a drink or an ice cream in the shade, we've sold every single raffle ticket and the donation tin is filled to the brim with money. It's been a hugely successful morning.

We are about to pack up when a yacht glides into the harbour and Chloe lowers her sunglasses to take a better look, as a handsome man around forty years old, with sun-streaked hair, appears on deck.

'Hi there, are you collecting for the dogs?' he asks, in what sounds like a French accent.

'We certainly are.' Liz beams, but Chloe pushes in front of her.

'We're about to pack up. Are you interested in donating something? It's for the Pine Forest Dog Rescue in the hills.' She twirls a strand of blonde hair around her finger and points up into the distance.

'Of course. I have three very spoilt dogs at home. They are very fortunate.' He smiles a mega-watt smile. 'I would like to help with the sanctuary. Would you take a cheque?'

He's deeply tanned and dressed stylishly in dark shorts and a crisp white shirt, an expensive watch on his wrist.

'You could pay us in pennies if you like, it all gets banked,' I say cheerfully.

The handsome man heads into his yacht for a moment, before returning with a cheque, which he folds in half and slides into the collecting tin.

'Thank you, my aunt will be thrilled with our fundraising efforts today,' I tell him gratefully, already wondering how much he has donated.

'Did you say you were just finishing up?' He looks directly at Chloe, before asking her if he can buy her a drink somewhere and she doesn't need asking twice. It's not too surprising, as she was clearly keen, and looks good in tiny shorts that show off her endless tanned legs, and has tied the loose T-shirt into a knot, revealing an inch of her toned stomach.

As they disappear together, Chloe saying she will take a taxi back later, I open the tin and take out the folded cheque. I'm astonished to find that the generous stranger has donated a thousand pounds to the dog rescue!

THIRTEEN

'I can hardly believe it.'

We've thrown the pop-up gazebo and camping chairs into the old truck and are sat in a café near the waterfront, gulping down cooling beers.

'I can't believe that guy actually donated a thousand pounds. He must be real a dog lover,' I say, hardly able to take it in.

'He must be loaded, more like.' Wes takes a sip of his beer.

'I know! Judging by the size of his yacht, he's definitely not short of a quid or two,' I reply.

'I bet the size of his yacht isn't the only thing Chloe is interested in.' Liz giggles.

'What an absolutely brilliant day. A thousand pounds, and that's not including what's in the tin that's stuffed with coins and notes,' I say, delighted by the generosity of the public today. The tin is in my bag beside me, firmly zipped up.

'I reckon there's at least four hundred euros in there,' says Wes. 'We sold two hundred euros' worth of tickets and some people were just dropping money into the tin as they walked past.'

. . .

It's just after four thirty when we return to the rescue; the sun is still so hot but we have work to do, feeding and cleaning. Lars has been busy these last two days building a large canopy as an extra shaded area for the donkeys. It's erected in the middle of the enclosure, complete with a water trough and straw-bale feeder. My aunt thought it might encourage the animals to do at least a little walking, rather than staying in their stables. It seems this weather is even too hot for worn-out donkeys.

'You're back! How did it go today?' my aunt greets us outside as soon as we are out of the pickup truck. 'Oh, and there's some fresh lemonade in the fridge,' she informs us.

Passing the donkey enclosure, I'm surprised to see Nicos talking to Lars, and also surprised to feel my pulse rate quicken. Especially as he is wearing denim shorts and no shirt again.

'You've met Nicos then?'

'I have indeed. He came over earlier to introduce himself properly and ended up helping Lars with the shelter for the donkeys. He seems really lovely,' says Judith as we stroll towards the kitchen with her.

'Tania thinks so, don't you?' teases Wes.

'How old are you exactly?' I roll my eyes at him.

At that moment Nicos finishes his conversation and heads over to join us. Please Lord don't let me blush.

'*Kalispera*. How did the fundraising go?' he asks me. 'Your aunt was telling me all about it.'

'I can't begin to tell you how wonderful it was. People were so generous today, especially one person in particular. We're about to count up and grab a drink, if you would like to join us,' I offer.

'Thank you.' He gives me a look that has those butterflies dancing in my stomach again.

Inside the kitchen, I place the money tin down onto the

long table. 'Feel the weight of that,' I say to Judith, whose eyes widen when she picks it up.

Over glasses of cooling, iced lemonade, we count out the takings for the day.

'Just over sixteen hundred euros including the cheque, I can hardly believe it.' My aunt claps her hands together in delight. 'I think that is worthy of some sort of celebration. And in anticipation of a good day's fundraising, I've put some champagne on ice to have with this evening's dinner. Where's Chloe?' she asks, suddenly realising she hasn't returned with us.

'She's out with the generous guy who donated the cheque. She said she will take a taxi back later,' I tell her.

'Well, I'll make sure to save her some champagne,' says Judith. 'Although it sounds like she might just be enjoying some of her own.'

'You could be right there.' I smile, and why not?

'I must be leaving now,' says Nicos, a short while later. 'Thank you for the lemonade. It was good to meet you today, all of you.' Nicos casts his eyes around the group and smiles.

'I must thank you for your help,' says Lars. 'We made short work of that shelter working together. It would have taken me days to do it alone in this heat.'

'It was my pleasure. Although maybe now I will have a siesta before I head out this evening.' I picture Nicos spread out on his bed, beneath crisp white sheets as a ceiling fan whirrs above him, before quickly pushing the thoughts away. What on earth is happening to me?

When Nicos leaves, I tell Judith all about the people we met today, and how Wes charmed the older ladies and she smiles and says she can easily believe that. The others go and check on the dogs before they head up to shower and change and I linger in the kitchen for a moment, looking through the window and watching Nicos walk back to his house. I also find myself wondering where he is going this evening, and who with.

. . .

We sit quietly outside in the evening, thankful for a very slight breeze. Chloe returns and asks Judith if she can have a word with her in the kitchen. A short while later, Judith returns alone.

'Where's Chloe?' I ask.

'She'll be down shortly. She's gone to pack. She's leaving us tomorrow.'

'Leaving?' Although if I'm honest, I'm not completely surprised.

'She is. I expect she will fill you all in shortly. We should manage, as we have a new starter next week and some of the dogs have been rehomed.'

'Wow, the French guy must have really impressed her with those meatballs,' says Liz, grinning.

'Pardon.' My aunt laughs.

'*Keftedes*. Greek meatballs. I heard him talking to her about some place down a side street that sells the best ones apparently. How could a girl resist?' She giggles. 'I'll miss her, though,' says Liz, taking a sip of wine.

'You will?' Wes looks a little doubtful.

'Yeah, she's alright really, a bit like an annoying big sister. I'll have no one to spar with now.' She grins wickedly.

'Would you nick your big sister's expensive conditioner too then?' teases Wes.

'I swear that was not me,' Liz insists.

'Well, it was not me.' Lars runs a hand over his bald, tanned head and makes us laugh, the only hair on his head being a well-trimmed grey beard.

'Come to think of it, Wes, your hair is pretty sleek looking?' suggests Liz.

'Definitely not me.' He holds his hands up.

All eyes turn to me, and my long brown locks.

'Nope. I have to use an anti-frizz serum, when my hair is not tucked beneath a cap, that is.'

'So that only leaves...'

Everyone points at Judith and choruses, 'You,' and she laughs loudly.

'I think expensive beauty products would be wasted on me.'

'Nonsense. You have beautiful hair,' says Lars with open admiration. My aunt strokes her hair, which is long and loose tonight, and thanks him.

We're tucking into a meze this evening. There's soft pitta bread, stuffed vine leaves, hummus and a selection of meats and grilled halloumi on the table. Huge baked jacket potatoes are wrapped in foil and crisp white wine is sat cooling in an ice bucket.

'Does it seem a bit cooler this evening? It's the first night I haven't had to use my fan,' I remark, as I take a bite of some salty halloumi.

'A little bit, yes. But, apparently, we have a few more days of this heatwave to come,' my aunt tells me.

Later, over the washing up with Chloe, I ask her why she is leaving early, although I think I know the answer.

'I was due to leave next week anyway, and as someone else is arriving then, Judith has let me leave early,' she explains as we load the dishwasher together. 'Phillipe has asked me to go sailing around the Med with him, and I thought, why the hell not? Life's too short, isn't it?'

'He isn't married then?' I find myself asking. 'I recall him saying he had three dogs at home, and wondered if it was a family home he was referring to.'

'I don't think so.' She frowns. 'What wife would put up with her husband going off sailing for a month without her? Although maybe they lead their own lives.'

She's quiet for a minute as she mulls it over. 'If nothing else, I'll have a great time sailing around the Greek islands. I certainly have nothing to rush home to in England,' she lets slip. 'I lost the rental on my flat as the landlord wanted to sell up. Trying to get another rental around London is a total nightmare.'

'Sorry to hear that. What did you do for work in London? I don't think you've ever mentioned it.'

I recall the odd time around the pool when we had discussed our lives back home, and Chloe was always a little evasive.

'I was a fashion model,' she tells me, which, given her looks, doesn't surprise me at all.

'My folks have a large house, so last resort I can always move back in with them. I think my dad would approve. He's always worried about me,' she confides.

'I suppose that's what parents do,' I say, even though my parents never looked back when they moved to Spain.

'I guess so. I knew how to look after myself but I did come across some unsavoury characters when I was modelling. My dad was probably right to worry at times, but I never told him that.' She smiles.

'It's not hard to imagine you being a model, you're gorgeous. Do you think you might do some more modelling in the future?'

'Thanks, but it's very doubtful. And it's a relief to be able to eat food again, if I'm honest. I used to be half the size I am now. You don't work if you get bigger, it's that simple. Besides, I'm too old now. There are always kids right behind you waiting for a chance.' She shrugs. 'It's a short career, unless you are a world-famous supermodel, of course.'

'It's good to know you have that safety net of going home, though.'

'It is, but I'd rather not at my age. It's hard when you've been used to your freedom. Anyway, we leave for Kos tomorrow. I guess I'll find out at the end of the journey what the future holds for me,' she says. 'I'll stay in touch.'

'Please do, and I hope things work out for you, Chloe, I really do,' I tell her, and mean it. I hope they both get their happy ever after; after all, isn't that what we all want?

'Thanks, Tania. I wish I was a bit more like you, you seem so together. And you always give the best advice.' She touches my arm.

'If only you knew,' I tell her.

When she goes to bed, I think about her comment. So, I appear to have all the answers? Maybe it's easier to be objective when looking in on other people's lives. It's surprising how someone can appear so outwardly confident and practical, whilst silently having no clue about the direction in which their own life is heading.

FOURTEEN

The next morning, we have just finished a breakfast of yoghurt, fruit and honey and I notice that Chloe keeps glancing at her watch. She's wearing a short, blue cotton dress, her blonde hair loosely falling over her tanned skin and, wearing just a slick of lip gloss, she looks naturally beautiful.

'I can't believe you are going off sailing on that yacht,' says Liz, grabbing a final slice of melon from the breakfast table before we head outside. 'The size of it! In fact, do you need any cabin crew?' She laughs.

'You're okay, thanks, he already has some.' Chloe grins. 'That's if he hasn't changed his mind. He's ten minutes late.' She looks at her watch once more.

'You're kidding, he'd be mad to leave you behind,' says Liz kindly. 'I don't think you have anything to worry about.'

Just then a car arrives, followed by the sound of Judith chatting as she appears with Phillipe. Chloe's face breaks into a huge smile, as Phillipe kisses her on both cheeks.

We all stand and chat for a while, before Phillipe takes Chloe's case to load into his car.

'Please stay in touch,' says Judith. 'And thank you for your hard work.'

'Thank you, and thanks for letting me sneak off a bit earlier than planned.' Chloe squeezes my aunt in a hug.

'Bye then, Chloe. I'm not jealous at all.' Liz grins as she gives Chloe a lingering hug before she departs.

'You shouldn't be jealous of anyone,' Chloe tells her. 'You have everything going for you. If anything, I should be jealous of you.'

'Thanks.' Liz looks a little surprised by her comment.

The handsome Phillipe loads Chloe's suitcase into his silver Jaguar and Judith thanks him earnestly for the generous donation to the sanctuary.

'I was happy to contribute. I love dogs,' he says in his seductive French accent. He smiles a broad smile and places his arm around Chloe, who looks as if she just might burst with happiness.

We all stand and wave until Phillipe's car disappears around a bend.

'I told you,' says Judith later as we are in the donkey pens. 'Love really can appear in the most unexpected of ways. Who would have thought Chloe would meet someone, and a wealthy yacht owner at that, whilst fundraising down at the harbour.' She shakes her head as she refills a water trough. Eric has sauntered over, two brown donkeys trailing behind him.

'I know. And to think she didn't even want to wear the T-shirt.' Liz laughs. 'Although she did customise it a little.'

'I hope Chloe will be okay,' I say. 'I think I'd be too cautious just going off with a bloke I barely know.'

'I know where she is at all times, so don't worry,' says Liz.

'You do?'

'Yep, she let me put a tracker on her phone. She said if she gets bunged in a car boot or something we can find her.'

'Oh my goodness, perish the thought.' I give a little shudder. 'And what if the phone battery runs out?'

'Ever the practical one, aren't you? I actually never thought of that, but I told her to ring me or text regularly so at least we would have her last location.'

'You two surprise me,' I tell Liz. 'I thought you and Chloe were arch enemies at first, but it seems you really do care about each other.' I laugh and she shrugs.

'I know. I was surprised when she said she ought to be jealous of me, who'd have thought it? She's okay really, and a hard worker, I'll give her that. A bit up her own arse sometimes, but no one is perfect, I guess.'

'You're right there,' I agree.

'And she did give me some of her make-up and half a bottle of that good conditioner before she left,' Liz reveals.

'She might as well have, as you'd already used the other half,' teases Wes and once more Liz protests her innocence.

'Are we ready then? It seems it's just us three now,' says Wes, glancing at his watch. 'We need to be at the harbour by ten and it's just after nine already.'

'Ready,' I say, really looking forward to being out at sea, enjoying the cooling sea breeze.

'Well, have a wonderful day. I'll have something on the BBQ this evening when you return,' says Judith. 'Lars says he will pick up some steaks.'

'Now you're talking,' says Wes, rubbing his hands together. 'We should be back around five, I think.'

Driving down to the harbour in the old truck, I spot Nicos walking up the hill, and can't help wishing he was coming with us too, swimming in the turquoise sea. I can't help but think of him bare chested, strolling out of the water.

'So, what do you think then?'

'About what? Sorry, I was miles away there.'

'And I can guess who with,' Wes teases.

'Well, he is pretty fit,' says Liz, turning around and watching him walk down the lane towards his house. 'Who could blame you for being a bit smitten, although I personally don't go for the strong, silent type.'

'I am not smitten,' I say, a little too defensively. Gosh, am I? I do know that I haven't felt this attracted to someone in a long time. 'And strong and silent? I'm not sure that's true, I think maybe he just likes to get to know someone first, and I don't see anything wrong in that.'

'If you say so. Either way, he is seriously good-looking.' She grins.

I don't have time to dwell on that too much, as soon enough we are down at the harbour and approaching the boat to take our trip.

An older guy, with a weather-beaten face and wearing a white cap, introduces himself as Captain Zeus, which is also the name of the boat. A younger version of him, presumably his son, smiles as he takes our tickets and welcomes us on board.

'*Kalimera!* Welcome! We hope you have the best day. We take you where no other boats go,' Captain Zeus declares proudly. 'Only the best place for swimming. And also an optional excursion,' he says, which has all glancing at each other and wondering what it might be. 'Please,' he continues, stretching his arm out and gesturing upstairs, 'you pay for the seats upstairs.'

We immediately climb the white metal steps, hoping it will have the best view of the sea, happy that we are the first to arrive.

'My son will be up shortly to offer drinks from the bar when we set sail,' he tells us.

'This is the life, hey.' I glance at the brilliant blue sea, before I settle down onto a sunbed. I put my sunglasses on, and stretch out in my shorts and cropped top, feeling the sun caress my face. Liz and I lie side by side, and Wes stands at the side of the boat just staring out at the vast sea, lost in his thoughts. I have one eye open just watching him, wondering why he isn't his usual jaunty self. He was the one who booked this trip, after all, and was really looking forward to it.

A short while later, once everyone has arrived and we are out at sea, Zeus's son skips upstairs and takes our order for three cold beers. When he returns with the drinks, Wes joins us, seemingly having left his thoughts behind, and is laughing and joking as he sips his beer.

We sail past rocks and coves, and swathes of sea that changes seamlessly from shades of jade green to sapphire blue. A white church here and there, a coloured villa high in the hills. Soon enough, there is nothing but sea ahead of us, the hot sun beaming down and caressing our bodies as we stretch out on the sunbeds, and I soon start to feel incredibly relaxed.

'I'm glad we booked the good seats,' whispers Liz. The seating below is white plastic chairs, or padded seating along the side of the boat.

'Me too. This is wonderful.'

We sunbathe, sip our drinks and just glance out to sea, chatting with the other passengers on the top deck as we navigate the sparkling water. It feels so free here, without a care in the world and I suddenly envy Chloe having the courage to just sail off into the distance without a plan.

An hour passes and Captain Zeus tells he will drop anchor soon for some swimming. I spy a small sandy cove in the distance that looks like the perfect place for our picnic.

Climbing down the rope ladder into the crystal-clear water, I see fish dart about below the surface and wish I'd brought my snorkel and swimming goggles. Liz and Wes follow me into the water and Liz starts chatting to a bloke from the lower deck. After a few minutes they are swimming and laughing together like old friends.

'She sure has a way with blokes,' notes Wes.

'I think Liz has a great way with everyone. Her enthusiasm for life is infectious.' I smile as I flip onto my back and stare up at the vast blue sky. I think of our conversations and how vague she is and won't be drawn about her past much, just living for the moment. Apart from revealing that she once worked as a mermaid, that is, which still makes me chuckle when I think about it.

We swim in the clearest of waters, before climbing back onto the boat, refreshed and happy, having enjoyed a wonderful respite from the burning sun.

'I really enjoyed that.' Wes towels himself dry, his physique attracting admiring glances from a couple of women sat opposite him. 'I'm starved now, though.'

'Me too,' says Liz.

'Surprise, surprise.' I raise an eyebrow and Liz laughs.

When the boat stops at the small beach, Wes and I carry the cooler box onto the sand.

'I see you've thought of everything,' says Liz, when I pull a picnic blanket from my beach bag and set it down. 'And enough food to feed the whole beach.'

'That's not true.' I laugh. 'Although there is plenty of quiche. You can ask your new friend to join us if you like,' I offer. The tanned, dark-haired bloke is already striding out of the water towards us.

'Great.' She calls him over and introduces him as Frank. He's on holiday from England and decided to stay on for another few days when his friends went home.

'Bit impulsive really, but I just didn't feel like going back yet,' he tells us as he takes a bite of quiche. 'I still have some holiday left, so I thought, why not? I decided to reschedule my flight and I'm glad I did now.' He casts an admiring glance at Liz.

He tells us he works as an art teacher in a college, hence the long holidays. He has his dark hair in a man bun, a tattoo sleeve on his arm and I can't help thinking that he looks vaguely familiar.

'Where you in Hersonissos the other night, by any chance?' I ask him, recalling the dark-haired bloke who gave Liz the eye as he walked past.

'He was! What are the chances of that?' says Liz, before whispering to me, 'It must be fate.'

'I was indeed. And you ladies looked the other way, when my friends and I glanced over. My heart broke.' He places his hand on his chest. 'At least fate decided to step in. I thought I might not see you again.' He smiles. 'Yet here we are, me planning to go out for lunch tomorrow with the one that got away. Or so I hope.' He looks adoringly at Liz.

I wonder whether or not Liz is going to disappear with Frank, just as Chloe did with Phillipe, but then she tells him that she will be busy at the rescue tomorrow, having been out today.

'Maybe we could hire a jet ski down at the beach in the late afternoon, though,' she suggests. 'I don't want to take advantage of Judith's good nature. She's been very good to me,' she says loyally.

'That sounds like a great idea, and late afternoon is fine. Although I have to warn you, I'm not the best driver. Be prepared to get flung in the sea.' He grins and I can't help thinking he has literally just blown his macho image right out of the water.

'Can I come along and film that?' asks Wes and Liz slaps him on the arm.

Liz and Frank head off for a stroll towards a nearby rocky cove, Frank gently taking Liz's hand in his as they walk.

Wes polishes off some more of the picnic, and we sit in companionable silence for a while, just watching the gentle waves roll onto the soft golden sand. Captain Zeus and his son are sat on deck of the blue and white boat playing cards.

'Are you having a good time?' I ask Wes as I open a can of gin and tonic and pass one to him.

'Do you mean right now, or being here in Greece?'

'Both, I suppose?'

He regards me with his big brown eyes, his hair still looking stylish, even though he's been swimming.

'I'm having the best time today. In life? That's another matter.' He pulls the tab on his drink.

'Do you want to talk about it?'

'And spoil the day? No, thanks.'

'It wouldn't spoil the day. Well, not for me at least. Everyone needs a listening ear now and then. And I couldn't help noticing you looked a little preoccupied earlier,' I gently venture.

'You noticed then?' He takes a swig of his drink. 'Hmm, not bad. These canned drinks have improved a lot.'

'I always notice things about people. The little things tell you a lot.'

Maybe it comes from watching people in the surgery back home. The ones lost in thoughts, leaving with prescriptions for anti-depressants. The stressed-out mums with sick children. The anxious types who make weekly appointments with various aches and pains. The lonely people who need to get out of the house and chat to someone. You become tuned in. Sensitive to people's needs in a place like that.

'Well, I guess I'm figuring things out whilst I'm over here. I'm dreading the thought of going home, to tell you the truth.'

'Are you running away from something?'

I'm expecting him to back off, tell me to mind my own business.

'Not running away exactly... Well, actually, maybe I am,' he reconsiders. 'Because I can't face going home and disappointing my father yet again.' His jaw tightens slightly.

'Disappointing him?' I leave the comment hanging in

the air.

'I don't want to work in the family business anymore.' He takes a swig of his drink. 'My father owns a large timber yard that he built up from scratch before me and my brothers were born, it's worth quite a bit now. Probably a couple of million dollars.'

'And he expects you to work there?'

'Of course he does. We had no say in our own life. Well, up until now that is. I told him recently that I want out. I'm not interested in the business anymore. I'm not sure I ever was.'

'How did that go down?'

'Take a guess.' He sighs. 'He told me I was ungrateful, and wouldn't most kids kill to be part of a successful family business? But it doesn't interest me. Being surrounded by piles of logs doesn't exactly fill my heart with joy.'

'Is there something else you would rather be doing?' I ask him, feeling for Wes and the situation he finds himself in. My own parents didn't mind what I did for a living. In fact, a little more encouragement to find my place in life would not have gone amiss.

'Music is the thing I'm really interested in,' Wes reveals. 'I play the guitar and sing a bit.'

'Sounds good. Surely your father knows that?'

'I think he sees it as a hobby, nothing more. I had a place at music college and everything, but ended up working in the family business anyway. My father just marched us all along to work for him when we left school, without even having a conversation to find out what we were really interested in pursuing.'

'I can imagine that being tough, family loyalty, and all that. How do your brothers feel?'

'Ah well, that's the thing. It suited my elder brother. Living in a small town, married at nineteen to his first love, it was the security he needed to set him up for life. My other brother was a bit of a tearaway. He might have gone down the wrong path with some of the company he was keeping, so being part of the family business was a gift to him. I should have learned the lessons from those two to spread my wings a bit, but I lamely accepted a role working for my father.' He sighs.

'Oh, Wes, that's so hard for you. It's not too late to pursue your love of music, though, you're still young. Could you return to college? You're only, what, twenty-two?' I take a stab at his age.

'Twenty-three. And, yes, hopefully. I get some gigs at a hotel in a nearby town from time to time, which have been pretty well received. Who knows, one day I might even get talent spotted.' He grins.

'It worked for Ed Sheeran,' I remind him, and he smiles.

'Anyway. I've made up my mind,' he says firmly. 'When I get home, I'm telling my father I want to pursue my music career and get out of the family business. I sure as hell don't want to marry young and get tied into the business. Love is off the radar for me. At least for now.'

Maybe that's the reason he resisted Chloe's obvious beauty.

Just then, Captain Zeus sails the blue and white boat a bit closer to the beach, and waves us all over to board.

'Looks like it's time to move on,' I say, packing up the bags.

'Thanks, Tania,' says Wes. 'You really are a good listener.'

'Anytime. No one should carry a burden around with them. Just remember, though, it's your life. Whatever you do, I'm sure your father just wants you to be happy.'

His slightly forced smile tells me that he doesn't feel too confident about that. It makes me think about the changes I have made in my own life, starting with quitting my job at the surgery. I'm not sure what's around the corner for me now, but then, do any of us? For a moment, though, I dare to dream that here in the gorgeous Greek sunshine, maybe romance could be on the cards.

FIFTEEN

'I really enjoyed that,' says Liz, who is sat beside me as we sail.

'Me too. We would never have discovered this place alone. I don't remember seeing it when I did a search of tourist attractions,' I say, thinking of all the local trips I googled on my phone.

Captain Zeus makes an announcement that we will soon be approaching the blue caves, where we will have the opportunity to disembark and head down some steps to the caves and be taken through a grotto in a small rowing boat. 'If you wish, of course, this is the optional extra,' he adds.

'I guess this is the surprise part of the trip,' I say. 'It does sound rather lovely.'

'After that, we will sail past a mansion belonging to someone very famous,' says Zeus. 'You may even see a glimpse of him in his garden or around his pool,' he teases, not revealing who the celebrity is.

'I just love it here.' I sigh contentedly. My curly hair is blowing wild and free, and I don't even bother putting it under a hat. Today is all about feeling liberated and having fun.

'Me too,' says Liz. 'I really want to stay here forever. Then again, maybe not. I do get bored quickly.'

'So, I take it you're not looking forward to going home?'

'Maybe. Not home exactly, as in my home town. But I'll have to head back to the UK eventually, I suppose.' She sighs. 'There isn't the work abroad these days. Especially since Brexit.'

'That's true. Is your home town that bad? Oh, I'm sorry, you were right, I do ask a lot of questions. Maybe I should have been an investigative journalist. I just like to learn about people, that's all,' I explain.

'No, it's alright. You've told me all about your life.'

We'd sat one evening drinking wine after the church visit, and I told her all about my life back home. I told her how my boyfriend had cheated, and about my parents moving to Spain. I even confessed that I was lonely at times, and she'd listened quietly and said you would never know I was lonely, as I chatted so easily to people. I confessed to feeling a bit abandoned as a child with no siblings, as my parents couldn't wait to be off on their biking adventures in the mountains. No place to take a child, with all those dangerous bends in the road, they'd told me. At times, Judith was more like a mother to me as a youngster. I spent so many gorgeous weekends at her large, welcoming house in the countryside, playing with the dogs and my friend next door.

'Anyway, my home town isn't exactly that bad, but there are people I want to get away from. I'll have to sort out a place to rent, in another town. And a job,' Liz confides. She stands and goes to lean on the boat rail as she gazes out across the water.

'Why would you need to get away from people?' I ask, joining her.

'I was into drugs.' She turns to face me.

'Drugs?'

'Yes. Are you shocked?' She regards me closely.

'Actually, no. I worked in a doctor's surgery, remember. I've seen it happen. For so many reasons.'

'I never intended to be an addict. I mean, who does? No one

wakes up in the morning and thinks, I'll walk along a path to destruction and ruin my entire life. I just smoked joints at the weekend, that sort of thing. Being introduced to cocaine by my boyfriend was the worst thing that could have happened to me.' She sighs. 'I just loved the buzz. I was soon an addict,' she tells me candidly.

'You're very brave to tell me this. You must have been through a difficult time.' I gently touch her arm.

'Thanks, Tania. I'll never go back there.'

'Do you attend support groups?' I ask. I've seen too many people at the surgery relapse, without the right support.

'I do, but in all honesty, I haven't been to one lately. I'm two years drug free and in a good place.' She smiles.

'Well, that's good. Have you thought about maybe going to college? Study dress making, or design?' I suggest. 'You have a real skill.'

'I do, don't I?' She laughs, giving a twirl in the yellow tie dye bikini she's wearing beneath a kaftan, one of her many creations.

'You really do. Don't let that talent go to waste.'

'Actually, going to college might not be a bad idea,' she considers. 'Maybe I'll ask my new friend Frank, he teaches in a college.' She drums her fingers on the rail of the boat. 'Thanks, Tania, you're a bit of a problem-solver, aren't you?' She cocks her head to one side and studies me.

'I don't think of myself like that. Maybe I'm just practical. Anyway, leaving your old crowd is definitely something you should do. Don't be too hasty about leaving your home town, though, why should you be pushed out?'

'Because maybe I'm not really as strong as I think I am?' she says honestly and shrugs.

As we've been chatting, the boat has started drifting slowly towards a huge cave and Captain Zeus moors up. A couple of minutes later, we enter the thick-walled sandy cave, the coolness washing over us. We pay a few euros to a lady at a kiosk, and she hands us each a ticket. Even though the trip was optional, all of the passengers have decided they would love to sail through the caves, rather than just sail past them.

We descend some steps that seem to go on forever, before we are rewarded with the sight of a sparkling lake, in shades of emerald and blue, the craggy cave walls rising up on either side. Several motor boats are lined up awaiting visitors, as the sun dances on the water from a shaft of sunlight above.

'Oh, my goodness, look at this,' Liz gasps. 'It reminds me of that scene from *The Goonies*.' She gazes around in awe.

'Minus the pirate ship,' I joke, although I have to agree. Who would have known this magical space existed below the ground? I take in my surroundings, completely hypnotised by its beauty.

We take our seats in the small boat and the engine purrs gently as it takes us slowly across the water. It feels so wondrous, watching the reflection from the water cast an almost purple hue onto the cave walls as we slowly chug along.

After a short while, we have driven through the cave into the waters of the blue lagoon, taking photographs of the marbled water, the sun caressing us once more. Everyone is quiet, absorbing the surroundings as we slowly make our way back through the caves to the departure point. The boatmen happily pose for photos beside their boats, as tourists snap away with their cameras.

'That was just amazing,' I say as we step out of the boat and begin our ascent of the cave steps to the entrance at the top.

'Worth every penny. In fact, I think they ought to charge more. I got some fantastic photos,' says Wes. 'It was so still and peaceful down there.'

'It really was,' I agree. 'Nature is so fascinating, isn't it? Creating such places of beauty.'

I've really enjoyed this boat trip, and Captain Zeus and his son are thrilled when we tell him what a great day it has been.

'I tell you I have a surprise.' He smiles. 'I knew everybody would like that.'

On our journey back to the harbour, we sail close to a large house, surrounded with a glass panelled balcony, halfway up a hill. A man with blond spiky hair, wearing sunglasses and a white T-shirt and jeans, appears on the balcony and waves.

'And now, another surprise. Rod Stewart.' Captain Zeus gestures towards the man and waves back and we giggle. I'm not sure it really is Rod, but it makes a good talking point.

Back at the harbour, we say our goodbyes and the passengers have all thrown some loose change for a tip into a dish near the small bar, and Zeus and his son thank us gratefully.

'Be sure to tell your friends,' calls a smiling Zeus and as I wander off, I can't help wondering whether Zeus is his real name, although I know the Greeks often keep traditional names, after the ancient gods.

Judith and Lars are playing cards sat at a table beneath a tree when we arrive home just after five thirty. The nearby BBQ has already been started up, smoke spiralling gently into the air.

'You're back? How was your day?' asks my aunt, smiling as she greets us.

'Oh, Judith, it was wonderful. We went through some glorious caves. You should go for a day out before the season ends, I think you would really enjoy it.'

'I'm sure I would,' says Judith. 'I'm so busy here, I often forget about the beautiful things on the island. When your uncle was alive, we did hire a boat occasionally and head off for the day with a picnic.' She smiles at the memory. 'Maybe when I've had my knee operation, I might visit those caves. I'm not sure I could manage all those steps at the moment.'

I tell her all about the rest of our day out as Lars places some steaks onto the smoking coals of the BBQ.

'Oh, and we saw Rod Stewart in his garden, didn't we?' says Wes, a grin on his face.

'Really?' She looks surprised.

'Probably not. Not unless Rod hasn't aged in the last thirty years,' Liz replies with a giggle.

Soon enough, the smell of sizzling steaks fills the air and has everyone too hungry to chat until it's served up.

'This is wonderful,' says Wes as he tucks into his food. 'What's the steak marinated in?'

'A sticky bourbon sauce. My own recipe,' says Lars proudly.

'My dad would love this. He enjoys a good steak on the BBQ,' says Wes as he makes appreciative noises over his food.

It's the first time he's mentioned his father outside of our chat about the family business earlier. It's nice to hear that their relationship has its good moments too.

Liz, normally ravenous, is more interested in her phone this evening, texting quickly. By the grin on her face, I can guess who she is talking too.

'Have the dogs all been out today?' I ask Judith as I sip a glass of ice-cold white wine.

'Yes, we had plenty of volunteers in today. I wasn't sure if it was a little hot, but the dogs seemed keen to go out. Especially Smudge and Annie, as usual.'

I imagine them trotting along together and hope Smudge wasn't too exuberant for the walkers.

'Nicos took a couple of the dogs out too actually. I kind of got the impression he would have liked to have walked with you,' she tells me.

The thought of it gives me a warm feeling inside.

'Really, what makes you say that?'

'Oh, he just asked if you were around. He said you had discussed maybe taking the dogs out together on a walk. I actually suggested he might like to rehome one to keep him company in that big house,' Judith tells me.

'And what did he say to that?'

'Something about him not being able to make the commitment, as he isn't sure whether or not he is going to sell the place or stay around.'

'Oh,' I say, a sudden feeling of disappointment in the pit of my stomach. It's not like I've decided to stay here forever either, but it was nice to imagine getting to know him more if I came out to see Aunt Judith again...

'It's a shame he couldn't stay until you got back, but he said he was busy again this evening,' Judith continues. 'He certainly seems to be making the most of being in the village for the moment, while he decides.'

This catches my attention. I wonder if he is seeing someone. I hope not, even though I feel a bit silly at the pang of jealousy Judith's words brought. Maybe I will find out a little more when he comes for lunch tomorrow.

'Well, Lars, that was amazing. I think you've missed your calling; you should have been a chef,' I say, sitting back and feeling stuffed. We've eaten our way through all the steak, as well as tasty chicken wings, and Greek salad.

'I'll second that, it was all fantastic,' says Liz, who soon tucked in when she had finished talking with Frank.

'Thank you. I did a little cooking in the army.' Lars has a proud look on his face as he listens to all the compliments.

Sitting around chatting, tired after our long day, Judith remarks that watching the flickering embers of the fire pit reminds her of going camping as a young woman and sitting around campfires singing. 'It's a pity no one can play the guitar,' she says wistfully.

'As it happens, there is someone who can do just that.' I turn to Wes. 'You don't have a guitar, do you, Judith?'

'As a matter of fact, I do. Would you believe one of the volunteers left one here.'

She goes inside and returns with a guitar, which she hands over to Wes, who gives a low whistle.

'Nice. I'm not sure I would have left this behind.' He strokes the side of the guitar in admiration.

'The guy was going travelling and didn't want to be lugging it about, apparently. He did say he might return next year and claim it, although he told me he had others at home.'

Wes strums the guitar lightly, before tuning it up.

'What would you like to hear?' he asks.

'How about something by Elvis? But I don't imagine that's your style, is it?' asks Judith.

'I could try.' He plays a few chords, then begins to sing 'The Wonder of You'. His voice is so mesmerising, it has the hairs on my arms standing on end. When he reaches the crescendo of the song, we have all joined in the singing and everybody claps loudly at the end. I think there might even be a few tears in my aunt's eyes.

'Oh my goodness, that was wonderful.' She's on her feet clapping. Wes does a little bow and smiles.

'Gosh, Wes, you truly are talented. You deserve a big break,' I tell him.

'Thanks. I'm not expecting fame and fortune, I'd just like to earn a living doing what I love.' He shrugs modestly.

'Well, I'm sure you could definitely do that. I'd pay to watch you perform.'

'Would you really?'

'One hundred per cent.'

After several more songs, we are sat enjoying a final beer before we head to bed. Across the field, I see the lights go on in the house where Nicos lives and wonder if he has returned home alone, or if the plans he mentioned to my aunt involved someone special.

I also wonder why he told my aunt he isn't short of company, despite him living alone. As I head to bed, it occurs to me that I spend a lot of time thinking about the handsome neighbour across the road.

SIXTEEN

Three of the dogs have been rehomed today, and even though there are plenty of them still needing attention, the place already feels a little quieter. It's nice to have a slightly slower Sunday. Judith is busy in the kitchen, putting the finishing touches to a huge roast lamb lunch she is preparing.

Every time I think of Nicos coming over to join us for lunch, I feel a fluttering of butterflies in my stomach. I realise I probably have a little bit of a crush, although it's hardly surprising. He's a good-looking Greek, somewhere in his thirties, who was asking about me when I wasn't here, yet I know little of his situation. He hasn't revealed much about himself, and last night he was heading off out for the evening, goodness knows who with. Then again, he happily accepted an invitation over here on a Sunday, didn't he? Surely, he would be spending the weekend with his other half if he had one? I can't seem to stop the questions going around in my head.

'Do you want me to do anything?' I offer. Lars is lending a hand with the cooking, and it would appear everything is under control. Wes is refilling the hay in the feeders for the donkeys and Liz has gone out on her bike to meet Frank, who Judith has also invited for lunch, telling Liz, 'The more the merrier.'

'No, darling. It's fine,' says Judith. 'But I thought we might have a G and T before lunch, and we could do with a few limes if you would like to grab some.' She opens the oven door, and the aroma of garlic hits my nostrils and my stomach gives a little rumble.

'Of course.' I head across the garden to a lime tree, smaller than the others but abundant with limes as they aren't used as much as the lemons. As I pull the fruits from the tree branches, I think how different things are out here. Back home, I would head to the greengrocer's to buy fruits that would often be thrown out before their sell-by date. The days, despite being busy, are filled with a contentment I haven't felt in a long while. The wonderful forests refreshing the mind, yet only a short drive to the glorious sea or nearby towns. I feel so lucky.

An hour or two later, with the animals all settled, I nip upstairs for a quick shower and to change for lunch. It's still hot outside, so I slip into a short, white cotton dress, then change my mind. Is it perhaps a little *too* short? In the end, I opt for a floaty maxi dress, in shades of green, that might be a little too dressy. Oh gosh, I can't believe I am overthinking what I should wear for Sunday lunch!

Annie the cockapoo is making a bit of a racket, barking and appearing a little unsettled, pacing her cage, so I head over to investigate.

'Hey, Annie, What's up?' I ask as she pokes her head through the bars of her substantial pen. I open the cage door and pet her for a few minutes and when she settles down, I relax a little. A few of the other dogs have been a bit restless this morning too, thinking about it, and I wonder why.

Sometimes, if a storm is heading across the island, the dogs can behave a little erratically, or even become a little noisy, my aunt tells me. There's no doubt a thunderstorm would definitely freshen the air, but maybe not until we have enjoyed our Sunday lunch outside. It is particularly hot today, so maybe that could be the problem, so I make sure the dogs all have iced water in their bowls.

Nicos arrives and when he kisses my cheeks in greeting, I inhale the smell of his gorgeous aftershave. He's wearing an open-necked pink shirt, the sleeves rolled up and smart, dark-coloured shorts. His style is understated, but I can't help noticing the designer sunglasses. Maybe today I will find out a little more about him.

He presents my aunt with a bottle each of red and white wine.

'Ooh, thank you, Nicos. I'm sure this will go down really well with the meal. For now, would you care for a gin and tonic?' she offers and he accepts.

Lars has set up a table close to the stone BBQ and is preparing the drinks. He drops some ice and a slice of lime into each glass, before handing them around.

'Is it okay if I propose a toast?' I ask Judith, just as Liz has returned with Frank, who is introduced to everyone and handed a drink.

'Of course, that's a nice idea,' she agrees.

'I just wanted to wish us all good health,' I say, glancing around at the assembled group. 'And I hope your operation next week gives you a new lease of life, Judith.' I raise my glass to my aunt. 'And may life always give us the opportunity to meet new people and make lasting friends. So, here's to friends old and new.'

'To friends old and new,' everyone choruses as they lift their glass and Nicos catches my eye and smiles at me.

Lunch is a wonderful affair; the food is fabulous – Judith serves up tender local lamb with a herb crust and fluffy roasted potatoes and vegetables from across the island. Wine glasses are filled and laughter rings out over the hills. I'm so happy I came here, and could happily lounge here all day with these wonderful people, one in particular who chose to sit beside me for lunch.

'So, what do you do for a living?' I ask Nicos. I don't particularly like asking people that question, as I always feel we make an immediate judgement about someone based upon their answer, despite it being the usual conversation starter. The last time I asked someone that question they had just lost their high-street business in an economic downturn.

'Take a guess?' he says as he twirls red wine around in his glass.

'Um. A business owner?' I suggest.

'No.' At this point, there is a pause in everyone else's conversation, so they tune in to ours.

'I'd say you were a property developer,' says Wes confidently.

'No,' he says. 'Although you are not a million miles away.'

'A builder?' says Liz.

'Close, but nope.'

'I didn't think so. Your hands are too smooth,' I say, then blush and wonder why on earth I just said that. 'But something to do with property?' I quickly ask and he nods.

Everyone takes a guess, but no one can come up with the right answer. Eventually Nicos tells us that he is an architect.

'Wow, really? Have you got any grand plans for the house?' I ask.

'Hmm. Possibly, yes. The first thing I would do is install floor-length windows to look across the valley. The view from the lounge is really something. Whether I decide to stay or not, it's an attractive feature I'd like to make the most of, for myself or a prospective buyer.'

'I can just imagine that.' I close my eyes, and imagine Nicos and I, sat on the outside terrace, fairy lights above, their reflection dancing across the valley as the sun begins to set. The fact he might sell up disappoints me slightly.

'What have you worked on recently?' asks Wes and Nicos searches for a picture on his phone. He shows us a stunning cream-walled restaurant with glass doors, overlooking a beach.

'A restaurant on a beach,' he says proudly, showing us the picture of the stunning building that has a patio and veranda looking out over the sea. 'That guy had some serious money. He owns a huge villa and an apartment in town too.'

'That looks beautiful,' I say dreamily, thinking of how I would love to go there one day. 'Are you working on something now? I take it you work from home?' I ask, as he appears to be around the area a lot.

'I am at the moment. I have taken some time away from the office to start clearing the house. It's a rather bigger task than I first thought.' He sighs as he takes a sip of his wine.

'Will you make a decision on selling or staying once the clearing is done?' I ask him, hoping that he might decide to stick around for at least a while longer.

I'm vaguely aware that Nicos and I seem to be having our own private conversation, as the rest of the party, having solved the mystery of Nicos's job, are chatting easily to each other. Frank has everyone laughing at something, whilst Liz glances at him lovingly. I think they make an adorable couple.

'Not exactly. It's complicated.' He refills both of our glasses.

'In what way?' I ask. 'Sorry, I ask a lot of questions.'

Although it's true, as Liz once said, it's often because I like to help if I think it's possible, in any situation.

'My sister wants to sell, but the longer I spend there, I'm thinking I might like to live in the house. There are so many attractions around here.' His hands brush mine as he slides my glass towards me, and I feel a crackle of electricity. I wonder whether he felt it too?

'Would it be a long commute to work?' I ask, feeling more mellow with every sip of wine.

'Around an hour. And I can work a lot from home, so that wouldn't really be a problem,' he explains. 'I still have my apartment in Heraklion at the moment as well, if I don't feel like the drive home.'

'What would your sister say to you living at the house?'

'I've been thinking of buying her out,' he continues. 'I think perhaps she needs the money, or at least that's what she told me over dinner last night. It's hardly surprising, though. She likes to spend.' He raises an eyebrow.

So, he was out with his sister last night? I'm surprised by the feeling of relief I feel, knowing it wasn't a romantic date.

Before we know it, the evening is almost upon us as the light begins to fade. We've eaten watermelon and sipped ouzo to end the meal and I stifle a yawn.

'Gosh, what a fabulous afternoon. I could do with a siesta now, though it's probably a little late, I would never sleep tonight.' I stretch my arms out, feeling relaxed after the food and wine.

'An hour or two in bed sounds like a good idea,' says Nicos and the way he stares at me makes my insides flip.

After carrying the dishes inside, Nicos asks me if I would like to take a walk. The thought of a moonlit walk with Nicos sounds super-inviting. Nicos told me he's disposing of some old furniture and unwanted items he has removed from the house tomorrow. I'm dying to have a look inside and would love to see whether there is anything that could be restored. I feel a bit cheeky asking, but I've been thinking about how nice it would be to be a bit creative with some of my free time. And, of course, to spend some time with him.

'That sounds nice, but we must do a check on the animals first,' I tell him.

Most of the animals are dozing, but Annie is lying on her side whimpering quietly.

'Hey, girl, what's the matter?' I bend down and stroke her and her head feels hot to the touch. Just then Liz calls me over to another dog. It soon becomes clear that a lot of the dogs seem a little listless.

'I think they're ill,' she tells me anxiously. 'Hardly any of them have touched their food or water.'

Despite the feeling of relaxation after the wine, everyone immediately springs into action. Judith calls the emergency vet and the rest of us sponge the hot animals down and race indoors to fetch some fans and rig them up to an extension lead.

'They were okay this morning. What on earth could it be?' My aunt wrings her hands anxiously as she tends to the animals.

'Don't worry, I'm sure it's nothing serious,' I try to reassure her, praying that it isn't.

SEVENTEEN

The emergency vet arrives within the hour. Nicos has stayed, helping make sure the animals are cool and comfortable. After his assessment of the animals, the vet asks us some questions. His English is not fluent, so Nicos offers to translate, and the vet speaks very quickly to him in Greek.

'Do the dogs go into the water?' the vet asks, removing his glasses and wiping his brow. 'If so, where?'

'Usually the stream further up the hill.'

'Anywhere different lately?' asks Nicos as he interprets the vet's questions.

'Um, actually, yes. We took some of them to High Point Nature Reserve. There is a large lake there.'

The vet is quiet for a moment, deep in thought.

'I will need to do further tests,' he says, finally. 'But I think the dogs may have leptospirosis.'

'Lepto?' My aunt seems familiar with the disease. 'But they were vaccinated against that, I'm certain.' She has a look of worry on her face.

'Different strains can appear and be resistant,' Nicos explains after translating. 'It can be caught from a diseased animal that often displays no symptoms and carries it into the water. If the dogs swam there, that is possibly where they picked it up.'

He explains that it is rarely serious if antibiotics are given immediately via injection, which the vet administers to the sick animals at once.

'Please, encourage them to drink fresh water. Call me tomorrow if things are any worse. But try not to worry,' he says.

'What about the dogs that are not showing any symptoms?' I ask.

'Keep an eye on them. I give them medicine too.' He pauses for a moment, searching for the word. 'As prevention.'

'As a precaution,' explains Nicos.

Judith is distraught, and the rest of us worry whether we have caught the symptoms early enough as, thinking about it, Annie and a few of the other dogs were behaving a little strangely earlier today. I'm praying a few hours won't have made too much difference. The vet tells us he will return tomorrow.

'That's us on night duty then,' says Wes, his commitment never in doubt.

'It's been a long day, so maybe we should have a bit of a rota so we can grab at least some sleep,' says Judith and we all agree.

Liz and I expect Frank and Nicos to be on their way, particularly Frank as he has only just become friends with Liz, but to our surprise they insist on staying too.

'The least I can do is make some coffee,' says Nicos and Frank joins him as they head to the kitchen. Nicos touches Judith's arm as he leaves and assures her that everything will be alright. I can only pray that he is right.

The vet returns the next morning, to hear that the dogs have had a settled night. He checks them over again and confirms that the antibiotics had probably been delivered at the right time. They don't have a temperature this morning. The rota worked out well, as we all managed to grab a few hours' sleep each.

Nicos leaves after breakfast to meet the removal people and tells me he will be in touch later.

'I'm so exhausted.' Judith is sat down with a cold glass of lemonade talking to Lars, who has never stopped working and mucking in, his devotion to both the dogs and Judith obvious to all.

'Put your feet up today, Judith,' I insist. 'There are enough of us here to keep things ticking over.'

'The timing couldn't be worse.' She sighs. 'I'm supposed to be going in for my knee operation in a few days' time.'

'You *will* be going for your operation. The dogs already seem a little brighter this morning. In a couple of days' time, I'm sure they will be feeling even better,' I say positively. 'And there are still enough of us here, as with some of the dogs being rehomed the numbers are manageable,' I remind her.

'It was fortunate that the adopted dogs were collected before the virus broke out. I do hope they are all doing okay,' she frets.

'I'm sure you would have heard if otherwise. I'll ring around later, just to be sure,' I assure my aunt.

'Thank you, Tania.'

The day passes quickly, thankfully with the dogs appearing no worse and if anything, a little better. By early evening they have even taken some food. I phoned the owners of the new dogs, and thankfully they are all okay, but I asked them to be aware of any changes in their health and call a vet if they do notice anything.

'Isn't it strange that some of the dogs seem absolutely fine?' I comment to Wes. 'Yet most of them swam in the lake.'

'I know. Maybe they are a bit like humans. You know how

certain members of a family can catch a cold virus, but not everyone does. My mum never gets ill when the rest of the family do,' he adds.

'I suppose so. Anyway, fingers crossed, it looks like they might all make a full recovery.'

Judith has been inside for over an hour having a nap, and just after seven o'clock she comes and joins us. She still looks exhausted, though, barely picking at her food. It's still light outside after we've eaten, so I take myself off for a walk to clear my head a little. There's a spot at the top of the hill that is a perfect place to watch the beginning of the sunset. As I head outside, I hear someone call my name and Nicos falls into step with me.

'Nicos, hi, how did your day clearing out the house go?' I ask him as we walk together.

'Pretty good. It would appear I am quite ruthless when it comes to throwing things away. I do not take after my parents, obviously.' He grins. 'I don't think I have ever seen so much stuff. Not just furniture, but newspapers, old ornaments. Even some of my old toys. Most of it has gone now. But I have kept some wonderful photo albums.' He smiles. 'And a skateboard. I remember my mother fretting over me having an accident every time I took it out,' he recalls. 'I keep staying up late, as I keep getting distracted looking through the photos.'

'Are you going to keep any of the furniture?'

'There are one or two nice pieces of heavy furniture I would like to keep. A cabinet and a solid wooden headboard that has some nice carvings on it.'

'I hope you don't mind, but could I take a look at anything else you are thinking of throwing away?'

'Of course.' He looks a little puzzled. 'But why would you want some old furniture?'

'I'd have a go at restoring it. Upcycling. I did a few bits and pieces at home.' I show him a picture of the lounge unit that I am proud of, and the bedside tables that are safely stored in my friend Angie's garage.

'You did those?' He sounds impressed. 'They look amazing. Come around tomorrow and have a look, we can have coffee.'

'Thanks, I'd like that.'

We head over a small bridge where already the glorious shades of pink and lilac are stretching across the sky as the sun begins to set. I take a seat on the bench and Nicos sits down beside me. Glancing out across the large lake in the distance, I can't help thinking of the dogs.

'I feel bad that the dogs might have picked up the infection from the water,' I tell him. 'We normally only let them splash around in the mountain streams. The lake is part of a wildlife reserve, so maybe other animals pass through.'

'You were not to know that. Don't blame yourself,' he says kindly. 'Besides, the dogs are eating and drinking again now. Maybe no long walks for a while, but I am sure they will be fine,' he tries to reassure me.

'Thanks, Nicos, I hope so. If they don't I'm worried Judith will put off her operation again.'

With that, talk turns to what brings me here. I tell Nicos about my life back home, including the split from my ex.

'He must be a fool.' He turns and gazes at me and I feel something pass between us.

'Well, I think so.' I manage a smile. 'So, what about you?'

'It's complicated.' His jaw twitches and I feel the atmosphere change.

'Most relationships are.'

I try for a light-hearted tone, but he doesn't smile, and I find myself wondering what complications he has in his life. I don't have time to dwell on things, though, as just then, my mobile phone rings. It's Judith.

'Judith, slow down. What did you say has happened?' I put

the speakerphone on so Nicos can hear. Thankfully we haven't wandered too far, so the signal is fine.

'It's Yolanda from the green house. She's had a bad fall; she's just telephoned me. She's in her seventies and lives alone. Her closest neighbours are elderly too, the wife not in the best of health.' She's babbling on. 'I really ought to go, but my knee is bad so I don't think I would be much help as I'm so exhausted.'

'Say no more. I'll head over there. Has somebody called an ambulance?' I ask.

'Yes, her neighbour Aristos has. But are you sure?'

'Of course I am.'

Nicos is already walking towards his house, mouthing, 'I'll get the car.'

'Oh, thank you.' Judith sounds relieved. 'Her other neighbours, who are a little younger, are visiting relatives in Heraklion, or I'm sure they would be with her.'

'I'll keep you posted. We're just getting Nicos's car.'

'Thank you, Tania, and give my thanks to Nicos, of course.'

The green house is at the top of quite a steep hill, so taking the car was definitely the right decision. A few minutes later, we pull up outside and are greeted by an elderly man who introduces himself to me, before ushering us inside. Nicos, who knows him, shakes his hand, and speaks in Greek. Inside a lady is lying on the floor unable to move. Once more Nicos talks and introduces her to me.

'This is bastard nuisance,' says the lady, her long black hair tied back. 'I cannot move.' She sounds frustrated more than in pain.

'Are you in pain?' I ask.

'Pain, yes, but what is a little pain?' She dismisses it, sounding more annoyed than anything.

She shakes her finger at me. 'Don't grow old.' She sighs.

She tells Nicos that one of her chickens ran in from outside when she left the door open, and she tripped over it.

'I'm not sure we should move her, something may be broken, maybe her hip,' I whisper to Nicos and he agrees. I place a pillow beneath her head to make her feel a little more comfortable. She speaks to Nicos, and he translates that she is telling me to stop fussing, but I notice her hands are cold. Nicos fetches a woollen throw from a nearby couch and covers her. She tuts but leaves the blanket in place. Her hands feel cold to the touch, but I don't want to give her a hot drink in case she needs surgery when she gets to the hospital.

'You have a beautiful house,' I tell her, glancing around the neat as a pin lounge. A huge red sofa dominates the room; a cream woollen rug in front of it sits on quarry tiles. 'I love your cushions,' I comment on the pretty tapestry cushions adorning the sofa.

'I make,' she tells me.

'Really?' I say in surprise, as they look so perfect and professional.

'*Nai.*' She nods, unable to hide the look of pain on her face as she tries to move.

'Please, try and stay still,' I say gently, and she huffs. 'I'm sure the ambulance will be here soon.'

I tell her all about the dogs at the rescue. I'm not sure how much she can understand, but feel the need to do something, even if it's only talking to keep her distracted. Nicos translates at various points, although he tells me her English is pretty good. Apparently she just chooses when to use it.

The next-door neighbour looks a little unsure of what to do next, so Nicos thanks him for his help and shakes his hand, telling him we will wait for the ambulance if he needs to go home to his wife. I ask Nicos to explain to Yolanda that my aunt sends her good wishes, but is having trouble with her knee today. And also about the dogs being ill.

'The operation. When she have?' she asks in her broken English.

'In a few days, actually. She might be running up that hill to visit you after that,' I joke.

'Good, good.' She smiles and it makes me think that my aunt ought to have a little more time with friends and neighbours, as her whole life revolves around the rescue.

Half an hour later an ambulance arrives, and the crew take charge of the situation.

'*Efcharisto.*' Yolanda manages a smile, as the ambulance staff gently manoeuvre her onto a stretcher.

She speaks to Nicos and asks if he could ask Aristos next door to look after her chickens whilst she is in hospital.

Noting Yolanda's long black hair and fine features, it is clear to see she was a real beauty in her day. In fact, she still is. I'm a little surprised when she reaches over and squeezes my hand and smiles as she is wheeled into the back of the ambulance. Nicos speaks to the staff, who say she will be taken to Hersonissos Hospital. He tells her he will let her other neighbours know when they return from their trip away, although I'm pretty sure Aristos will do that.

'Gosh, I hope she will be alright. Are there no relatives to contact?' I ask Nicos, concerned for her welfare. Thank goodness they have the WhatsApp group to at least get some help from neighbours.

'She has a son. I will tell Aristos to phone him when I ask him to look after the chickens. I am sure he will appreciate being of some help.'

'Do you know her son?' I ask as we walk to the car.

'Yes. We were friends when we were young,' he recalls.

'Are you still in touch with each other?'

'How many people stay friends forever?' He shrugs.

I'm not sure if I'm imagining things, but he appears a little tense when he talks of his old friend and neighbour, so I don't continue the conversation.

Back at the rescue, we tell my aunt that Yolanda has been taken to hospital.

'Oh, thank goodness. I really ought to pop over and see her a little more, especially as she is on her own now, but I'm always so busy with this place. I shouldn't really rely on the fact that she has good neighbours close by. She's a nice lady, who can be an absolute hoot. We had some fun times together, once upon a time.' She smiles fondly.

'Well, you haven't exactly been able to run around lately yourself, have you?' I remind her. 'Although once your knee is fixed, you should maybe try to see some of your neighbours once in a while. You deserve to have a little fun.'

'You mean I should get a life.'

'Well, maybe spend a little more time doing the things you enjoy. All work and no play and all that.'

'Haven't I been telling you the same thing?' adds Lars. 'And when Yolanda is better, I will drive you both somewhere nice for a day out, if you like,' he offers.

'Thank you, Lars.' She smiles warmly at him. 'And you're so right, Tania. The people in the village were so kind when me and your uncle Ray first came to live here. Some of them have moved away now. But it's true, we should communicate more in person, and not just through the online group.'

It's been such a long day, I crash into bed after checking on the dogs, who thankfully seem to be sleeping peacefully, having picked at some more food and drunk some water. Before we parted ways, I told Nicos I will call over tomorrow and look at some of the furniture he is thinking of disposing of. Before I drop off to sleep, I realise that I am in no hurry to head back to England. Even with the ups and downs of the day, I feel quite fulfilled and I think, maybe, I could get used to this.

EIGHTEEN

News from the hospital reveals that Yolanda has in fact not broken her hip but one of her ribs, and a tiny bone near her pelvis. No surgery is required thankfully, but she needs complete rest when she returns home. Her son has been in touch with Judith and tells her he will visit his mother at home when she is discharged from the hospital.

'Yolanda reminded me that it's no fun growing old and with my creaky knees, I would have to agree with her,' Judith says with a deep sigh.

'Your best years are yet to come,' says Lars. 'Just you wait until that knee of yours has been sorted out,' he adds positively.

'I hope you're right.' My aunt rubs at her knee. It's only a few days before Judith's operation, and it couldn't come soon enough. I'm pleased to see that the dogs are continuing to improve, which ought to reassure her as she prepares to go into hospital herself.

There will be a new face when she returns, as Wes is due to head home next week and another volunteer is arriving soon. I know I'll miss Wes a lot, as we quickly became good friends.

· · ·

It's late afternoon when I head over to see Nicos, where I spy several items of furniture in the garden, including a long wooden unit and a dark wood chest of drawers. There's a handsome wing-backed chair that looks a little tired and ripe for a refurbishment.

'How did you get these down here?' I ask, as they look heavy.

'The house clearance guy helped. He took some of the bigger items away and gave me a hand to bring these down. What do you think?'

I glance at the beautifully carved wooden chest, and think it would look good in the house, maybe against white walls with some colourful paintings on and I suggest this to Nicos.

'Hmm, maybe. The whole house needs repainting and decorating. Maybe you could help me,' he suggests.

'I'd be glad to,' I tell him, feeling excited by the thought of us leafing through interior design magazines together, or maybe even heading into the city to browse some shops.

'Are you planning on keeping this?' I run my hands along the wooden chest of drawers.

'I don't think so.' He shakes his head. 'The room it came from was already overcrowded.'

'In that case, may I have it? I could definitely do something with it. I'd pay you something, of course,' I offer.

'Be my guest. And it is not worth much, so you don't need to pay me. I will be intrigued to see what you do with it.' He smiles. 'I will bring it over to the rescue. Unless, of course, you would like to work on it here?'

'And the chair?'

'Surely that is definitely past its best.'

'Nonsense.' I give it the once over, before sitting down, happy to note that it doesn't sag in the middle. 'Actually, Nicos, it would be great if I could work on the furniture here, if you really don't mind.'

There aren't many outdoor areas that the curious dogs don't access at the rescue. I have a vision of Smudge and Annie rolling in paint and darting off through the gardens, recolouring the trees.

Nicos tells me there is a DIY shop in a large village nearby that sells everything needed for restoration and decoration.

'I could take you there, if you like.' He glances at his watch. 'I know a lovely restaurant not far from the shop. If you would like lunch afterwards?'

'I'd like that. If you're sure you don't have any work to do?' I hope he doesn't. This day just keeps getting better.

'A little. But I am ahead of schedule on something I am working on, so a few hours out will be a nice break.'

'In that case, thank you.'

Climbing into the car beside Nicos, I'm surprised by quite how happy I feel spending time with him. He has proved to be hands-on and helpful, stepping up when there have been problems at the rescue, and heading to Yolanda's place after she had her fall. And, of course, there is no doubt he is very easy on the eye. It's all I can do to stop myself staring at his very handsome profile.

The sun is beating down as we drive along the familiar mountain roads with the roof down on the car, enjoying a light breeze as we drive. Nicos turns the radio on, and hums along to a Greek tune.

'I see the *kafsonas* is still continuing,' I remark.

'You see...' He turns to glance at me, with a broad smile. 'You remembered. One word at a time, and the words will build up slowly.'

'It's true, but I really ought to make an effort to learn at least a few more phrases.'

'Maybe a word each day. Today, you could try and remember the word *panemorfi*.'

'What does it mean?'

'It means "beautiful".' He turns to look at me, and I feel my cheeks colour.

Twenty minutes later, we arrive at the busy village and Nicos parks the car not far from the sea, the sun dancing upon it like a million silver stars.

The shop is down a nearby side street, and stepping inside I discover it's almost Tardis-like. Narrow aisles are packed with paints, wallpapers and varnishes. There is also a good selection of pretty handles for doors and drawers.

Half an hour later, loaded down with bags, we are outside in the bright sunshine once more, and I'm armed with everything I need.

'Well, that was a successful shopping trip. I can't wait to see how the drawers turn out.'

I'm thrilled at how reasonably priced the goods were and can hardly wait to get started on the furniture. My mind is already considering the possibility of doing some more projects in the future, wherever that may be.

'Me too,' says Nicos. 'So, are you a creative person then?' he asks as we walk back to the car.

'In some ways, I guess. I always thought of myself as more of a practical person, but maybe we all have a bit of a creative streak in us. I quite like baking too.'

'You do? I can't resist cake,' he tells me hopefully.

'Yes, but I haven't done much in this weather. I only stay in the kitchen long enough to chuck something in a pot to simmer.'

'Well, if you do feel the desire to bake, I can't resist fruit cake. My mother used to make it.'

'Duly noted,' I tell him, although I would feel nervous about having my baking compared to his mother's. 'I guess you must be a creative type too, being an architect?'

'Not especially. A lot of the time is spent drawing other people's plans. I enjoy it, though. My dream would be to design and build my own house eventually, but, of course, that costs a lot of money.'

'Your parents' house is so beautiful, though. Perhaps you could just make some alterations to the place?'

'Maybe.' He shrugs. 'If I decide to stick around.'

His comment makes my heart sink a little, which annoys me slightly. He's as free as a bird after all. He can do whatever he pleases.

After placing my bags in the car, we walk further along the coast road and arrive at a restaurant overlooking the sea. The outside space is filled with colourful flowers in pots surrounding a water feature.

'What a pretty place,' I comment as Nicos requests a table for two.

'And the food is as good as the surroundings,' he tells me as a friendly waiter ushers us to a table.

'This is nice.' I'm sipping a cold Mythos beer and glancing out across the sparkling water. 'We were lucky to get a table with such a beautiful view.'

I feel a tiny bit guilty sat here in the sunshine with the sound of the sea lapping at the shore, while the others are hard at work at the rescue. Although I did my work for the morning before heading out.

'So, tell me, are you enjoying your time here in Crete?' Nicos asks as a waiter arrives with a basket of fresh bread and some gorgeous olive oil to dip it in.

'More than I thought I would. I've been out here regularly, to visit Judith. This time feels a bit different, though. I'm happy to be busy. Being busy distracts me from my thoughts,' I find myself saying.

'What thoughts do you want to be distracted from?' he presses, as he tears a piece of bread.

'Oh, I don't know. The fact that I wasn't exactly living the dream back home, I suppose.'

'Do you think anyone is really living a dream?' He takes a swig of beer from his bottle and regards me closely.

'I don't suppose so, no. I know everyone has their troubles. But it's good to at least have an idea of what you want to do with your life. To at least think you have things figured out.'

'And you haven't figured out what you want yet?' he asks.

I never really did have a plan. Obviously, me and my ex weren't meant to be together forever, yet I thought we were, caught up as I was. I've realised that if one person is more committed to the relationship than the other, sooner or later the less invested person will leave if temptation arises. I found that out the hard way. I truly believe wild horses couldn't drag you away from the person you really love.

'No. I know I needed a change, though, hence my coming here.'

'Could you make a living from furniture restoration? Is it a big thing in England?'

'As a matter of fact, it is, and, yes, possibly. Recycling is in everyone's consciousness, saving the planet and all that.'

'Then why not? Wes has told me how much you have encouraged him to pursue his music. Maybe it's time to think about what you want for yourself in life.'

Perhaps he's right. I also suggested Liz go to art school. I think sometimes we are oblivious to our own talents that other people see in us.

'I don't know, maybe I find it easier to help with other people's problems.' I smile, but his comment has brought a lump to my throat. Is that what I do? I wonder. Try and fix other people's problems? Does it make me feel good inside or am I just avoiding my own worries? It sounds a bit sad when I think about it, but maybe there's something inside of me that wants to feel people's gratitude. A counsellor would probably have a field day with me.

'There's one problem,' I tell him, before I pop some warm,

soft bread into my mouth. 'You need money and a workshop for restoration projects, and I have neither of those things right now.'

Just then our main meal arrives, mine a chicken dish in a creamy white wine sauce. Nicos has ordered a moussaka, and they both look mouth-watering. For a few minutes we are silent as we tuck into our delicious food.

'Good choice,' I say, wiping my mouth with a napkin and finally taking a breath. 'The food is really wonderful.'

'I'm glad you think so. It's a little less crowded here, less touristy. And I know a lovely path for a walk later alongside the beach, if you like?'

'I might need to walk this food off, but I don't want to be out for too long. My aunt has things to do before her operation tomorrow.'

'Of course.' He smiles. 'That was a little thoughtless of me. She's very lucky to have you around.'

'It was one of the reasons I came over, to help out so she could have her operation. We've always been close.'

'Maybe we can do the walk another time,' he suggests. 'I know a beautiful place to sit and watch the sunset at the end of the harbour.'

I imagine myself there with Nicos, strolling along hand in hand, and stopping to steal a kiss on a secluded beach.

'I'd like that.' I pull myself back to the present, realising there is work to do back home. I'm also excited by the prospect of working on the furniture and seeing what I can create.

We finish our food and decline a dessert, although the owner comes out and serves us a small shot of local brandy that really hits the spot. Nicos refuses to let me pay my share and soon we are back in the car ready for the drive home. In all honesty, I would have loved to stay here all afternoon, taking that walk along the beach path, my hand wrapped around Nicos's. The thought of it fills me with warmth.

We drive back and when we climb out of the car, Nicos invites me over for a drink later this evening.

'Thanks, Nicos, but I think it will be an early night for me. I'm taking my aunt to the hospital tomorrow morning.'

'I understand. Another time then. I will give you a tour of the house.'

'That would be lovely.' I smile.

'I hope everything goes well tomorrow for Judith. Bye, Tania.'

I still like how he says my name.

When I arrive home, the vet is just leaving with a smile on his face, which is reassuring.

'Well, he seems happy,' Judith tells me. 'He seems to think that the non-infected dogs are likely to remain so. It's a weight off my mind, I can tell you,' she says, wincing slightly as she climbs the front step to the entrance of the house.

'The sooner you get that knee sorted the better,' I say, and she agrees.

'Talking of hospital trips, I phoned the ward earlier and Yolanda is doing well today.'

'Oh, that's good to hear.' I'm pleased Yolanda is receiving good care, especially with Judith's operation coming up.

'Maybe we can have a walk together when she's up and about. We actually used to take walks with the dogs, once upon a time. It could help both of our recoveries to start that up again,' she tells me.

'Did you? Well, I'm sure you will soon be able to do it again. Maybe without the dogs at first, though, and especially not Smudge and Annie.' I raise an eyebrow.

'Oh, don't worry, I know.' She laughs. 'It will be nice to take a gentle walk, though, maybe sit on a bench chatting in the forest like we used to.' She smiles as if recalling a happy memory. 'Oh, and her son is arriving tomorrow.'

'Do you know him?' I ask.

'A little, but he moved away many years ago, so I only really came across him when he comes to visit. Nicos probably knows more about him than I do, as they grew up around here together apparently.'

'Nicos told me that. Although I kind of got the impression Nicos isn't his biggest fan,' I reveal.

'Really? Yolanda has never mentioned any problem between them.'

I think of how pleased she was to see Nicos when we went to her aid after the fall and wonder if she misses her son being around.

'Maybe it was nothing more than childhood stuff.' I shrug. 'As he said, not many people stay friends forever, I suppose. Anyway, enough about that, I'm pretty sure I'm on dinner duty with Liz.'

'Not today, it's all in hand. Liz has gone off with Frank to watch a band play in a bar somewhere. There will only be four of us this evening, and a chicken casserole is already on the go. Unless you've got somewhere else to be, that is?'

I think about it for a moment, but decide to stay for dinner at least. It will be nice to have a bit of a catch-up with Wes too, see what his plans are after he leaves in a few days.

'No really, it's fine. I'm more than happy to have dinner here,' I tell her. 'And I imagine it's an early night for you. Are you all sorted?'

'Yes, my hospital bag is packed. I won't lie, though; I can't help feeling a little nervous,' she confides.

'You'll be fine.' I reach over and take her hand. 'But don't expect an easy ride when you get home.' I wink. 'We need to get you moving as quickly as possible.'

'Gosh, I'd better enjoy the rest in hospital while I can then,' she teases.

Dinner is a relaxed affair, everyone happy that the dogs are continuing to do well. When the dishwasher has been loaded, Wes and I sit chatting with a coffee.

'So, are you looking forward to heading home next week?' I ask him.

'Not exactly looking forward to seeing my father, but I've managed to secure a gig at a pretty big venue in a nearby town.'

'Oh, Wes, that is brilliant!' I'm so thrilled for my friend.

'I must admit I'm pretty excited.' He sips his coffee. 'I hope I'm ready for a large audience, though.' He pulls a face.

'Of course you are! Your voice is amazing, you have a real talent. How could they not love you?'

'Thanks.' He grins. 'The guy who runs the place has heard me sing before, he used to work in a smaller bar I performed at. He manages a large city venue now, so I thought I'd give him a call.'

'Well, I'm thrilled for you, honestly, I'm sure it's the start of something big.'

'Thanks, Tania. You've been a real pal. I'll miss you. All of you. It's been a blast being here.'

'I'll miss you too. I'm glad you're figuring things out, Wes. I'm sure things will take off after the gig, just you wait and see.'

'I hope so.'

'Right, that's me.' I stand up and stretch my arms. 'It's an early start tomorrow. I'll do the morning feed before I take Judith, I—'

'We'll sort it,' Wes interrupts. 'Me and Liz can do that. You just get Judith to the hospital.'

'Thanks, Wes.'

We step forward and hug each other like the oldest of friends.

As I head off to bed, I feel so blessed to have met such great people this summer, and I like to think we can be friends for life.

NINETEEN

The next day the dogs look a lot happier, and Annie has even been leaping up at her cage, wagging her tail furiously in greeting. Smudge has been whining theatrically, hoping to be let out for a run, but he's not quite ready for that yet.

'Hey, not long now. I will walk you around the grounds later, but first I have to take Aunt Judith to the hospital,' I tell the dogs.

'I'll see you all soon.' Judith blows kisses to the animals, who bark in unison, as if they have understood every word.

'I will come and see you tonight,' says Lars to Judith. 'Good luck with everything.'

Although Lars would have liked to have driven us to the hospital, he knows he is needed here in Judith's absence.

'Thank you, Lars.' Judith embraces him, and I notice him give her a squeeze.

'Lars is a nice man,' I say to Judith as we drive. 'And it's obvious he thinks the world of you.' I turn to gauge her reaction.

'Do you think so?' she replies, almost coyly. 'I mean, we've become friends, obviously, but I think he might want something

more. I'm not sure I do at my age, and men, well, you know...'
She sounds a little shy.

'You're worried he might want sex?'

'Exactly. Men don't stop having the desire, do they? At least
that's what I've read. I know women do too, of course, but me?
Well, I haven't thought about that for years. Ray was my one
and only,' she confides.

'Do you feel physically attracted to him, though? Sorry,
Aunt Judith, I'm sure this isn't a conversation you want to be
having with me.'

'Who else would I speak to about it?' she asks with a laugh.
'I'm glad you broached the subject actually. And, yes, I do find
him attractive, but the thought of being intimate with someone
again terrifies me.'

'Well, I say just let things happen naturally. Lars is a lovely
man. I'm sure things will work out. There's plenty of life in you
both yet!' I reassure her.

Arriving at the hospital, Judith is quickly settled into a bed.
A doctor comes and explains, in very clear English, that she will
be taken for her operation in around an hour.

'Gosh I'm ravenous,' says Judith, who hasn't eaten since last
night. 'It's a shame I couldn't sneak a bacon sandwich in,' she
jokes.

'And have your operation postponed? Don't worry, it will
soon be done, and I'll be here waiting,' I reassure her.

'You're staying?' She looks surprised.

'Of course I am. I squared it with Wes, and Liz and Lars are
happy to help. Frank has volunteered to come along later too
and give them a hand.'

'That's wonderful. What would I do without you all?' She
smiles as she places her belongings into a bedside cupboard.

'I'm sure you'd manage. But it's an ideal time to have your
op. Don't forget it's the main reason I came over.'

· · ·

Later, as I wait for news of Judith's operation and with a coffee in hand, I find myself thinking about my own love life, Nicos, and how much I enjoy his company. I find that his handsome face pops into my mind often and how when I'm in his company something stirs inside of me. I think of how lucky he is to have inherited such a beautiful house, despite the sadness over losing his parents, and wonder whether he will decide to stick around. He's hinted at maybe buying out his sister's share of the house, but nothing is certain. Come to think of it, though, nothing is certain about my own future here.

I pull a book from my bag and settle into a comfortable chair, immersing myself in the story. Before I know it, Judith is being wheeled back to her bed. She is still under the anaesthetic for a little while longer, but soon enough she is sat up sipping some tea, a plate of buttered toast beside her.

'How are you feeling?' I ask.

'A bit groggy, hungry as a horse.' She laughs, picking up a slice of the toast.

A doctor approaches to check in and tells Judith that the operation has been successful.

'A day or two here, and then you must get moving quickly,' he advises. 'Although not too much initially.' He turns to me. 'Maybe a gentle assisted walk to begin with.'

'Don't worry, Judith, I won't be taking you mountain climbing. And maybe no bending down to the dogs, but we will get you moving with some gentle walks. Maybe down by the sea when you're ready?' I tell her.

'That sounds lovely. And, of course, I haven't forgotten what you said about me getting a life,' she says, but with a smile on her face.

'I never said that exactly.' I'd only reminded her that she ought to have a little fun sometimes, as her whole life is dedicated to the animals.

I hope she doesn't think I was being rude, but she deserves to have a little fun away from the rescue from time to time. We all need a little downtime.

'Don't worry, I'm glad you did. Yolanda and I once saw each other regularly. In fact, when I've finished this I'd quite like to go and see her, if you don't mind assisting me. She's on the floor above.'

'Of course I don't.'

With the agreement of the nurse on duty, who organised a wheelchair, we take the lift to the first floor. When we arrive at Yolanda's bed, there are several people sat around it laughing as she deals some cards on her food table.

'Judith.' She beckons her over when she spots her, and says something in Greek. Judith replies in Greek also, which surprises me a little, although it shouldn't do as she has lived here for many years after all.

'You've met my niece, Tania.' Judith beckons me over and Yolanda hugs me tightly and thanks me for coming to her rescue with Nicos on the evening of her accident.

'It was my pleasure, I'm glad you are on the mend. There will be no stopping you two when you are up and about.'

I try and recall a few Greek phrases that I have been practising, and hope I have told Yolanda that she looks very well. Until I hear raucous laughter from the people around her bed, that is.

'What's so funny?' Oh gosh, I hope I didn't just spout a bunch of nonsense to Yolanda.

'You told her she looks like a mountain goat,' a nurse who has been nearby refilling Yolanda's water jug tells me, laughing.

'Oh my goodness, I did what? I'm so sorry.' At least I know how to apologise, repeating the word *sygnomi* several times.

'*Ella, ella.*' Yolanda pats the side of her bed and invites me closer, still smiling.

'Laughing is good. Best medicine,' she says. 'And also

efcharisto. For helping me. My neighbour, Aristos, he good, but as useless as mud, and his wife she is a little crazy.' She taps her head.

'How are you feeling?' I ask.

'Okay. I laugh with my new friends, they cheer me. I have a crack somewhere here.' She points to her hip. The nurse explains that Yolanda's bones are actually very good, so the break will knit together naturally with plenty of rest.

Yolanda and Judith chat away, as the other people filter back to their beds. I leave them chatting together, heading off to the café on the ground floor in search of a snack, where I bump into Lars in a corridor, clutching a bunch of flowers.

'Lars, hi! Judith is upstairs, visiting her friend. I'll bring her back down shortly, now that you're here. I'm just grabbing a coffee; would you like to join me?'

'Yes, okay, that would be nice.' We walk along the tiled corridors to the café.

'Judith's having a good chat with Yolanda,' I explain as we sip our drinks and I dive into a sandwich, having skipped breakfast this morning. 'It seems they are both recovering well and I think they will be good medicine for each other, judging by the laughter I heard when I left. Although part of that was down to my poor grasp of the Greek language,' I admit, and he laughs when I explain my gaffe.

'It's such a relief to know that the surgery went well. And it's good that Judith is talking with Yolanda. Maybe you were right in saying that all work and no play can't be good for her.'

'You're very fond of my aunt, aren't you?' I broach the subject as we are alone.

'I am.' He stirs his coffee. 'She is a wonderful woman. We get along very well, but I'm not sure...' He hesitates for a moment as he takes a sip of his drink.

'Not sure what?'

'If she feels the same way about me. I know we are friends, but I think she is a very attractive woman.' He looks at me and smiles.

'I know she thinks a lot of you too, Lars. We talked about how much she appreciates your company. I told her she should let things happen naturally.'

'You did?' He looks surprised, and I hope he doesn't mind the fact that we have been discussing him.

'I did. Remember, she was married for many years and hasn't had a relationship since. She's probably just a little nervous.'

'Of course, I understand. It is the same for me,' he reveals. 'I had forty years with my wife until her death three years ago. After she died, I sold up and went travelling. My love of travel and exercising kept me sane, I think. I never thought I would develop feelings for anyone else,' he tells me.

'Well, I think you would make a wonderful couple,' I reassure him. 'You'd definitely have my blessing.'

'Thank you, Tania, that means a lot to me.'

I'm thrilled for them both, finding such a connection. Yet I can't help wondering whether I will find the love of my life just once, never mind twice.

Finishing our drinks, we take the lift to the next floor and Judith's eyes light up when she sees Lars beside me, clutching the flowers. Yolanda gives her a nudge and winks, and I can't help laughing.

Introductions are made, and a few minutes later, we are in the lift taking Judith back to her bed. The huge floral display is placed in a vase on her bedside table.

'Oh, Lars, thank you, they really are beautiful,' says Judith, taking in the arrangement of gorgeous purple and white flowers.

My phone rings, and I leave Judith and Lars alone for a moment as I go outside and take the call. It's Nicos.

'Hi, Tania, how is your aunt?' he asks and his gorgeous voice melts me just a little.

'Hi, Nicos, she's great, thanks for asking. The operation went well. Hopefully she will soon be up and about.'

'I'm glad things went well.' I can picture his handsome face at the other end of the phone.

'In fact, I took her to see Yolanda, who is also doing well.'

I tell him about Yolanda's strong bones and her not requiring any surgery.

'That's wonderful news. I think I am right about her being made of strong stuff.' He laughs. 'I would have suggested dinner this evening, but I imagine everyone else will already have prepared something.'

I hesitate for a moment, before I reply. Maybe the other guys wouldn't miss me tonight? I could invite Nicos to join us, but perhaps he wants us to spend some time alone?

'You're welcome to join us,' I find myself saying. 'Unless you were offering to cook for me, of course.' I try for a casual tone.

'Actually, that was exactly what I was thinking. I was looking for an excuse to spend some time alone with you.'

It suddenly feels a little hot in here, and I clear my throat before I answer. The thought of dining with him, alone, thrills me.

'In that case, what time would you like me?' I ask.

'Maybe seven o'clock?'

'Perfect. I'll see you later. Thanks, Nicos.'

When I return to Judith's bedside, I clearly have a beaming smile on my face.

'Someone's happy,' says Judith, glancing at Lars.

'Nicos has invited me over for dinner,' I tell her, still grinning.

'How lovely. Enjoy a nice, relaxed evening, you deserve it.'

'Oh, and he asked after you and sends his best wishes. I told him we had seen Yolanda too, and that she is doing well.'

'Well, you two have a nice evening. Liz and Frank have prepared dinner for everyone. Liz messaged me earlier.'

'Yes, go and enjoy yourself,' adds Lars. 'Nicos is a nice man.'

Suddenly I can't wait for this evening to arrive.

TWENTY

Driving home later, I take a detour for a walk along a beach as the *kafsonas* continues, slipping off my sandals and feeling the silky sand massage my feet. It's glorious here and very quiet today, apart from a few people swimming in the sea and one or two like myself, strolling along the sand. A boat sailing in the distance reminds me of the day out when we visited the caves. I long to do something like that with Nicos, stopping somewhere secluded for a picnic, swimming in the clear water. I shake myself as my mind wanders, and I imagine us lying down in the sand as he reaches for me and kisses me passionately.

I'm surprised at how Nicos has managed to get inside my head so quickly. It's not even as if we have kissed or anything, but I definitely felt something as our hands touched when he slid the wine glass towards me the other evening. There's no doubt he has been very attentive, but there hasn't really been a hint of anything romantic, or even that he is attracted to me. At least not yet. Maybe that's what this dinner invitation is all about.

But I can't help worrying. Am I just someone he is whiling away the time with whilst he sorts his parents' house out? What possible future could there be for us when his plans are so uncertain? Maybe he will head back to Heraklion and stay there, deciding to put his parents' house up for sale after all, so I must push any thoughts of romance firmly to the back of my mind. The stars are not exactly aligned for us, living so far apart. And I certainly don't want to risk being hurt again.

The sun is so warm, I feel like diving into the sparkling sea myself to cool off. Maybe I'll have a swim when I get back to the rescue. I smile at a little black cockapoo that reminds me of Annie, splashing about in the water. I should see what work needs to be done first if I'm out for the evening.

I stop at a beach café and sit with a frappe beneath a striped canvas shelter and just stare out to sea. I'll be on my way soon, but the cooling breeze is so wonderful here, I savour it for just a moment longer. The quiet stretch of beach is the perfect place to gather my thoughts.

I'm interrupted by the sound of the phone ringing in my pocket. It's my dad.

'Hi, Dad. How are you?'

'Not too bad, thanks. How are you doing?'

'I'm well, thanks.'

'And your aunt Judith?'

'She's okay, recovering well from her op.'

'Ah, yes, your mother spoke to her last night I think.'

'Is everything okay, Dad?' I ask as Dad isn't normally one for talking on the phone without a reason.

'I'm okay, thanks, but your mother has had a bit of a fall.' I hear a deep sigh.

'Oh no, what happened? Is she okay?' I can feel my heart racing, wondering what he is about to tell me.

'She came off her bike.'

'Gosh, is she alright? Has she broken anything?' I ask, concerned.

'No, thankfully, but she is pretty battered and bruised. She's getting about on a walking stick for now,' he tells me.

'Oh well, thank goodness nothing is broken.' I breathe a huge sigh of relief, yet can't help thinking that maybe their mountain biking days should be over. Or at least they ought to be looking for gentler cycling routes, rather than continuing cycling the roads with lots of bends.

Dad takes groups of people up into the hills of Andalusia on bike tours of the region. It's given him an extra income and it also keeps him remarkably fit. Sometimes Mum joins him but she prefers to bike alone and has groups of female friends that she often goes to lunch with after a ride. Maybe after her accident, she will favour coffee with friends over mountain bends.

There's a bit of a pause in the conversation, before I think about what to say. Even though I feel a little guilty for not offering to head over, Mum hasn't broken anything, whereas Aunt Judith has had fairly major surgery. She needs me right now. Dad could rearrange the bike tours, surely, and take care of Mum. He's certainly fit enough, although by his own admission, he isn't much of a cook.

'Actually, Dad, can I speak to Mum?'

'She's having a lie-down at the moment. The fall has shaken her up, that's for sure. But if you need to be with Judith, then that's up to you,' he says, managing to make me feel like the worst daughter in the world.

'Well, when she's awake, could you tell her I'll call her later?' I tell him, thinking that this couldn't have happened at a worse time.

I finish my frappe, and walk back towards the car, my thoughts whirring. Maybe I could go to Spain next week, when Judith is mobile again, but Mum might also be back on her feet by then. I'd planned to go and visit them in the autumn as they rarely come to the UK anymore.

Absorbed in my thoughts, I'm not really looking where I'm

going, and I collide with the black cockapoo that's leaping into the air after a frisbee, who manages to knock me off my feet.

A Greek woman rushes over and apologises.

'I'm fine, it's okay.' I brush sand from myself as she helps me to my feet.

'I wasn't looking where I was going,' I tell her. 'It's a good job I love dogs, hey?' I pet the friendly dog, and it wags its tail.

Suddenly I can't wait to be back amongst my four-legged friends. They can be hard work sometimes, and, yes, they get sick, but they do not have the complicated emotions that us humans have. And there's a lot to be said for that.

Everything seems to be under control when I arrive back. I go and say hi to the dogs in their pens, as even though there is an area to run around, it's reserved for early evening as it's still far too hot right now and the dogs would risk dehydration. The dogs have been out earlier with volunteers and Liz and Frank are now sat beneath the trees on an outdoor sofa, arms wrapped around each other.

'Hi, guys.' I flop down on a nearby chair.

'How's Judith?' asks Liz, untangling herself from Frank and sitting up.

'She's okay. Her friend is in the same hospital, so they've been having a long overdue catch-up.' I tell them about Yolanda. 'Judith should be home in a couple of days.'

'I'm glad she's okay,' says Liz.

'Right, I'm going to have a swim, before I melt,' I tell them and go upstairs to change.

Wes is stretched out on a sunlounger at the poolside when I arrive, his body glistening with water, suggesting he's just had a swim.

'Hi, Wes,' I say, and he sits up and asks me all about Judith. I fill him in, before diving into the glorious water, just as Lars is climbing out. Even though it's hot outside, the pool is exactly the right temperature and I feel the water washing over me and cooling me down at once.

I concentrate on my breathing, swimming energetically, feeling the need to release the sudden tension that has appeared in my shoulders and throughout my body. With every stroke, I feel the tension release a little, and when I eventually climb out, I feel a little less stressed.

'Are you in training for the Olympics?' asks Wes. 'I've never seen you go for it like that before.'

'It was either that or start on the wine,' I tell him as I towel myself dry. 'Probably the lesser of the two evils, at this time of day.'

'What's up?' he asks.

I tell him about my mum having a fall.

'I'm going to ring her before dinner. Obviously, I'm concerned about her, but the timing couldn't be worse, what with Judith.' I sigh.

'I see what you mean. I would have stayed on and helped out, if you wanted to go see your folks in Spain, but I have the concert at the weekend.'

'It's very kind of you to offer, Wes, but you have your own life to live. And I know Lars will be here helping Judith, but he's getting on in years too.'

'And probably fitter than all of us,' he reminds me.

'That's true, but he's here to pitch in and look after the dogs, not look after my aunt. Anyway, I'll figure it out.' Although frustratingly, I'm really not sure how.

I paint a bright smile on my face as I head off to shower before I give Mum a ring.

Mum insists she is fine and tells me that Dad is just fussing and that there was no need for him to have called and worried me.

'Yes, I get a little tired, it only happened two days ago and a fall can shake you up a bit as you get older,' she tells me. 'But nothing is broken and I'm pretty fit for almost seventy. I'm sure I'll be just fine.'

'Well, I promise I'll be over just as soon as Judith is up and about, but it might take a week or so.' I feel so torn over where my loyalties lie right now.

'No, really, stick to your plan of coming over in the autumn, it isn't too far away. I'm looking forward to us taking gentle walks in the cooler weather,' she reassures me.

I feel better having chatted to her. And Dad only has two tours booked, and although they take several hours, I'm sure Mum will be alright. She has a good friend who lives next door, so maybe I shouldn't be worrying quite so much, but at the same time I can't help feeling a little guilty.

'I called Judith earlier at the hospital,' Mum says. 'She seems in good spirits. She's very lucky to have you there.'

I know it isn't a pointed remark, yet her comment succeeds in making me feel bad once more, although I know it wasn't Mum's intention to make me feel that way.

My heart feels a little heavy as I get ready for my evening with Nicos and, after showering and changing into a long white cotton dress, I join the others for a pre-dinner glass of wine outside.

Everyone is tucking into a delicious-looking beef stifado.

'That looks amazing, I kind of wish I was just going for drinks with Nicos now,' I joke.

'Are you okay?' asks Liz, maybe noticing I don't seem my usual self.

'Yeah, just tired I think.' I don't feel like discussing what's on my mind, and Wes smiles knowingly as he tops up my wine glass.

'Anyway, you look really nice,' she says kindly. 'Nicos is a lucky man.'

I cross the road to Nicos's house and as I approach the garden, I notice white fairy lights draped all around the front porch. A table for two has also been set, with a flickering chunky candle at its centre.

As Nicos sees me approaching, he walks down the path to greet me, opening the gate.

'You look beautiful,' he says, taking in my white dress accessorised with colourful jewellery.

'Thank you.'

'I thought we'd eat outside on the front porch. We have the best view across the valley from here.' His eyes flick over my body again and I can feel my cheeks burn. Hopefully that's not the only view he enjoys tonight.

The valley in front of me is pretty stunning too, I can't help thinking. Nicos is wearing a black shirt, and dark jeans and an air of effortless sex appeal.

'This looks amazing.' I glance at the perfectly set table; a vase of white flowers sits beside the candle.

Like a true gentleman, he pulls my chair back for me to sit down, before he pours a glass of champagne that is sitting in an ice bucket.

'Champagne? What's the occasion?' I ask.

'You're here, the night is beautiful, what more reason do we need?' He locks eyes with me and I feel my heart rate quicken once again.

'How has your day been?' I ask after I've answered his questions about mine, leaving out the bit about the phone call with my parents. I don't want to ruin the mood by discussing the dilemma I suddenly find myself in.

'Busy. I've done quite a bit inside. It's pretty dusty, hence the idea to eat outside on the terrace.'

'Does that include the kitchen? Will I find dust in my food?' I joke.

'Definitely not. Or at least I hope not.' He pulls a face.

'Well, you chose well, setting the table out here. It looks wonderful.'

The twinkling white lights above our heads stretch across the full length of the porch, casting a soft glow and meeting the grass beyond that is bathed in the soft moonlight.

When Nicos disappears into the kitchen for the starter, the sound of smooth music suddenly fills the air. I recognise the Frank Sinatra song from the opening bar, as he is a favourite of Judith's.

'"Strangers in the Night".' I smile as I take a sip of my champagne. 'Is that what we are then?'

'Of course not. Trust that to be the first song on the compilation.' He laughs.

I make short work of the delicious pâté starter and by the time the main course is served, I've drunk two glasses of champagne and feel pleasantly mellow.

'This is all so delicious. Where did you learn to cook?' I ask, tucking into the melt-in-the-mouth steak.

'Here and there. Watching TV programmes, the odd cookbook. My ex-wife taught me a thing or two as well.'

'Oh, you never told me you were divorced?'

'You never asked.' He smiles. 'And it's maybe not the very first thing I would tell you.' He shrugs.

'I guess not. How long have you been divorced?' I ask, and for some unfathomable reason my heart sinks a little. I hope he isn't newly separated.

'Coming up for two years,' he tells me, and I feel a little reassured. Two years is quite a long time to be out of a relationship, I suppose, so hopefully he's moved on. I wouldn't want to get involved with someone who is recently single, then wonder why I am even thinking that way.

'Do you have children?' I ask, realising I know almost nothing about him, yet here I am dining at his home.

Nicos takes a long glug of his champagne.

'One. A boy called Lucas. He is nine years old.' He seems to be toying with his food as he speaks.

'That's a nice age. Do you get to see him much?' I'm suddenly aware that I'm asking him a lot of questions. I could kick myself. But I have no idea where this is going, if anywhere. I'm simply enjoying dinner, getting to know a friendly neighbour.

'As often as I can, yes.'

After a pause, we leave the subject of his ex-wife and son and talk turns to food again.

'Now, tell me truthfully, what do you think of the pepper sauce? I added a little brandy, but I was worried maybe too much?'

'Not at all, it's delicious. Like a steak Diane.'

We finish up with some of the brandy he mentioned and I'm beginning to feel delightfully relaxed.

'Would you like to dance?' Nicos extends his hand and I take hold of it as he pulls me to my feet. Beneath the twinkling lights on the porch, we dance to a slow number and when he circles his arms around my waist and pulls me close. I feel as if I'm walking on air.

We dance beneath the stars, listening to the music and Nicos runs his fingers gently up and down my back. I'm anticipating what might happen next, when he lifts my chin towards him and kisses me softly on the lips. I drape my arms around his neck and kiss him back, as my whole body responds.

'I'm glad you came here,' he whispers in my ear when we finally pull apart.

'Me too,' I mumble, barely able to string a sentence together. The kiss was so perfect and somehow everything I imagined it would be.

There's a sofa on the porch. And after a while, I kick off my shoes and we sit down together, cuddled up, looking at the white moon.

'This evening has been wonderful.' I sigh with pleasure. 'I wish I could stay here all night.'

'You could if you like.' He turns to look at me, a longing in his eyes.

It's an exciting prospect, but I've never been one who is into casual affairs.

'I probably shouldn't,' I tell him. 'I have an early start tomorrow, then I'm going to visit Judith at the hospital.'

Half an hour later, I reluctantly prise myself away from Nicos, and pull my shoes on ready to head back home. Nicos walks with me and, at the gate, he kisses me goodnight, more deeply than the last time and I almost take him by the hand and drag him back to his bedroom.

'Goodnight, Nicos, thank you for a lovely evening,' I tell him, feeling deliriously happy.

'The pleasure was all mine,' he tells me, before I glide inside, floating on a cloud.

TWENTY-ONE

Two days later, Judith has arrived home and is making remarkable progress already. Yolanda must stay in hospital for a while longer, so I've agreed to take Judith to visit her friend in a couple of days' time. While she was in the hospital I took some fabric Judith had here at the rescue, and covered the wing-backed chair from Nicos's house. Yolanda donated one of her beautiful handmade cushions, as a finishing touch.

'But for now,' I tell Judith, guiding her to the newly refurbished chair with a plumped-up cushion, 'we are going to spoil you. Lars has baked an apple pie.'

'You can bake?' She looks at Lars in admiration. 'And apple pie just happens to be my favourite.'

'I know,' says Lars, with a wry smile.

'Gosh, I feel a little spoilt, especially sat here in this beautiful chair.' She runs her hands along the fabric and smiles.

Once she is settled, I serve her a pot of tea and a slice of warm apple pie, with ice cream.

'I could get used to this,' says Judith, forking a mouthful of pie into her mouth and making appreciative noises.

'Don't get too used to it. You need to get moving. But as it's your first day home, I guess you deserve a little TLC,' I tell her.

'Don't worry I won't take advantage of your good nature; the whole point of this operation is to give me a new lease of life, remember. I intend to get moving as soon as I can. Maybe after I've read a few chapters of my book, though.' She winks.

I leave her settled and walk outside to chat to Wes, who will be leaving in around an hour and I've offered to drive him to the airport. He's chatting to Liz as she bundles hay into the donkey feeding troughs. As I approach the enclosure, my number one fan Eric sidles over and shoves his head under my arm.

'Hi, Eric, how's things?' I ask, and I laugh as he brays loudly as if in response. I swear these animals are half human. 'That good, hey?' I stroke him and he enjoys it, nuzzling my hand. 'Well, behave yourself. And don't forget to thank Liz and Wes for refilling your hay feeder. Wes is going home shortly,' I say, and I kid you not, Eric walks over to Wes and nudges his back. Wes turns around and pets Eric, who for once doesn't back off and walk away.

'What did you say to him?' Wes laughs.

'I told him you were leaving today. He was just saying goodbye.'

'And, of course, he understood you.' He laughs again. 'Maybe you should get out of the sun for a bit.'

'I'm telling you, he knows every word you say. Donkeys are highly intelligent animals.'

'There's one thing you've forgotten. He's a Greek donkey, so won't have understood a single word.'

'Don't be too sure,' I tell him, feeling irrationally disappointed by his remark.

It hits me then, how much I am going to miss Wes. We bonded really quickly, and the place just isn't going to be the same when he's not around. I will miss him so much.

After hugs all round, Wes loads his case into the boot of

Judith's car as we prepare to head off for the airport. Nicos approaches and shakes Wes by the hand and wishes him well. I can feel my heart start beating faster, as I recall the kisses we shared last night, the ones that I've relived over and over again since the moment I woke.

'You're welcome to come and make a start on your furniture project,' Nicos offers, coming over to me as Wes continues his goodbyes before we set off. 'I have a meeting today, but I'll be home later in the afternoon. Come over whenever you like.' He smiles that gorgeous smile, and a part of me wishes he didn't have the effect he does on me, yet each day I find myself looking forward to seeing him more and more.

'Actually, making a start on the furniture this afternoon might not be a bad idea. A new volunteer is arriving this evening, so I will need to be around to show him the ropes and might not have time after that.'

'Perfect. I'll see you later.'

'It's so beautiful here, I don't think I'll ever forget this summer,' says Wes as we drive through the forest roads, taking in the familiar route.

'I know what you mean. It does stay with you, doesn't it? When I was in a bit of a rut back home, the memories of Pine Forest drew me back once more. And, of course, it's always a joy to see my aunt.'

'She's a great woman,' agrees Wes. 'Those animals are so lucky to live in a place like that.'

We enjoy the drive in appreciative silence, before Wes turns to me. 'It was good to talk to you about my music. I think you gave me the courage to tell my father it's something I really want to pursue as a career.'

'I did?' I turn to him and smile. 'Well, I'm very pleased

about that. Although I'm sure you would have figured it out yourself.'

'I'm not so sure. After a while I think I might have just accepted my fate being a part of the family business,' he muses. 'My music would probably have remained nothing more than a hobby.'

We say a final goodbye at the airport, with promises to stay in touch. Even though people often say that, I think I have a friend for life in Wes.

'Get someone to record your concert and send it to me if you can, I'd love to see it. And good luck.'

'Thank you, Tania, I'll text you soon.'

I watch Wes walk towards departures, pulling his case, his good looks getting admiring glances from a group of women who are stood chatting. If he makes it in the music industry, I get the feeling he will attract a whole lot more female admirers. I wish him all the luck in the world.

TWENTY-TWO

When I return to the rescue, a group of volunteers have arrived to walk some of the dogs. Smudge and Annie are champing at the bit to get outside, having been inside for several days now, and a young couple are keen to walk them.

'I hope you'll be okay with these two, they are not for the faint-hearted,' I tell the couple, who look young and fit enough to hopefully cope with them.

'Don't worry. I'm sure we'll be fine,' says the muscular, dark-haired bloke.

'Oh, and if they're off lead, maybe avoid the nature reserve.' I tell the couple about the dogs recently being ill. 'The water has been tested, and came back as uncontaminated, but just to be on the safe side.'

'No worries. There are enough freshwater streams if they need to cool down. We've found some gorgeous spots up in the mountains on our hikes so far,' says the pretty young woman, who bends down to pet Smudge, who laps it up and makes a very contented noise. Annie is being petted by the bloke, and is wagging her tail like crazy.

'Do they come back okay, if you let them off the lead?' asks the girl.

'I'd say pretty much, yes. But use the extendable leads if you don't feel comfortable doing that,' I advise them as we get the dogs ready. 'They can be a little lively.'

'Well, maybe we will use the extendable lead. We want to return the dogs in one piece,' says the young man.

When the morning work is done, and I've helped Judith take a short, tentative walk around the grounds on her sticks, I arm myself with some DIY paraphernalia and head across the road.

Nicos is pacing the back garden, talking on the telephone when I arrive. I retreat into the background for a moment, when I hear him raise his voice a little. Maybe now isn't a good time. I'm almost at the gate, when Nicos calls me over.

'Tania, please come in.' He plasters a smile on his face.

'Are you sure this is a good time?' I ask a little uncertainly.

'Yes, yes, of course. I've just been sorting a few things out,' he tells me, not elaborating. 'Would you like a coffee?' he offers.

'Coffee would be nice, then I'll get on with sanding down the chest of drawers.'

After coffee, Nicos says he needs to head out to attend to some business, and I feel a little sad. I had thought we would have some time together.

I begin sanding the drawers, finding the mindless, repetitive motion quite soothing. I'm soon in a rhythm and after an hour I take a break. It's harder work than I remember, especially in the heat. I'll apply a base coat of paint later, and maybe the rest tomorrow. I cannot wait to see how it turns out with the pretty handles I've bought for the drawer fronts.

I gulp down some water from the fridge, which Nicos told me to help myself to, then find myself wandering around the large rear garden. It is so peaceful here, the only sound being a dog's occasional bark coming from the rescue. At the end of the garden, beyond the old stable block, is a row of trees, the sound of water gushing gently in the background. I make my way through a clearing, to the sight of hills and mountains rising in the background.

It's almost like a secret place beyond the garden. Glancing around, I spot a bench between two tall trees and as I head closer, I can see that it's a memorial bench that looks as though it's been quite recently installed. A bronze plaque has the inscription of two people's names, and I wonder whether it might be a memorial for Nicos's parents.

Back at the house, I cover the drawers in a dust sheet once the base coat is done and dry enough. It's unlikely to rain but I know from experience that the weather can change quickly, especially up in the hills. I resist the urge to explore the house, visualising how it might look if it were transformed into a modern style with some elegant soft furnishings.

Back at the rescue, feeling disappointed at missing Nicos for most of the afternoon, I busy myself again. The volunteers have returned the dogs, all in one piece thankfully; Lars and I are making a late lunch when Aunt Judith tells us the new volunteer will be arriving in around an hour.

When everything has been put away, I head up to my room and get changed. It's been a lovely day, and I can't wait until tomorrow to get back to refurbishing the chest of drawers. I'm beginning to feel that my life here is falling into an easy routine and wonder what there is at home for me, when I return.

Back downstairs, I pass Lars in the kitchen and he tells me Judith is just welcoming the new volunteer, so I go along and say hello. And I'm shocked when the new arrival shakes me by the hand with a huge smile on his face.

'Euan,' I say in total surprise. 'What are you doing here?'

TWENTY-THREE

We're sat having a cold drink outside after Euan has been shown to his room and had a look around the rescue and met the animals.

'I still can't believe you're here.' I'm so shocked to see my airport friend sat in front of me.

'Ah well, you inspired me.' His manner is just as friendly as I remember. 'My friend's bar was a bit quiet, if I'm honest. I almost felt guilty taking any wages from him.' He pauses to take a drink of beer. 'Anyway, as I was finishing my time there, I remembered our chat about the rescue, so I looked it up online and got in touch with your aunt.' He beams that winning smile. With his blond hair, tanned skin and wide smile, he reminds me of one of those Australian surfer types I've seen in the movies.

'Well, it's really good to see you, Euan. And you will certainly earn your keep around here, that's for sure.'

'Excellent. I like to be busy.'

It's as if we have been friends forever and I recall feeling that way when we chatted at the airport over coffee. Euan begins telling me a funny story from his time in Stalis.

'My friend runs an English pub in Stalis, think draught beer and Sunday roasts,' he tells me. 'Anyway, there was an Elton John tribute planned one evening, but the bloke failed to turn up and my friend went into blind panic. The place was packed out.'

'Oh no, what happened?' I can just imagine a load of expectant punters awaiting the Elton tribute on stage.

'I stepped up and did it.' He starts laughing at the memory.

'You did the tribute? I didn't know you could sing?' He really is full of surprises.

'I can't really.' He laughs. 'But never knowingly being one to turn down a few quid, I thought I'd have a go. Turns out I can mimic Elton John's voice quite well, though. By the time I had all the gear on, the huge glasses and outfit, I actually managed to pull it off.'

'Oh my goodness!' I can hardly believe what I'm hearing, and find myself laughing loudly. 'How did it go?'

'The audience apparently loved it. They were on their feet,' he recalls. 'Although it helped that I didn't go on 'til ten o'clock, so most of them were probably half-cut.' He laughs.

After dinner, we're playing a card game when my phone pings. It's a text from Nicos asking if I would like to take a drive down into Hersonissos tomorrow if I have any free time. I had hoped to continue with the drawer refurbishment if I have a spare minute, yet the thought of spending time with Nicos at the harbour sounds very tempting. I reply that it sounds like a nice idea, and I will call him in the morning.

A little after ten thirty, it's time to turn in.

'I'm glad we met up again, Tania.' Euan steps forward and gives me a hug goodnight.

'Me too,' I tell him, really meaning it. I think the next few weeks are going to be a lot of fun.

.   .   .

The next morning, after a good walk around the rescue, and Judith getting accustomed to moving about with her new knee, we're both taking a break sipping a cooling lemon drink beneath the trees. I tell her all about the chat with Mum.

'I feel a bit guilty not going over right now,' I admit. 'But Mum assured me she was fine, and at least she hasn't broken anything. I think Dad was keen because he didn't want to rearrange some bike tours.'

'I can't imagine your dad being a very good nurse,' says Judith. 'Maybe that's why he suggested you go over and stay.'

'Whatever happened to "in sickness and in health"?' I ask.

'I know, but your dad has never been the type to dish out the sympathy, he's more the practical type.'

'I think they both are,' I find myself saying, thinking of how rarely they showed compassion in a situation, but rather rolled up their sleeves and sorted things out in a hands-on way. Once, in the street where we lived, a ceiling came crashing down on a neighbour, and they set about clearing the debris whilst the other neighbour held hands and soothed the old gentleman until the ambulance arrived.

'You were well loved, you know,' says Judith as if tapping into my thoughts. 'I just don't think your parents were the affectionate type.'

'So why did they have children?' I don't feel any anger or judgement towards my parents; I'm just trying to understand them a little.

'Well, I guess your dad is like a lot of blokes of his generation who don't really express their feelings and your mum, well, maybe she took after our mother.' Judith sips her drink.

I don't remember Gran much; I was very small when she died but I'm keen to know more.

'In what way?' I ask.

'Our mother, Mary, was a little cold. She never showed affection, but she'd had a really hard life,' she explains. 'So maybe she just got on with things, never really letting her emotions rise to the surface and get in the way. Our father was in a wheelchair after an accident during World War Two. She looked after him and three children. In a tiny house. It can't have been easy.

'There was also a brother who died in his teens, so that must have been an awful thing for the family to deal with too.'

'I suppose it explains Mum's distant nature, if that's what she was shown, but you had the same parents and you're so warm.' I feel tears prick my eyes when I think of all the love she has shown me over the years. Judith reaches over and clasps my hand in hers.

'There is a lot to be said for our DNA.' She smiles. 'Maybe our mother was just built that way, as is your mum. Don't be too hard on her, she truly does love you, albeit in her own way.'

I think about how unselfishly Mum told me not to dash over, knowing I was looking after Judith. Maybe over the years she has realised how she was when I was young, leaving me with Judith so often. But Judith's right. Sometimes we are the way we are, not just because something has been modelled to us, but because it really is in our genes. I feel better after talking to Judith. Nothing in life is black and white and I guess we are all just muddling along, doing the best we can. I suddenly feel like speaking to Mum, and head off to give her a call.

TWENTY-FOUR

The Greek sun is beating down. Thankfully the dogs seem to be completely back to normal, eating voraciously and happily being taken out on walks by volunteers in and outside the centre.

Nicos is coming to collect me and take me for lunch in a couple of hours, so I chat to Euan while waiting for his arrival. I tell him about my mum coming off her bike, as it's on my mind after calling her. He reassures me I did the right thing staying here, and soon we are talking about accidents we have sustained over the years and showing battle scars.

'I got this when I fell off a mountain.' Euan lifts his vest and shows me a scar that runs down the side of his body.

'You fell off a mountain?' I ask, aghast.

'Oh yeah, but I was near the bottom. About four foot from the ground. Landed on my side, got away with a few broken ribs.'

'This scar is from when I came off a swing as a kid.'

I show him the scar beneath my knee, which is a faint line now but still visible.

'This one was really painful.' He lowers his pants just a

fraction to reveal the scar just above one of his buttocks. 'I fell onto some broken glass at a party.'

'Ouch. Well, I have this when I came off a moped.' I lift the skirt I'm wearing, revealing the scar on my upper thigh, just as Nicos approaches, looking gorgeous in a black T-shirt that hugs him in all the right places. He also smells divine.

'I hope I'm not interrupting anything,' says Nicos as he takes in the scene, and I'm completely mortified.

'Gosh, no.' I quickly brush down my skirt, wondering what on earth he must be thinking. 'We were just comparing battle scars. Nicos, this is Euan.'

'Nice to meet you, Euan.' Nicos smiles, but it doesn't quite reach his eyes.

'Right, see you later,' I tell Euan as I walk to the car with Nicos.

'You seemed very at ease with the new arrival, I couldn't help noticing,' says Nicos, staring at the road ahead as he drives.

'I can imagine how it might have looked. But he's not exactly someone I've only just met. I got to know him a little on the way here,' I explain.

'Ah, I see. Well, he seems like a nice bloke,' he says, turning to smile at me.

'Oh, he is. Some of his stories are so funny. I think you would really like him.' I can't help but smile when I think of the Elton John tribute.

Driving along, I feel proud to be sat next to Nicos in his stylish car, and I notice an attractive woman check him out when we sit at traffic lights.

'So today, I thought we could do something a little bit different,' Nicos tells me.

'Sounds intriguing.'

'I thought it might be fun if we hired a couple of quad bikes and drove along the coast road to a quiet section of beach I know.'

'Oh amazing. I'm definitely up for that. You don't want me to ride pillion then?'

'I thought we might have a race at the beach. I warn you, I'm quite competitive,' he lets slip.

'Really? Bring it on.'

After picking up the bikes from a local hire shop, we drive along, me following Nicos, until we pull into an almost secluded beach.

'So, you're a bit of a thrill seeker then?' I ask, revving the engine of my bike and he laughs.

'It's hardly an F1 circuit. And I wouldn't say I'm a thrill seeker exactly, although I do enjoy waterskiing from time to time and I have been paragliding. I find outdoor pursuits very relaxing, especially when I have been at my desk all day.'

'I've been telling Judith she ought to get out and have a little more fun. Work can consume you, if you're not careful.'

'That's true. Meetups with friends tend to be centred around food and drink, don't they? Not that there's anything wrong with that, but we should never forget to try something different every now and then. Have a little fun.'

We fasten our helmets again and are soon zooming along the sand. Nicos is hanging back, ready to make his move and overtake me but I'm ready, and I accelerate as he approaches. Maybe I ought to have fessed up that I used to ride an ex-boyfriend's moped around the hills of Lancashire, speed being something I was never afraid of. With the end of this stretch of the beach in sight, I'm way in front and feeling triumphant, when suddenly, from nowhere, Nicos overtakes me. I battle to keep up with him for the final stretch, but he just pips me to the post.

'I never realised you could drive so well. Maybe you were keeping something from me.' He looks at me a little suspiciously.

'I've never ridden a quad bike before, but I was always quite comfortable on a motorbike,' I confess.

'Ah, I see. Well, that makes sense. I believe you were trying to trick me into thinking it was something you would be very feeble at.'

'Feeble? That's not something I have ever been called, thanks very much.'

'I can't imagine it would be. Maybe that was the wrong word.' He grins. 'Come along, let's see if you can beat me at crazy golf then. I know a place not far from here.'

We take a short drive up into the resort of Koutouloufari, a place I haven't visited in years, but holds happy memories for me. Judith and Ray took me there once and we had lunch and played crazy golf, at the place we are visiting today. The little cobbled streets of the pretty village have restaurants running through a main street and pots of flowers outside, some with hanging baskets above canopies, others with elevated wooden terraces set with tables that give a distant view of a beach. Mopeds are leaning against the walls of some of the bars and down a side street, I glimpse a ginger cat sat on a stone step outside a house with a blue painted door. As I walk, a host of memories comes rushing back.

'I remember this place,' I tell Nicos, recalling a time Mum and Dad actually came over and we spent a week together, before I remained with Judith for another week when they went to Spain. I loved every minute of that summer and treasure those memories of going to the beach and having ice creams when the day's work was done at the rescue.

Clutching our scorecards, we play a fun game, and I beat Nicos fair and square.

'Okay, so now we're even.' He laughs. 'Do you have time for a drink before we leave?' He nods towards a café across the road that has red flowers in blue pots outside.

'Of course.'

. . .

Sitting at a table on an elevated balcony that overlooks the busy road, I ask how the house renovations are coming along.

'Pretty well. I will show you how the bedrooms are going next time you come over.'

He holds my gaze for a second longer than is necessary and I try to keep my composure and not to picture Nicos lying in bed. He is just showing off the house. Isn't he? Even if he was implying more, would it go anywhere? I wish I knew if he was staying here. Or that I knew what I was going to do next.

'Lovely,' I say, sipping the froth from my drink. 'It's been so much fun today, thanks, Nicos. And if it's okay with you, I was hoping to maybe do the first coat on the drawers later before the light fades. After I have checked on the animals.'

'Of course. I've enjoyed myself today too. I always enjoy spending time with you.' He reaches for my hand across the table, the touch of it thrilling me.

Later, as we approach the village, I notice a car outside the rescue and Judith chatting to someone. After we get out of the car and draw closer, I realise Yolanda is in the back of a car.

'Nicos?' A dark-haired man shakes Nicos by the hand and speaks to him in Greek. Nicos introduces us. It's Yolanda's son, Artemis.

'Hi, pleased to meet you.' I smile. To my surprise, he kisses me on both cheeks, not something anyone else around here has done so far. This guy oozes confidence and it's pretty obvious he likes himself. With his undeniable good looks, he is obviously accustomed to women falling under his spell.

The reunion chat between the men is very brief, I notice, Nicos excusing himself quite quickly, telling me he will see me later as he leaves.

'We must be off also, Judith. I will see you tomorrow,' says Yolanda.

'Two invalids together. I'll bring some scones over,' Judith replies, with a wave goodbye.

'I'll bake the scones,' 'I tell her as we walk inside. 'I don't want you overdoing things.' Though I am happy to say, Judith is making great progress in her recovery.

'If you insist.' Judith pats my arm. 'Your scones are better than mine anyway.'

I check on the animals and have a cup of tea with Liz, as Euan saunters over.

'How was your day?' he asks, flopping into a chair beside us.

'Good, great actually, it was a lot of fun.' I tell them about the quad biking and the crazy golf.

'We were meant to do that, weren't we?' Liz reminds me. 'Before we got a bit distracted.'

'Speak for yourself,' I tease.

'I know, Frank's wonderful.' She sighs. 'Although you've been spending a fair bit of time with Nicos too. How's that going?'

Euan is listening to us both and smiling. 'You two have been busy, haven't you?'

'Cheeky. So how are you enjoying being here?' I ask Euan.

'Loving it so far, this place is pretty amazing. It runs like clockwork, doesn't it?'

'It does. The rescue took a little while to build up, but it's like a well-oiled machine now. Judith makes sure the volunteers are real animal lovers. They don't stay if they're not fully committed, which can be a right headache.'

'I can imagine. Anyway, it seems like a great place. I think I'm going to enjoy the next six weeks.'

'What are your plans after that?' asks Liz.

'Not sure. I might head to Cyprus, actually. It's a bit easier for English people to get jobs there. I have a contact at a car hire place at the airport.'

'Do you know people all over the world?' I ask, thinking of his friend who runs the bar in Stalis.

'I wish. No, actually, although I did meet a lady in France last year who offered me a bed if I ever needed one.' He gives a cheeky smile.

'I bet she did,' says Liz, saying what I was just thinking.

'She's sixty-five. And if you must know it was in exchange for looking after her garden,' he admits.

'Lady garden.' Liz coughs the words out and has us both roaring with laughter.

'You're a right one, you,' Euan says with a laugh. 'I've only been here five minutes and you're already suggesting I'm a gigolo.'

'Don't mind me, I'm teasing,' says Liz.

'I don't mind you. Not at all.' He gives her the kind of look that Frank usually gives her.

'Right, I'm off,' I say. 'I'm going to do a little work on some furniture before sunset.' I find myself asking Liz if Frank is calling over later. Frank and Liz make a great couple, but there is no doubting Euan's charm. She is leaving soon, and I would hate anything to ruin her blossoming relationship with Frank.

'Yeah, in about an hour.' She stands. 'I'm going to grab a shower. Catch you guys later.'

Euan walks over to the donkey area. I watch as he approaches and shake my head in disbelief as Eric saunters towards him and nudges him with his head and Euan strokes him. It seems even animals are not immune to his easy charm.

TWENTY-FIVE

With the drawers beautifully sanded, I begin painting them in an Air Force blue shade. I can't wait to see Judith's face when it's all finished.

'It was good to see Yolanda is back home. It must have been nice to see Artemis after all this time,' I say as I concentrate on the brushstrokes.

'Not especially. We were friends so long ago.' He shrugs. I can tell there's more to it, but I don't push. I'm trying to break the habit of asking too many questions, something I became accustomed to doing at the doctor's surgery, I guess.

Nicos disappears then, and returns a minute later and hands me a bottle of water. I'm surprised when he picks up the conversation.

'Artemis and I were good friends as kids. We went everywhere together on our bikes, made rope swings over the streams, that kind of thing,' he recalls. 'There were only a few children around here.' He pauses to take a drink of water.

'What changed between you?'

'We grew up.' He gives a rueful smile. 'I first noticed him becoming competitive towards me when we were teenagers.

When I got my first motorbike, he got a bigger one. He got his first car before I did, first girlfriend, everything and relished telling me so. When I became engaged, he decided he would take my fiancée from me, just because he could.'

'Oh, that's awful, Nicos. I'm so sorry.'

No wonder he hasn't exactly welcomed Artemis here with open arms.

'It's ancient history.' Nicos shrugs. 'Although it is sad because I have so many wonderful memories of our childhood years,' he tells me.

'I can imagine. It must have hurt.'

'It did at the time, but looking back I was eighteen and about to start university, we were just kids really. He did me a favour. I went to university and married in my late twenties, although that did not turn out the way I expected.' He pulls a garden chair over and sits down. 'Artemis ended up leaving the village too, for a sales job in the city with his new wife. Things were never the same between us,' he confides. 'I've seen him occasionally over the years and we manage to at least be civil to each other now.' He shrugs again.

'At least you have the grace to be civil to him these days. It's a shame, though, as you were such good childhood friends. It sounds like he was jealous of you.'

'Jealous of me? He was taller, better looking, good at sports.'

I put my brush down and look at him. 'Maybe he was better at sports than you, but better looking? Never.' I stroll over and kiss him on the cheek and he pulls me onto his knee. Suddenly he's kissing me with such passion that I almost abandon all thoughts of finishing the drawers. After a minute, he takes me by the hand and leads me inside.

'I never did show you how the bedrooms are going, did I?' he says, as he quietly leads me upstairs.

'Nicos, stop.' I release my hand from his at the top of the staircase.

'I'm sorry,' he says, holding me close. I can smell his masculine scent and almost change my mind and follow him into the bedroom.

'It's not that I don't want this, but I don't want to rush into anything.' I keep reminding myself that my life is not here in Greece, and however the idea of a long-distance relationship sounds, in reality they rarely work.

'Of course. I understand if you are not ready for this. But I care a lot about you, Tania. I can barely control myself when I'm around you.'

He releases me from his embrace and looks into my eyes.

'I care a lot about you too, Nicos.' I can hear my own heart thudding inside my chest.

'Well, as we are up here, I will show you the rooms anyway.' He smiles, and I feel a mixture of desire and annoyance with myself. I'm a grown woman; what the hell is stopping me? So what if this is little more than a holiday fling? The moment has passed, though.

I gasp as I enter the largest bedroom, which has a large window overlooking the garden, with tall pine trees in the background, rising towards the sky. The walls are painted a soft buttermilk, pairing perfectly with some dark furniture. There is a large wooden bed with a carved headboard, and crisp, expensive-looking white bedding on the bed.

'I had the basics here, I just spruced things up a little. A new mattress and bedding, a coat of paint on the walls,' he explains as I glance around, taking it in. The room is south-facing and flooded with light from outside, giving it a soft, golden glow.

'Well, it's absolutely beautiful.' I glance around, thinking of how tasteful it looks.

'So are you.' He pulls me to him and kisses me, gently on the top of my head, this time. 'And now, I really must control myself, so how about I give you a tour of the rest of the house?'

He shows me the large bathroom, which he says will be updated and two further bedrooms that are spacious and simply in need of a little TLC. Walking downstairs, I slide my hand along the dark wooden banister as I go, visualising the stairs with a rich red carpet and the large hall with the black and white tiled floor, housing a stylish, maybe antique, table and set with a vase and some fresh flowers.

Back downstairs, Nicos makes coffee and I continue painting the drawers until it's completely finished, trying to focus on the task in hand and not dwelling over my decision not to sleep with him.

It's late evening when I slip back into the rescue, my head reeling from what almost happened this afternoon. I haven't known Nicos a long time, yet the attraction between us is so strong, I almost slept with him. I'm confused and a little annoyed with myself for falling for Nicos so easily. Coming here and falling in love wasn't part of my plan. Is that what this is? I wonder. Love? Or an intense physical attraction, nurtured by the idyllic surroundings of the forest. There's no doubting Nicos is also a good person. I think of how he helped Lars with the building in the donkey area and how he took me into the village to buy the paint supplies. He is there whenever I need him and has shown concern for Judith too, asking after her when she had her operation. Men like Nicos don't come along too often, that's for sure.

It takes me ages to get to sleep; I toss and turn, and the next morning I climb into the shower exhausted. What on earth am I so worried about? I wonder. We are both single, free to do what we desire, yet I just can't seem to let him completely into my heart.

I head down to the kitchen, where Lars is making coffee and

the others are sat around the long pine table, and I'm shocked to see that it's nine thirty.

'Morning, sleepyhead. Coffee?' Liz grabs a mug and fills it before passing it over.

'Thanks. Gosh, I'm sorry. Why didn't someone wake me?' I sip down the delicious strong brew, hoping it will have the desired effect.

'It seemed a shame, you were flat out earlier when I knocked on your bedroom door,' Liz tells me.

'I can only apologise. I had a bit of a restless night. I tossed and turned for hours.'

'Chill, the morning's work is done,' says Liz. 'Everyone is entitled to a lie-in every now and then, you know,' she says kindly. 'Anyway, as I go home tomorrow, I thought we might have a girlie afternoon down at the harbour, what do you think?'

'I think that sounds just perfect. A girls' day is exactly what I need. Although I'm taking Judith to see Yolanda at lunchtime.'

'I can do that.' Lars steps in. 'If that's alright with you.'

'Of course, if you're sure, Lars, thanks. I did promise to make some scones, so I'd better get on with that.'

I jump and whip up a batch of scones that takes no time. When they are cooling on a rack, Euan comes into the kitchen and eyes them. 'Ooh they look amazing.'

'Eyes off, they're for Judith to take to her friend's house,' I warn him.

'They won't eat all those, surely, they're huge.' He looks at me with his large puppy dog eyes and I find myself saying he can have one. 'But don't tell the others. I'll make another batch tomorrow for everyone here.'

'Nice one.' He winks before he grabs a scone, furtively glancing over his shoulder as he butters it, which has me laughing. He then practically shoves it in his mouth.

'That was the best scone ever,' he declares, wiping crumbs from his mouth with a paper napkin. 'Anyway, probably better if someone tastes it first, especially when it's for a friend.' He winks again.

'If you say so.'

He gives me a big hug. 'Thanks, Tania.'

He's such a force of nature, warm and loving. I hope he can settle when he gets home and find someone nice to build a life with. If that's what he wants, of course.

Animals walked and fed, it's early afternoon when Liz and I head off down to the harbour. Euan asks if he can tag along, but we tell him it's strictly a girls' afternoon out and he has plenty of animals to keep him company and he laughs.

'Actually, I think I'll enjoy hanging around with my four-legged friends for a bit, maybe take a swim.'

'Sounds good. And don't forget you are on dinner duty with Lars this evening,' I remind him.

'Oh, I know. I'm cooking my speciality. It's quite filling, so don't eat too much.'

We take the familiar paths, slowly navigating the bike past a dozen or so mountain goats who are stubbornly stood in the middle of the road.

Down at the harbour, we decide to find a lively bar with music playing and sit outside in the sunshine, the music pumping outside. After ordering cooling beers, talk turns to returning home.

'Have you figured out what you are going to do next?' I can't believe that Liz is leaving tomorrow. I am going to miss her so much.

'I have.' She takes a sip of her beer. 'Frank has asked me to move into his apartment back in the UK.' She almost squeals with excitement.

'Oh, Liz, I'm so happy for you.'

'Thanks, Tania. I know it's a big step, but it feels like the right thing to do. I'm going to enrol at night class and take a design course.'

'That's fantastic, Liz. I know you will make a success of it.'

'Thanks, I hope so. How about you? How long are you staying with your aunt?'

'I really have no idea.' I sigh. 'Obviously I'm welcome here indefinitely, but I must earn a living. My savings won't last forever. They were modest to start with.'

'Maybe you could sell the drawers you are working on. It could be the start of something. You're pretty good at helping people to develop their talents, maybe you should take your own advice?' She picks at a few nuts from a bowl.

'I've actually been giving that some thought. I'm just not sure where things are going with Nicos,' I confide.

'Are you saying that is all that would keep you here?'

'I really don't know. I love being in Crete, who wouldn't, but it's pretty quiet here for a single woman,' I have to admit.

'Maybe you should just take one day at a time and see what happens.' She sips her beer. 'Life isn't always part of a plan. I came here to get away from a life I vow never to return to. I never dreamed I would meet someone and end up going home to live in another town. I mean, meeting someone was incidental, I've never needed a man. But it's kind of nice having some male company on my terms,' reflects Liz.

'You're right, of course, and I'm still figuring out whether I could settle in Crete, with or without Nicos. I've lived alone for a while, and I'm fine with it. He's so bloody fit, though.' I smile.

'No argument there.' She winks. 'I'm sure you will figure things out,' she says confidently. 'Right, drink up, we're picking a speedboat up in fifteen minutes.'

'You've hired a speedboat?'

'Yep. Well, actually Frank organised it for us. He told me to go and have some fun with you before I leave. I thought we could have some fun exploring.'

'I think a speedboat sounds just perfect.'

'I've got a little map.' She retrieves it from the pocket of her shorts. 'There are a few beach coves we can call into. I've found one with a restaurant that does a great fish dish.'

'Lead the way.'

We pop to one of the many tourist shops nearby and buy a pair of goggles and snorkels, before collecting the boat from an older Greek guy.

'This is the life, hey.' I'm sat with my face turned towards the sun, enjoying the feel of it as Liz takes the wheel. The gentle bobbing of the boat at it skims the waves, along with the warm sun beaming down on me, almost has me falling asleep, especially after my restless night.

'Don't get too comfortable there,' says Liz. 'You're taking over in a bit.'

'Do I have to?' I pout. It feels so wonderful to be sat here, I could selfishly be driven for hours.

'There's a small cove up ahead. We could stop and chill on the sand for a bit, if you like?' suggests Liz.

'No, it's fine, we've only been out for a short time. Besides, I'd probably fall asleep on the sand. I'm fine here really. I'll take the wheel soon, I promise.'

Liz drives the boat as confidently as she does the bike, and we pass tiny islands, verdant green with sandstone cliffs rising up from the sea. Squawking seagulls fly above occasionally puncturing the stillness of the tranquil open water.

As I stare out to sea, I find myself wondering whether a life out here in Greece would be possible for me. Could I really make an income selling upcycled furniture? Maybe set up an internet page. Perhaps Nicos could point me in the direction of some stores in the city who might be interested in stocking some of my work? I realise I'm daydreaming, getting ahead of myself, but it doesn't do any harm to visualise something.

Two guys in a speedboat drive past us, and wave, reminding

me for a moment that I am young, free and single despite my attraction to Nicos. When we pull up at a sandy cove a while later, we see the same two blokes sat on bar stools at a tiny beach bar and they offer to buy us a beer.

'Lemonade would be nice. Can't drink and drive, I'm afraid, and we've had one beer,' explains Liz.

We spend the next hour laughing and chatting to the two blokes who are here on holiday. It really does feel good to be having fun, acting like a young woman who is free from the constraints of any sort of relationship. Maybe being one half of a couple isn't all it's cracked up to be after all. At least not for the moment.

TWENTY-SIX

An hour later, after I enjoyed taking my turn at the wheel, we've dropped anchor and are swimming in the delightfully warm sea. Shoals of small fish can be seen beneath the crystal-clear water, and we fasten on our goggles and snorkels, enjoying spying the sea life below. I spot colourful fish and, diving down a little deeper, I think I spot a small squid, nestled between some seaweed and a rock.

'That was amazing. This is definitely not something we can do back home.' I think of the often freezing-cold beaches in the North of England, more suited to bracing walks than swimming in the sea.

We're sat on the boat drying off in the hot sun, wrapped in towels. I reach into my bag and rub some anti-frizz serum through my hair, before tying it back once more and putting on my cap.

'Shall we find that fish restaurant now, I'm starved,' says Liz, already pulling on her shorts.

'Let's go. Although I think squid is off the menu for me after the snorkelling,' I say.

As it is now late afternoon and with Euan cooking his

speciality tonight, we order just a Greek salad and some sparkling water. The wooden terrace stretches out over the water, making me feel like I am on an island in the middle of nowhere. As the water seems to stretch out forever in front of us, I feel a bit like Robinson Crusoe, although, thankfully, I don't have to hunt for my own dinner.

A yacht sails past in the distance and I think of Chloe. 'I wonder how Chloe's getting on with the handsome French guy and where they are now?' I muse as I sip my mineral water.

'I know they were heading for Elounda, according to the tracker. It's not really showing where they are at the moment, but maybe the signal gets a bit lost at sea.'

'It was a brave thing she did going off like that. I do hope she's alright,' I say.

'She is. I forgot to mention that she messaged me the other day when you were out with Nicos. She's having the time of her life, apparently.'

'Good to hear,' I say, finishing my water and savouring every last moment of being here in this beautiful spot. It was such a great idea to get out and spend some time on the water.

'I'll miss you,' I find myself saying to Liz. 'We really must stay in touch. I know people say that to each other when they meet on holiday, but I mean it.'

'Ah, of course we will keep in touch, I'll miss you too. And you call this a holiday? I've never worked so hard in my life.' She laughs.

'You've enjoyed being here, though?'

'What do you think?' She casts her arm around her surroundings. 'I've loved every minute. I've met the best people.' She reaches over and squeezes my hand.

By the time we've returned the boat to the bloke at the beach, I feel totally refreshed and energised. I feel as though I've been on a mini cruise, even though it's just been a few hours out at sea.

'Right, best get back for the evening feeds and see how Judith got on at Yolanda's today,' I say.

'And after that I must go and pack. I can't believe I'm leaving tomorrow,' says Liz. 'It's been so good for me coming here.' She sighs happily. 'And I've really enjoyed today too. So many happy memories made.'

'So have I. And we've been lucky to have you here, Liz,' I say, and she links arms with me as we walk to the bike park and return to the rescue.

The evening feeds done and the donkeys checked on, I catch up with Judith and ask how her afternoon went with Yolanda.

'Oh, Tania, it was wonderful. We drank tea and laughed all afternoon. Then she brought the ouzo out, but I suggested only one, or she'd be falling over again.' She giggles. 'I think her son was horrified.'

'Oh gosh, I can imagine. I think I'd be horrified by the thought of an intoxicated invalid too.'

'She made short work of your scones, and said they were wonderful. She would like your recipe.'

'Of course.'

'How did your day go?' she asks.

I tell her all about hiring the speedboat and getting out on the open water. 'It was just wonderful. I'm going to miss this place so much.'

'There's no rush to be on your way, is there?' asks Judith.

'No, but I need to be working and earning money. I can't survive on your generosity forever.'

'It isn't generosity. You're working here, and I provide bed and board, as I do for everyone. But you are a young woman, of course you want your independence. But, honestly, you can stay here for as long as you want.'

I tell her about maybe upcycling furniture to create an income.

'Actually, you might have something there. I was talking to the couple who own the holiday cottage, and they were talking about updating the place a little,' she reveals. 'The furniture came with the house sale, but I don't think it's quite to their taste.'

'Really? Maybe I could offer to revamp it a little. When are they out here again?'

'Next month, I believe. And I wonder how many other expats would use the service? You could have an internet page and display a few pieces.'

'That's exactly what I was thinking of doing. Oh, Judith, it has to be worth a try, doesn't it?'

'It certainly does. Now would you like a cup of iced tea?'

'Sounds good.'

As we step into the tiled kitchen, a familiar smell hits my nostrils. Inside, Euan is placing a huge pie onto the table, alongside a mountain of vegetables.

'Steak and ale pie.' He beams, looking really proud of himself.

'Oh, Euan, that looks amazing. How on earth have you managed to cook that in this heat?'

'No sweat.' He grins. 'Well, there may have been a bit, to be honest, but don't worry, it didn't go anywhere near the food.' He laughs.

'This is wonderful, Euan, I love a good pie. I can't wait to see what you come up with next,' says Judith.

'Don't get too excited. It's my one and only dish. Probably a bit too heavy in this weather really, but I thought it might make a nice change from Greek food.'

We tuck into the tasty pie, and Euan was right, it really did make a nice change.

'That was delicious,' says Judith and we all agree.

'I'm definitely getting that recipe from you before I leave,' says Liz. 'That's if it isn't some closely guarded family secret.'

'It might be. But as it's you, you can have it.' He winks.

Later that evening, Judith takes a call from some volunteers who ask if they can call over tomorrow with a view to maybe rehoming two of the dogs. The number of dogs is getting smaller, as we haven't taken in any more strays, which is obviously a good thing. Maybe it is time for Judith not to take in any more dogs as she deserves a little freedom in her later years, even though she adores the animals. Another shelter has opened up around three miles from here, run by some younger people. She deserves to have some time to develop her blossoming friendship with Lars; she has worked so hard all of her life, after all.

Liz holds back tears the next morning, as she hugs us goodbye, before saying her farewells to every single one of the animals, and there's a cacophony of barking and braying. Even Eric allows himself to be petted briefly, before he saunters off. I think he's getting a bit soft in his old age.

'Oh, Liz, I'm going to miss you. Good luck with everything. Let me know how it all goes.' I give her an extra-long squeeze.

'You know I will. I'm definitely going to focus on a design course, and see what the future holds. Bye, Tania. And don't forget to follow your own dreams,' she says, before she climbs into Frank's hire car and they head for the airport.

I get the feeling they will make a good life together and I hope she never returns to her old ways. I admire the fact that she is at least prepared to try and develop her fashion skills. She is definitely stronger than she realises.

It's a busy morning, and Judith is a little teary when two of her favourite small dogs are rehomed today.

'Oh, it's always so bittersweet,' she says when the couple

have left. 'I know they must have their forever homes, but certain animals you just become so fond of.' She takes a tissue from a box in the kitchen and blows her nose.

'I understand. It's like being a foster mum in a way, isn't it?'

'Yes.' She smiles. 'I suppose it's exactly like that, although maybe only animal lovers would agree. Anyway, the new owners have promised to send me lots of photos and videos to reassure me that the dogs have settled in okay.'

The couple only live five miles away in a small village. Their elderly dog died recently, and when Judith told the couple that the terriers are inseparable, they decided to take them both.

Euan and I muck out the donkey stalls, as Lars walks around with Judith, who seems to be getting accustomed to her replacement knee and is walking a little further each day. After the dogs have been fed and watered, I grab the handles for the chest of drawers I'm transforming and head across the road. I'm still thinking about yesterday and hoping Nicos doesn't think I'm childish for resisting him, although maybe he would be respecting me less if I'd slept with him. Gosh, I'm a grown woman; why am I thinking like a teenager?

There's no sign of Nicos outside, so I knock at the door but there's no answer. I walk around the back of the house, and begin prising the old handles from the drawer, when a few minutes later Nicos appears, startling me a little.

'Nicos, I thought you weren't at home.'

I feel like an intruder for a second, and hope he doesn't mind me being here.

'I was working upstairs; I've commandeered the smallest bedroom as an office. Nice view from the window,' he explains. 'Later I have to go and meet a client in Heraklion. I'm thinking I might stay there overnight.'

Unsure what to say in reply, I smile at him and turn to continue fitting the new handles.

'Well, I must get back to my work. I can't wait to see how the drawers turn out, they look amazing already.'

'Thanks. I'm really enjoying working on them.'

Despite the passionate kisses we shared yesterday, there is no affectionate gesture today, no kiss on the cheek, nothing. I can't help feeling a little puzzled, as well as disappointed. There is no time to dwell on it, though, as I immerse myself in my project, taking my time as I fix the pretty floral handles. When it's finished, I stand back to admire my handiwork with satisfaction.

I don't want to disturb Nicos whilst he's working, so I slip out and will ask him later if he can help me transport the drawers over to the rescue. As I cross the garden, I can hear him talking on the phone, his voice raised once more and I hope that everything is okay in his life. And if it isn't, I will leave him to tell me about it in his own time.

Back at the rescue, I'm surprised to see Yolanda sat in the kitchen with Artemis, who is dressed in a suit and glancing at his expensive watch.

'Sorry if I keep you.' She waves her arm at her son. 'Go off and do whatever you have to do.'

Artemis rolls his eyes. 'I have a meeting. I told you about this, I cannot be here all of the time.' He sounds a little frustrated.

'I will take Yolanda home, don't worry,' I offer. 'Go to your meeting,' I tell Artemis, who is on his feet right away.

'Thank you.'

I walk him to the car and he confides that he wishes his wife was able to help, as she is a very nurturing woman, but she is away with her sister.

'I suppose you think that's sexist, huh? But my wife is so much better than me at fussing over people. And my mother is not the easiest of patients to look after. She is supposed to be resting.' He sighs.

'I can imagine she won't be told what to do. Although from what I have observed, she doesn't like too much fussing.'

'You've noticed.' He glances at his watch. 'Now, I really must go. Thank you so much for taking my mother home. Are you sure it is not too much trouble? She has the wheelchair to go in the car.'

'It's fine, really.'

He thanks me again, then disappears.

Back in the kitchen, Yolanda grips her large walking frame, a look of steely determination on her face as she pulls herself to her feet.

'Are you okay?' I rush to her aid, and she lifts her hand.

'I need the bathroom. And I don't want help,' she informs me.

'Well, I will wait outside the bathroom, just in case you do,' I insist, and she tuts, but I'm not going anywhere. I hover outside and though it takes a little while, she eventually emerges and gives me a triumphant smile.

An hour later, after more tea and laughter, Yolanda decides it is time to leave.

'I'm getting a little tired now. It's the opium,' she tells us, referring to the codeine the doctor has prescribed. 'I must have the scone recipe, though,' she remembers as she slowly gets to her feet.

She reluctantly sits in the wheelchair for the short journey to the car parked outside the gates, and Lars loads the chair and walking frame into the back of the car once she is seated inside.

'*Efcharisto*,' she tells me when I finally manage to get her settled inside her house.

'Are you sure you will be okay? Maybe you should have stayed for dinner?' I feel a little uncertain leaving her here alone.

'My son will be home in two hours. I will be fine, he will make us dinner later. I will rest now.'

I can't help smiling as I imagine Artemis fussing over his mother and wishing his wife was around.

Yolanda asks me to switch the radio on that sits on a windowsill, and she settles down on the sofa, surrounded by her comfortable cushions. I bring her a bottle of water and place it on a table beside her.

'*Efcharisto*, Tania, you are a good girl.' She closes her eyes, telling me it's time to leave.

'Bye, Yolanda. Please call if you need anything,' I tell her as I close the door behind me.

TWENTY-SEVEN

Later that evening Judith calls Yolanda to make sure her son is home and she tells her that he is, and that he bought a takeaway from a chicken shop, so maybe she ought to have stayed for dinner after all.

After the evening feeds and clean-ups, I glance at my phone to see if I might have any messages from Nicos, but there's nothing. I find myself wondering who he was talking to with a raised voice on the telephone. Just then, I'm distracted by Euan, who appears with a bottle of wine and two glasses. Lars has taken Judith out for a drive as it's a beautiful evening, saying they might stop at a café near a viewing point to watch the sunset.

'Just us two then.' Euan pours me a glass of white wine. 'I'm pooped, when is the other volunteer starting?' he jokes.

'It does get very busy. You do notice when we are a volunteer down, especially with Judith not getting about as much just yet. I don't think anyone is coming for a while, though, so we will just have to work extra hard.'

'That's not a problem. How long has your aunt had this place?' Euan asks as he sips his wine.

'Coming up for fifteen years now. It was in a right state

when she and my uncle took it on, although an absolute bargain. It was a real labour of love.'

I remember being here with my parents before they headed off on one of their bike tours during some of the renovation. The sound of diggers and machinery, the long days in the sun, drinking lemonade, watching it slowly take shape will stay with me forever. It had been an animal rescue in the past, but had fallen into disrepair, the gardens overgrown and the buildings tired and damp when they took it on. I feel so proud of how my aunt and uncle transformed the place.

'Well, it's amazing. What a beautiful place to live, up here in the forest. It's so peaceful, yet not too far from the coast.'

'It's the best of both worlds, I guess. Did you enjoy exploring the other day?' I ask Euan.

'I did. I walked to Forest Point where I had a great view of the sea. From there I walked down a valley and cut through a village on the way back, I'm not sure what it was called but it was really tiny. At least there was a shop, though, so I managed to grab a cold drink.'

'You should always take water with you in this heat,' I suggest.

'I realise that now.' He grins. 'I'm really looking forward to exploring more. You're welcome to join me anytime. I'll pack the drinks next time.'

'I might just do that. Walking is fine, I enjoy that, but I'm not much of a hiker, though. I don't think I'm fit enough for uphill climbs.'

'You look pretty fit to me.' His eyes flick over my body. 'Although I won't be doing too much climbing myself, not in this heat.'

We chat easily, sharing the bottle of wine, when talk turns to Nicos.

'He seems like a nice bloke,' says Euan. 'I'm not sure what he must have thought when he came over the other evening and you had your skirt hiked up showing me your scar, though.'

'Oh my goodness, I know! I told him I knew you a little, as we had met at the airport.'

'And he was okay with that?' He looks doubtful.

'He was. At least I think so.' Perhaps he wasn't okay with it really.

'So, what's the story? Is it serious between you two?'

I find myself confiding in him that I'm really not sure about our relationship status.

'He's considering selling the house, and as I'm not into holiday flings I guess I'm just being a little cautious,' I confide.

'Can't really blame you for that,' he agrees.

I place the empty wine bottle and glasses onto a tray. 'Right, I think it's time for us to go to bed.'

'I thought you weren't into holiday flings?' Euan jokes.

'Separately.' I raise an eyebrow. 'Sleeping with co-workers would definitely be off-limits.'

'Good job I don't fancy you then,' he says, and I roll my eyes.

'Night, Euan. See you in the morning.'

I wake early the next morning and, after doing the usual tasks, I take a walk outside. Judith tells me she is going to take a gentle swim later, and I'm happy that she is so determined to be fully back on her feet again as quickly as possible.

Finishing a circular walk in the glorious early morning sunshine, I call on Nicos to tell him I will collect the chest of drawers later. He is in the garden looking a little tired, watering some of the plants when I arrive.

'*Kalimera*, Nicos.'

He gives me what I perceive to be a strained smile. '*Kalimera*, Tania. How are you?'

'I'm good, thanks. I've just been for a lovely morning walk. How are you?'

'A little tired,' he admits. He finishes watering a plant, before turning off the garden tap. 'I never slept too well last night.'

'Is everything alright?' I ask tentatively.

'Do you have time for coffee?' He gestures to the kitchen and I follow him inside. I glance around the kitchen as he sets about making coffee; the dark beams contrasting with the cream units give it a homely feel.

'Remember you asked me about my son the other day?' He places a coffee down in front of me.

I nod.

'Well, I suppose I never said too much about him, because I felt a little guilty,' he reveals.

'Guilty?'

'Yes. About not seeing my son enough. Although, please believe me, I have tried.'

'Go on.'

'We used to live in a large village, not too far from here. When we separated, she went to live with her parents in Heraklion and took my son with her. She made it difficult. Whenever I arranged to see him, she would not be home.' He picks his coffee up and paces the room with it.

'Why on earth would she do that? Did you split on bad terms?'

'You could say that.' He doesn't elaborate. 'My contact has been a little sporadic. I'm ashamed to say that at times I have almost felt like giving up, but I didn't.'

'You must never do that.' He sits down and I place my hand over his. 'A child needs both parents. I spent a lot of time with Judith as a child and missed mine. And they weren't even separated.' I tell him all about my life growing up. 'You want your son to have memories to look back on of spending time with you, don't you? You must fight harder for him.'

'Of course, Tania, you are right.' He runs his fingers through his hair, and sighs deeply. 'I love my son. Maybe I thought he was better off without me, I—'

Just then my phone rings. It's Euan asking me how to get Eric out of his stall whilst he mucks it out. It seems Euan's charm didn't last long, and Eric has returned to his stubborn ways. I tell him I will be back in ten minutes.

'I'm so sorry, I have to go. Donkey emergency. But I would love to hear more about your son.'

'Will I see you tonight?' ask Nicos as I stand to leave, and I tell him I would like that.

'I'll call you.' He presses his lips softly against mine and I can't wait for this evening to come. I also wonder why he thinks his son might be better off without him.

Eric is lured out of his stall by some carrots and Euan sets about cleaning it.

'He's so stubborn, him,' says Euan.

'As a mule?' I grin. 'Although he usually saunters outside when it's mucking-out time. Maybe he just can't be bothered as it's so hot today.'

'Maybe he's just making an ass out of me.' Euan grins.

Judith is walking around with a stick, really happy with how things are progressing. Lars is taking her to see Yolanda later. Hopefully things are going really well between the two of them as well.

We tackle all the usual jobs, including clearing up rather a lot of donkey poo.

'What on earth have they been eating? Especially Eric,' says Euan, just as Eric saunters towards him and places another mound of dung at his feet. I can't help but burst out laughing.

'I have no idea. Unless someone has been secretly feeding them treats, which seems unlikely.'

Eventually, the chores are finished and I'm taking a break sat beneath the shade of a tree, when Euan returns from a walk in the forest.

'I passed a group of young blokes down near one of the streams not too far from here. Tourists, I think,' he says, sitting down next to me and glugging down some water.

'One of the forest hiking trails used to be quite popular with tourists, although we don't get as many people up here these days. It's usually just locals, or us lot walking the dogs,' I comment.

'I thought that. Nice for tourists to get out in the forest, though, as a change from the beach, I guess.'

With quite a few of our dogs finding their forever homes recently, and the chores for the day complete, Euan asks me if I fancy a drive to Malia to make the most of our free afternoon.

'I'm told there is a shop there that sells really good electrical stuff at a discount price. I could do with a decent set of earbuds.'

'Sure,' I say, thinking I might have a browse of some of the clothes shops there. There won't be anyone left at the rescue, but the dogs are all sleeping in their pens and the donkeys are in their shelter, so a quick trip would be lovely.

Malia is bustling when we arrive; holidaymakers are out in force, walking through the main street with its plethora of bars and restaurants. Things seem pretty tame at this hour, but in the evening it turns into a neon-lit party place with music blaring out from bars and clubs.

Walking away from the main drag, we soon arrive at a large store with all things electrical on display in the window. A few doors down is a ladies' fashion shop, so I head in there and we agree to meet outside later. There is a sale on in the shop, and although I probably shouldn't be spending money, I can't resist a floaty orange dress that is heavily discounted and will look good against my nicely developing tan.

'Sorted,' says Euan outside later, lifting a carrier bag. He's also bought himself a gadget that locates lost keys. 'There's all sorts of stuff in there, gadgets and bits and pieces that I can't resist. I even bought this.' He shows me a SpongeBob Square-Pants mouse mat and has me laughing.

'How old are you exactly?'

'Young at heart.' He laughs. 'I started watching the cartoon with my nephew and now I think I like it more than him,' he admits.

We take a walk along the seafront and Euan buys us both an ice cream that we eat on a bench looking out over the water. Talk soon turns to work.

'Do you enjoy your job in IT?' I ask as I enjoy my pistachio ice cream.

'I do, most of the time, anyway. It's a large company, so the social scene can be pretty good too. I could probably earn more money if I moved to London, though.'

'But then everything else is more expensive,' I remind him. 'Do you fancy living in London then?'

'Not especially, although there are more job opportunities. But you're probably right, with the extra cost of accommodation it wouldn't really make sense. And I suppose the pay is decent enough, although saving a deposit for a mortgage still hasn't happened.'

'Maybe if you stopped the wanderlust,' I suggest. 'And all the socialising.'

'Probably, but I'm not ready for that yet,' he admits.

'I'm not sure when I'll have saved enough money for a house deposit either.' As I say it out loud, I realise that it's as far away as it has ever been. It's so much harder for our generation to get a foot on the property ladder these days.

'You could always live here with your aunt.' He turns to me. 'At least it's a possibility for you.'

'That's true. And I do actually have the offer of a room back home.'

I tell him all about my friend Angie.

'Oh well, you're sorted then.' He smiles. 'Or we could rent a place together.' He nudges my arm. 'Split the rent and save a deposit for a mortgage together. In fact, shall we make one of those pacts, that if we are still single in five years we should go for that?'

Looking at Euan's handsome face, and with his charming manner, it's unlikely he will be single in five years, so I laugh and say, 'Sure, why not?'

Euan must be joking; he doesn't seem the type for settling, pact or no. And I'm still hopeful that, by some miracle, me and Nicos could have a future together. Everything is so unsure that it's nice to have something approaching a plan, though, even if it is just friendly banter.

As we drive home, I think about Euan's comments. Could I really live out here in Crete? I'm pretty sure Judith would welcome me with open arms, as she has already said I can stay for as long as I like. But is there enough for me in the tiny village? It would be a completely different story if things progressed with Nicos, but I have no idea where that is heading. He still isn't sure whether or not he is going to put the house on the market and his decision has me trying hard to not let my heart rule my head.

We're almost home, when with the window down, I smell the unmistakeable smell of smoke outside. I imagine it might be someone having a BBQ, but climbing the road towards the rescue, we are greeted by the sight of spiralling smoke and my heart stops. There's a fire in the forest. A line of orange flames is approaching the donkey shelter and as we draw closer, I gasp at the reality of the situation.

TWENTY-EIGHT

Racing out of the car, we arrive to a scene of chaos. Nicos is herding the donkeys across the road to his place, but Eric is refusing to move. There is a cacophony of noise from the animals, and spiralling smoke seems to be inching closer.

'Nicos! Oh my God, I am so glad you are here!' My heart is thumping wildly.

'The fire service are on their way. But maybe we can try and get the animals out, then get the fire under control,' he advises.

I take over herding as Euan and Nicos spring into action, attaching the garden hose to an outside tap and dousing the grounds, to stop the fire spreading. It appears to be moving along the back of the shelter away from the dog pens, thankfully, following a line of trees, although the grounds are thick with smoke.

Somehow, between us all we manage to get the dogs across the road to Nicos's place and into the large, fenced garden. Nicos houses the donkeys in his old stables, several in each stall.

Before long, Judith has arrived back with Lars. She covers her mouth with her hand as she takes in the scene, surveying the charred remains of the donkey shelter, and the blackened hay.

'Don't worry, Judith, it looks worse than it is,' I try to reassure her. 'And the dogs are across the road.'

'We saw the flames from higher up in the hills,' says Judith. 'I prayed it would not reach here.' Tears are forming in her eyes and my heart breaks for my aunt. 'How are the animals?' She is already striding across the road to Nicos's house, and I remind her not to walk too quickly.

'Slow down, you're still recovering.' I take her arm and lead her across the road, whilst Nicos and Euan attempt to spray the fire more, but to little avail. Thankfully, it doesn't take too long until the fire services arrive and an hour later the fire in the forest is under control.

Judith is sat in the kitchen sipping brandy, barely able to take it all in, although relieved that the animals are unharmed.

'I was only gone for a couple of hours, I can hardly believe it.' She shakes her head. 'The whole place could have been destroyed.' She sobs.

'Well, thankfully it wasn't, and thank goodness for you too, Nicos.' I turn to him. 'It was quick thinking leading the animals over to the stables. Thank goodness Eric was on his best behaviour.'

'And for acting quickly and hosing the dog area down with Euan. I can't thank you both enough,' says Judith, turning to them both.

The fire crew speak in Greek to Nicos, who tells us that they found the remains of a disposable BBQ in the forest near the lake.

'No doubt that caused the fire.' He shakes his head.

'I wonder if it was the group of blokes I saw mucking about in the stream earlier?' says Euan.

'Very likely. What absolute idiots not extinguishing a BBQ

properly in this heat. The forest can be a tinderbox.' I'm astounded by people's thoughtlessness sometimes.

'How can someone be so irresponsible?' Judith shakes her head. 'I dread to think what might have happened had the fire spread.'

'People don't think, do they? But you're right, especially given the extreme temperatures here lately,' says Lars.

'Well, thank goodness the fire is out now and the damage seems to be restricted to the donkey area.' I take hold of her hand. 'Try not to think about what might have happened. The animals are safe, that's the main thing. And us lot, of course.'

'Of course, you are right.' She manages a smile as she squeezes my hand. 'It's going to take a little while to put right, and we will have to sort out the insurance. Oh, what a mess. It's so lucky you were home, Nicos, and able to raise the alarm so quickly.'

'I was working in the garden, when I noticed the fire,' explains Nicos. 'I could see the direction it was heading in, running along the back of the rescue. I could see the donkey area was likely to be hit before the emergency services arrived, so I got the donkeys out first. They are perfectly happy in the old stables. Thank goodness you guys arrived to help with Eric and the dogs.' He turns to me and Euan. 'The smoke was pretty thick by then.'

'We will sort everything out,' says Lars soothingly to Judith. 'It's nothing that can't be fixed. The main thing is that all the animals are okay.'

'You're right, I know things could have been a whole lot worse.'

'And in the meantime, the donkeys will be fine in the old stables until their shelter is rebuilt,' Nicos reassures Judith. 'Once the smoke has completely cleared, and the dogs have returned to their pens, they can also use the enclosed rear garden.'

'Thank you, Nicos, that's very kind of you. They do need an inside shelter, especially in the heat.'

'Not at all. Anything to help out.'

When the fire crew have left, we take straw bales across for the donkeys, who seem to be none the worse for being rehoused, even Eric, surprisingly. Luckily, they also have the large garden to wander around.

'I'm sure it won't take long for the enclosure to be rebuilt. I can lend a hand,' Nicos offers.

Judith and Lars spend time in the small office, getting in touch with the insurance people and an inspector will call over tomorrow to assess the damage. Yolanda has also phoned offering her son's services, but Judith declined, no doubt thinking he has enough on his plate looking after Yolanda. She managed to make Judith laugh, saying it was a good job they both weren't there and caught up in the fire, or they would have been running away on crutches and Zimmer frames.

'I think we could all do with an evening away from here to gather our thoughts,' I suggest. 'What say after we've sorted the animals later, we drive down to Hersonissos and have dinner at Vasilis's restaurant?'

'That sounds like a wonderful idea,' says Judith.

'I don't mind driving,' says Lars, and Nicos offers to take his car too.

Vasilis's seafood restaurant is busy with diners when we arrive, but Vasilis finds us a table promptly. He welcomes us all warmly, saying it has been far too long since we have been, which is probably true. Judith tells him all about the fire.

'Those fools.' He raises an arm in anger. 'They have no respect for the forest. Surely they know how hot it is, and there is a chance of fire. I hope they are found and arrested.'

'I don't think there is much chance of that, they could be

anywhere by now,' Judith replies with a deep sigh. 'I understand people wanting to enjoy the beauty of the forest, but having a BBQ and obviously not extinguishing it properly is foolish beyond belief.'

Despite the circumstances of the day, we enjoy a wonderful meal together. Plates of fresh sea bass, red mullet and squid are placed down in front of us, alongside Greek salads and fried potatoes. We enjoy cooling beers as a breeze wafts in from the nearby sea.

'I think this is exactly what I needed,' says Judith, wiping her mouth with a napkin. 'And I don't just mean after the knee operation and the fire. It's made me realise I ought to get out more.'

'I'll start a crowdfunding page,' says Euan, taking his phone from his pocket after dinner. 'People can be quite generous with animal fundraising.'

'That's a great idea!' says Judith. 'It would give us some instant access to funds. Before the insurance payout. It would be great if the building work can start sooner rather than later.'

'Thanks again for today, Nicos,' I tell him as we arrive back at the rescue.

'It was the least I could do to help. It's been a long day. Get some sleep, I will see you tomorrow.' He kisses me lightly on the lips before he heads home.

TWENTY-NINE

Half an hour later, I'm getting ready for bed when I'm alerted to a message on my phone. It's a video recording of Wes at his concert. I sit down on the bed and watch it with a huge smile on my face. He's simply brilliant and by the sound of the applause at the end of his performance, it would seem that the audience thinks so too. I tap out a message of congratulations and he asks if it's alright to give me a call.

'Hi, Tania. I wasn't sure if you would be in bed, with the time difference.' It's so good to hear his voice.

'No worries, it's so great to talk to you. Oh, Wes, your performance was fabulous! Did you enjoy it?'

'Every minute of it. I felt a little sick with nerves before I went on as it was a huge crowd, but thankfully, they seemed to like it.'

'They loved it. I heard the whoops and cheers. And I'm not surprised, you sounded fantastic.'

'Thanks, Tania, and I have a repeat booking next week so I'm thrilled.' I can hear the excitement in his voice.

'You deserve it. I'm sure it could be the beginning of something big.'

'You never know,' he says modestly.

'I'm certain of it.'

I don't think he has any idea how good he really is. He asks about things here, and I tell him about the fire.

'But don't worry, no human or animal has been injured. Just the nuisance of having to rebuild the shelter.'

'That's awful. I'm glad everyone is okay. All things considered, it sounds like the animals had a lucky escape.'

'Tell me about it. The fire ran in a straight line along the back of the rescue, just catching the donkey area. There was a lot of smoke, but the dogs were evacuated, which was chaotic, I won't lie, but luckily they were quickly able to return a few hours later.'

'It must have been pretty scary.'

'It was for a while. Thank goodness the emergency services arrived so quickly and were able to contain the fire before it spread further.'

I tell him about Euan starting up a fundraising page. 'I also have a friend in England who does a lot of charity walks. If she isn't currently fundraising for something in particular, maybe I could suggest she does a fundraising walk for the shelter.'

'And maybe it's time to go and shake the tins at the tourists again,' suggests Wes, and I think he might be right.

After the call, I nip downstairs for some water and Judith is in the kitchen sipping a cup of tea.

'Hey, Judith, are you okay?'

'Yes, fine. Just a little overtired, I think. I thought a cup of camomile tea might help make me sleep.'

'I'm sure it will. And you know, we're going to be just fine. Everyone springs into action when there's any sort of crisis, don't they?'

'They certainly do,' says Judith, gratitude written all over her face. 'I'm so lucky to have you all. I'm just trying to stop myself from thinking what might have happened had Nicos not been at home.'

'Well, he was, so you mustn't think like that. And Euan and I were not far behind. Try and put it out of your mind.'

'You're right, of course.' She smiles. 'But it would have to happen when I can't get about properly yet. You just don't expect something like this to happen.' She sighs.

'You'll be just fine. As long as you aren't tempted to overdo things, and I shall be keeping a direct eye on you to make sure you don't,' I tell her firmly.

'Thanks, Tania. Now maybe we ought to get to bed and try and get some sleep. Tomorrow will be another busy day.'

THIRTY

News of the fire has travelled fast and when we are down at the harbour fundraising, people are generous. Even the people in the hamlet and the regular dog walkers have chipped in, their generosity astounding Judith. Nicos has arranged for a builder friend to rebuild the wooden structure for the donkeys, and Lars will give a hand to keep the costs down. Hopefully it won't be too long before the donkeys can be returned to the rescue.

'I probably could have given a hand with the building work too, but I'm coming towards the end of a work project so I need to give it my full attention,' Nicos tells me. It's late in the evening and I'm sharing a glass of wine with him at his place.

'I'm not sure the donkeys will ever want to return. They love your stables,' I tell Nicos. 'You must be treating them far too well.'

'Their needs are simple, aren't they? A place to roam and some food.' He takes a sip of wine. 'If only humans had such simple needs.'

'Sometimes humans create their own drama, though,' I suggest, thinking of a few people on social media who like to make a drama out of a crisis. And he agrees.

'And other times, situations are forced upon them that they aren't really happy about.'

'I'm sorry, Nicos, but I have to ask you. Are you talking about your son?' I tentatively broach the subject.

'What makes you think that?' He turns to look at me with an expression on his face that I can't quite read.

'I heard you talking on the phone the other day with a raised voice. Not that I was eavesdropping, I'd arrived to work on the drawers,' I add hastily. 'But you did kind of tell me your ex makes things difficult, so I guess I put two and two together.'

'I was hoping to take him away for a few days, when this project I'm working on finishes,' he tells me. 'But then she tells me she is out of town. Maybe I should see a lawyer about putting something firmly in place. It was something I was hoping to avoid.'

'Well, you may have little choice, if your ex is being so difficult. Is it because she is with someone else, do you think?'

'Possibly.' He sighs. 'She did move over a hundred miles away. I can hardly just nip over when I feel like it.'

'I'm sorry things are difficult for you.'

'Me too, but I will never give up on my son.'

We are sat on the veranda on the outdoor sofa as the sun begins to fade and Nicos refills my glass.

'What happened between you both, if you don't mind me asking?' I ask gently.

He runs his hands through his hair, his regret obvious. 'I fell in love with my wife quickly. Or at least I thought it was love. As time went by, I realised we had nothing in common, but Lucas had arrived by then. I was determined we would stay together as a family, I wanted to make it work.'

'But your ex-wife didn't?'

'No. And maybe it was foolish of me to think we could stay married because of our son, when it was obvious we were so unhappy.' He sighs again. 'When she moved away with Lucas, it was almost as if she thought I would forget about him, but I would never do such a thing.'

'I can imagine how awful that must have been. For both of you. It can't be an easy decision to separate when you have a child.'

'He was seven years old at the time.' He looks into my eyes. 'It was difficult, I missed him, although I saw him whenever I could, despite being very busy with work.'

My heart goes out to Nicos. And I can't help thinking that maybe his ex shouldn't have moved so far away from him.

'When we split up, I told you she made things difficult,' he goes on. 'One time she even went on holiday without letting me know. I drove almost two hours, and there was no one home. A neighbour informed me she had gone away for a week with Lucas.'

'Oh, Nicos, that's awful. But you must fight for him, and make sure he knows you are there for him.'

I tell him all about my parents not always being present when I was a child.

'You don't want your son to have memories of you not being there when he was growing up.' I squeeze his hand and he pulls me towards him and hugs me tightly.

'You are right, of course. I will try and speak to her before I involve a lawyer. Lucas needs to know that I will always be there for him.'

'Don't be too hard on yourself. Things will work out, I'm sure,' I try and reassure him.

'Thank you, Tania. Tomorrow I will call my ex-wife. It's time I sorted this out properly.'

'I think you must,' I tell him. 'Time passes so quickly. And you don't want to live with regrets.'

'That's the last thing I want,' he agrees.

THIRTY-ONE

The next day, Euan and I take half of the dogs out in the truck, as we can't walk around the woods for a little while. We will take the remaining dogs tomorrow.

Heading out along the coast road, we soon arrive at a stretch of rocky, deserted beach and park up. As soon as the doors of the truck are opened, the dogs leap out and race across the beach towards the water.

'I felt a bit guilty leaving the other dogs behind,' I tell Euan, even though we couldn't have managed them all at once, just the two of us.

'I know. I swear some of them had a sad expression.' He laughs. 'But they will get their chance tomorrow.'

We find some pieces of driftwood on the beach and toss them into the water and the dogs race in after them. It's so peaceful here, the area hardly visited by families and tourists who prefer the sandy stretch of beach a short walk away. Standing here and staring out to sea beneath the brilliant blue sky fills my heart with joy. In the distance, a boat sails past, heading towards the port of Hersonissos. As I stand there, I find myself wondering if Nicos ever brought his son to the beach, or took him out on a boat trip. It's such a lovely place to bring up a child with the good weather and wide-open spaces. I hope he manages to sort things out soon.

'Penny for your thoughts?' Euan asks as he throws another piece of wood into the water for the dogs.

'What? Oh, I don't know, I was just thinking what a lovely place this is to bring up a child.'

'Do you want kids one day?' he asks as we walk.

'I'd like to think so,' I tell him truthfully. 'But it's hard to imagine at the moment, if I'm honest.'

'I don't know if I will.' He picks up a pebble and tosses it into the water. 'I think I'm too much of a free spirit. Or maybe selfish is the right word.'

'I don't think it is selfish to live the life you want. Besides, the planet is already overpopulated,' I tell him and he smiles. 'It's different for blokes anyway, if you change your mind further down the line you still have time. Look at George Clooney.'

'Oh yeah, the handsome millionaire actor? I wonder why he still attracts younger women.' He gives a wry smile.

'So, you might not be a millionaire, but—'

'I am handsome?' he interrupts. 'Thanks.'

'You're impossible.' I can't help laughing.

'Come on.' Euan suddenly grabs me by the hand and races with me towards the water.

'Wait, I don't want to get my shorts wet,' I protest, but a minute later I'm paddling in the water, the dogs barking in delight beside us. Soon enough, I'm being splashed by the dogs but find myself throwing my arms in the air and laughing loudly, wishing I'd brought my swimming things. Could I ever tire of living in the sun? Although as Nicos said, no one's life is perfect.

Suddenly, one of the dogs jumps up at me and I lose my

footing and land squarely in the water. Euan can barely contain his laughter.

'You'll soon dry off in this heat.' He laughs as he eyes my soaking wet clothes. The dogs are jumping for joy and despite being wet through it would be hard not to laugh and feel happy in this moment.

Later, when the dogs are dried off, we are sat in the van, enjoying a takeaway coffee that Euan has bought us from a nearby café.

'Thank goodness we brought extra towels,' I say, a large one wrapped around me inside the baking hot van. It's an old truck with no air con, so Euan is right about me drying off quickly.

Driving home, with the window down and the warm breeze washing over me, I feel a real sense of well-being. Today was a lot of fun and has reminded me that we should always make some time to connect with nature and just be free of our thoughts.

'Thanks for today, Euan.'

'Not a problem.' He reaches over and squeezes my hand and I'm surprised to find that I let it sit there for a second, enjoying the moment.

When we arrive home, I shower and change before checking on the animals. Lars is walking with Judith around the grounds when we return, and I'm happy to learn that some volunteers turned up earlier and walked the remainder of the dogs further down the mountain, away from the areas destroyed by the fire. Judith tells me that two dachshunds will be rehomed tomorrow.

'I can't believe how much they have come on since arriving here,' Judith says of the two small dogs who had been abandoned together and found wandering on a beach looking for food. 'It's always lovely to see them rehomed. It makes all the work we do here worthwhile.'

I'm happy that the two dachshunds are being rehomed together and although people have expressed an interest in taking Annie the cockapoo, I don't think she would like to be separated from her best buddy Smudge. It would appear he is a bit much for people when they have taken him out. I can't help feeling a little sorry for him; he's such a wonderful, loving dog who is just a little over-enthusiastic.

'You and Uncle Ray did a wonderful thing starting the rescue centre, that's for sure.' I smile at her with pride.

'Thank you, Tania. I have been thinking about limiting the numbers of animals I take in, although, of course, I would never turn away an animal in need. With the fire and my knee, it's been a reminder that I can't do as much as I used to. If the dog numbers are reduced, there will be less need to rely on volunteers.'

'I understand that. Would you ever give it up completely and just keep a couple of dogs as pets?' I ask her.

We're sat outside now, enjoying a cooling drink in a shaded area of the garden.

'I have thought about it, but only recently. The volunteers and the dogs have kept me company in the past. It's been my whole life.'

'And now?'

'Well, now that I've met Lars...' She hesitates for a moment. 'I dare to believe that I might have a future with him. Live a little before it's too late.' She smiles.

'Oh, Judith, I'm pleased things are going so well with Lars. That's wonderful. And if anyone deserves to spend some time relaxing, doing the things they want, it's you. You have devoted years of your life to looking after the animals. And being a wonderful aunt to me.'

'Did you enjoy your time at the beach today?' she asks, changing the subject as we sip an iced tea.

'I did. It felt so lovely. The beach was very quiet, which is just as well with the dogs. It was so wild and rugged. I even went in the water with Euan.' I chuckle when I think of how I never had much choice.

'I really like Euan, he's like a breath of fresh air,' says Judith. 'He doesn't seem like an office type, although I'm not sure what an office type really is, I suppose. Maybe I'm being a bit stereotypical.'

'I do know what you mean. Although he is very outdoorsy too. A man of two halves.'

I tell Judith all about him losing his best friend. 'So, I guess he's travelling around, clearing his head, seeing what he wants from his life. He's taken a sabbatical so at least he has a job to return to. Unlike me.'

As I say the words, I let them sink in. I have no job waiting for me, and even though I can probably find something, not knowing what makes me feel a bit like a teenager again, not someone who is approaching thirty. Maybe I ought to move to Spain with my parents, as Dad suggested. But living in Spain has never really been something I desired, and if I was to move at least I'd have some purpose if I moved out here permanently...

That evening in bed, I think about Nicos again and I wonder whether he has contacted his ex-wife today and managed to sort something out with his son. Despite trying to resist him, my heart beats that bit faster whenever he's around. I also think of the warmth I felt with Euan when my hand was in his in the van, and just how easy it feels spending time with him. Life can be so complicated. I roll over and attempt to empty my head of these thoughts and try to get some sleep.

THIRTY-TWO

The next morning after breakfast, a lorry arrives with a huge delivery of timber, much to the surprise of Judith.

'I think we need to start work on the shelter sooner rather than later,' says Lars as he signs for the delivery. 'Otherwise the donkeys might get a little too comfortable over at the stables.'

'But I don't understand.' Judith looks puzzled. 'Did you order the wood?'

'I did. You know how slow insurance policies can take paying out.'

'Lars, how can I ever thank you.' She looks thrilled and completely surprised.

'It is my pleasure. I have been so happy since I came here.' He looks at my aunt with such affection that it makes my heart happy. I never thought Judith would find love again, and I know she didn't think so either. 'I would do anything to make sure everything gets back to normal and runs smoothly again.'

'What's this then?' Euan has strolled over, munching on a piece of toast, eyeing the stack of wood.

'It's the timber to build the new donkey shelter,' Judith tells him.

'Great. When do we start building?' he asks enthusiastically.

'I think Nicos has a friend who is coming to help, although I think he's busy with another job at the moment.' Given Nicos's own personal problems, it's not something I want to bother him with right now.

'We don't need to wait for him, let's get started,' says Euan. 'Maybe you should cancel him altogether.'

'Don't tell me you're a joiner as well as an Elton John impersonator?' I say and Judith and Lars look puzzled.

'As a matter fact, I am. Well, okay, not qualified exactly, but you don't need to be. I built a garden shed from scratch for my dad once,' he says proudly. 'With step-by-step tuition on YouTube. It was massive too. I've always had an interest in woodwork.'

'You really are a surprise.' I shake my head and laugh. 'A man of many talents.'

'Nicos can help out when he has the time, and I know you are handy, Lars. We will have the shelter up in no time,' Judith says with delight.

'We need to put the fences up first,' says Lars. 'And I have built many fences in my time.'

The fencing is the most important job to tackle first as it separates the donkeys from the dogs and, although still standing, has needed repairing for a while, the fire charring it a little and probably weakening it further.

Euan's positivity is infectious and a couple of hours later the wood has been laid out in preparation to start work.

'It is pretty basic stuff,' says Euan. 'It's no grand design, so it shouldn't take more than a few days, maybe a week. Maybe even less if it wasn't so hot.'

I help with brushing down and hosing the area, collecting any final charred remains from the old shelter in preparation for the building work and Lars and Euan set to work almost imme-diately, measuring and selecting pieces of wood.

I feed the animals and set off across the road to check on the donkeys as I do every morning, when I notice a car pulling up outside Nicos's house. Standing back a little, I see a tall, dark-haired woman step out of the car and wonder whether it might be his ex-wife. I retreat to the shelter hoping that, if it is his ex, the meeting goes well.

An hour later, Euan and I take some straw bales to the stables for the donkeys and give them a clean-out. There doesn't appear to be anyone around, so Nicos must have gone out. I find myself wondering whether his ex-wife is still with her partner. And if his son is able to visit him, does this mean he might be thinking of putting some roots down around here? As I'm loading old straw into bin sacks, I feel a little confused and heavy-hearted. Suddenly, I'm happy I never took things any further with him, even though I really wanted to at the time.

'Right, no rest for the wicked,' says Euan as we pack up to leave. 'I want to start on the frame for the shelter.'

'Do you ever stop?' I smile at the whirlwind that is Euan.

'Just to sleep. We all have to do that, I suppose.' He grins.

'I must admit, I can't imagine you sitting for too long behind a desk,' I tell him as we walk back to the rescue.

'That's because I don't. I'm a computer engineer, so I flit about fixing problems. There's no way I could sit in one place all day.'

'Well, that figures.'

Lars and Euan work tirelessly throughout the day and by the evening, a fence has been erected and the frame for the animal shelter. Everyone is flopped down having an early dinner around six, when I receive a text. It's Nicos asking me if I would like to call over for a drink. Despite my reservations, I can't help but feel excited by the thought of spending time with him.

'I was going to see if you fancied a walk up to the bar tonight?' says Euan.

'That would have been nice, maybe another evening. I'm going to see Nicos,' I tell him. 'But you do know the bar closes as the sun begins to set. Its main trade is during the daytime from tourists visiting the church.'

'Oh right. I'm pretty pooped anyway, it's been a busy day. I might just stay here and play a card game. Solitaire, as I'm all on my own.' He pulls a sad face.

'I'm sure you'll survive. And I'm pretty sure Judith and Lars would love to play a game of cards with you. Judith is a bit of a dab hand at cards.'

Nicos is sat on the porch when I arrive, the lights above lit once more and a bottle of white wine and two glasses on the table. He stands and kisses me on the cheek in greeting.

'Tania, it's good to see you. I wanted to say thank you.' He can't disguise the smile on his face as he pours me a glass of wine.

'Thank me for what?'

'For making me see that things needed to be sorted out with my son. My ex came over today and we managed to have a civil chat together. I am hoping we can avoid lawyers, although I told my ex it will happen if she disappears with Lucas and changes any visiting arrangements in the future. Lucas is coming to stay with me next weekend. I can hardly wait.'

'Oh, Nicos, that's wonderful news! Is it going to be a regular arrangement?' I feel so happy for him.

'It is. Only every other weekend, which works for us all. When I am at my office in town, I will take him for dinner, or swimming after school. Whatever he wants. And I have said he can stay here whenever he likes over the holidays as well. I feel so relieved.'

He looks like a weight has been lifted from his shoulders.

'I'm happy it's all sorted, Nicos, I really am. You have to make the most of the time you have with kids, while they are young.'

He regards me with his large brown eyes that I could so easily lose myself in.

'When did you get so wise?' he asks. 'I tried to convince myself that everything in my life was good. I buried myself in my work, and now the house. But none of that matters if you are estranged from the one you love, I realise that now,' he says. 'I will do everything I can to make sure my son is a big part of my life.'

'I'm sure you will. Your son needs you,' I say gently. 'Children have to rely on the adults in their life to fight for them.'

'Of course they do. I need him too, I realise that.' He smiles. 'And I am excited to introduce him to you.'

'Really?' It gives me a warm feeling to know that Nicos would like us to meet.

'Of course. It is only right that the people who are important to me get to know each other,' he says, and my heart soars.

When Nicos walks me home, it's just before eleven and the place is in darkness, everyone seemingly gone to bed. We stop at the gates and stand together under the moonlight. It's so peaceful here, only the sound of the crickets and their almost hypnotic sound can be heard.

'Goodnight, Tania. And thank you.'

'You have nothing to thank me for, really.'

'I disagree,' he says as he circles his arms around my waist and pulls me to him. As his lips land gently on mine, I think someone must be letting off fireworks down at the harbour. No one has made me feel this way in a long time, and as I stand, entwined in his arms, I don't want this moment to ever end.

'Goodnight, Nicos. I'm happy things have worked out with your son.'

'I like to think that things are working out for me in other areas of my life too. At least, I hope so,' he says, before he moves in for another kiss.

THIRTY-THREE

Lars works tirelessly on the shelter with Euan's help. Even Nicos lends a hand when he has the time, but he has been busy working on a project, with a visit to his office in Heraklion. When he returns, he asks if I would join him for a drink up at the bar.

'If you don't mind the uphill walk? Or I could take the car, if you like,' he offers.

'No, let's walk. It's only a short climb. The cold beer will feel well deserved if we walk.'

'How is work going?' I ask as we stroll beneath the trees in the late afternoon.

'All finished. I've been working on the plans for some new apartments. It's good to know that business is good in the tourist resorts. There is a new hotel being built near the harbour too.'

'I'm not surprised. Greece is such an ideal holiday destination; you really feel like you can relax here.'

'Are you feeling relaxed now?' He turns to me.

'Most of the time, yes. I do love being here. My future just feels a little uncertain right now,' I tell him.

'Could you see yourself living here?'

'Here in the village, or here in Greece?'

'Both.' Am I imagining something in the way he looks at me?

'I'm not sure. I need a job eventually, I can't live off my aunt.'

'What about furniture restoration? That chest of drawers was really impressive,' he says kindly.

'I would need money to buy some furniture, not to mention a workspace. I don't really have either.' I shrug.

At the bar, the young couple who run it greet us and their elderly grandmother, who is dressed in black and sat near the bar bottling dried herbs, nods her head in greeting. There a few groups of diners at the wooden picnic-style tables sat outside, including a middle-aged couple; the flushed-looking woman has one of those portable fans in front of her face. A young couple are kissing, unconcerned about making a public display of affection, clearly in the first flush of love.

When we are seated and sipping our ice-cold beers, Nicos picks up the conversation of my furniture restoration.

'If it's a workspace you are after, I think the stables would make an excellent work room.' Nicos takes a sip of his beer as he gauges my reaction.

'The stables at your house?' I'm completely surprised by the suggestion.

'Yes. I think it would make an ideal space. What do you think?'

'Well, I agree, it's perfect, but what would happen when you sell the house?'

'That was part of the reason I went to Heraklion,' he tells me. 'It wasn't just for work purposes. I went to put my apartment on the market with an estate agent. I've decided I'm going to live in the house here in the village.'

'You are? That's great news.'

The thought of staying on here just got a whole lot more promising.

'I'm buying out my sister's share of the house and, with the sale from the apartment, I will be able to refurbish the house. First on the list is a room for Lucas. He is already excited, thinking about what theme he would like, although that appears to change constantly.' He smiles, with obvious affection for his son. 'Next on the list are those floor-length windows I talked about.'

'It's already a beautiful house, and I can imagine what it will look like with those windows. I must be honest, though, won't you find it a little quiet here after living in Heraklion for so long? It's quite a different setting.'

'I'm ready to embrace the change,' he tells me. 'I like the idea of spending time here with Lucas. He loves being outdoors, and I have happy memories of my own childhood here. It's a nice place to bring up a child, should any more come along one day.' He looks at me in such a way that suddenly everything feels warm and fuzzy all around me.

'I'm glad you're going to be seeing your son more. And that you're staying,' I tell Nicos as we walk home, having enjoyed a second drink. We're walking downhill as the sun is beginning to disappear over the hills. It really is beautiful here, the sky turning a soft orange as we walk.

'So am I,' says Nicos as he wraps his hand around mine and we walk back towards the rescue. 'I remember how wonderful it all is. I'm seeing it through different eyes, and I think that's because of you, although I regret not visiting my parents more in their later years.'

'I think we are all a little guilty of that,' I say, thinking of my own parents in Spain. 'But life gets busy, doesn't it? I imagine you were always there when they needed you.'

'It's true, I was, but my sister did the lion's share of looking after my parents as she lived closer. She was very close to my mother. Burying myself in work after me and my wife split didn't just take me away from my son...' he muses.

'You like to beat yourself up about things, don't you? I'm sure you were a wonderful son.'

'Once more, you make me feel better about myself.' He smiles. 'And, yes, I like to think I was a good son.' He nods his head as he considers it. 'I did my share of full days at the fishing lake with my father, even though I hated fishing.' He smiles. 'Or weekends walking around shops with my mother.'

'Please don't tell me you hate shopping.' I look at him in horror, thinking of how much I like browsing shops, especially large department stores.

'Would it be a deal-breaker?' He raises an eyebrow.

'Not really. I'm teasing.'

'Good. I actually don't mind shopping in large stores but taking my mother food shopping to the market could be draining. She would stop and talk to everyone, and I mean everyone. I never thought there could be so much to say about the quality of a tomato or the size of a watermelon.' He smiles good-naturedly as he recalls the memories, although there is a tinge of sadness.

'It sounds like you had some lovely times, though. I'm sure Lucas will love to hear more about his grandparents when he comes to stay.'

'Yes.' He smiles. 'He loved the visits he had with them. He's looking forward to decorating his room too.'

'You will have a full house if you are still happy for me to work there. The stables would make a wonderful workspace. Maybe I could look for a few pieces of furniture to upcycle for Lucas.'

'I might be able to help with that. There is a warehouse just outside town that sells second-hand furniture. I could take you there some time, if you like?'

'Sounds good, thanks. Judith suggested the couple who have

the holiday home might need their place refurbishing too. I might suggest revamping some of the furniture they already have, if they are interested.'

I'm suddenly spurred on by the possibility of doing some work and making some money. It's easy enough to post things online in buying groups.

Outside the rescue, I stifle a yawn.

'Am I boring you?' Nicos teases.

'Gosh, I'm sorry, it feels like it's been a long few days with the fire and worrying about Judith. You could never bore me.'

'It's a shame you are so tired. I was going to invite you in for coffee.'

'Coffee, really? Before bed?'

'Or whatever you like.' He wraps his arms around me and kisses my neck and I lose myself in the moment, tingling all over. That's just before the dogs start barking and a security light comes on at the front of the house.

'I think that's my cue to head inside.' I sigh.

'Goodnight, Tania, I will see you tomorrow. Until then, sweet dreams.'

There is no danger of anything else, I think to myself. Nothing but sweet dreams about you, Nicos.

THIRTY-FOUR

Euan is making me laugh so much when we take the dogs out the following morning, I almost have to stop and catch my breath.

'That's when I knew my days of playing cricket were over,' he says, finishing a tale of how he smashed a cricket ball through the windows of the club house, knocking a cup of tea out of the team captain's wife's hand and mentally scarring her for life apparently.

'Is that why you stick to your rock climbing and solo stuff then?'

'Maybe. At least I can't hurt anyone but myself.' He laughs.

We pass the nature reserve and even though the water has been tested and deemed safe after the dogs became ill, I'm reluctant to let them in any water other than mountain streams and the sea.

Pausing, we sit on a patch of grass in the unofficial dog park, sipping water as the dogs run free.

'How long do you think you will be staying out here in Crete?' asks Euan as one of the dogs drops a ball at his feet, which he picks up and throws.

'Not sure. As I've said, I've pretty much burned my bridges at the doctor's surgery.' I shrug.

'Do you regret that?'

'Honestly? No, not really. If I didn't get away from the village and see something of the world at this point in my life, I'm not sure I ever would have,' I tell him truthfully.

'I don't think you need to worry about your future, you have it all going for you.'

'I do?'

'Sure, you do. You're beautiful, clever, funny.'

'Keep going,' I say, and he laughs.

'Seriously, you have a room back home, folks in Spain and a very handsome admirer right here in Greece. And I'm not talking about Nicos.'

'Is that right?'

'It is.' He looks at me seriously for a moment with those gorgeous blue eyes. 'Nicos is a lucky man.'

'Is he?'

'Of course he is. But don't forget you have other admirers too,' he says, with genuine feeling.

'Well, I'm flattered, Euan, thank you.'

'I have to admit you and Nicos make a very handsome couple, though. Obviously, I think you would look better with me, but hey.'

I roll my eyes and laugh, knowing that a fling would be exactly all that Euan is looking for. There is no doubt there is a spark of attraction between us, but I watched him flirt with Liz when she was here, and can just imagine how he would have carried on around Chloe had she still been around.

'And don't forget, we still have our pact if things don't work out. Five years.' He winks.

'That's very reassuring,' I tell him as he extends his hand and helps me to my feet. I'm lucky to have options in my life, which, I realise, so many people don't.

As we walk on in companionable silence, the dogs are running around in circles chasing each other. Annie goes haring off after something in the undergrowth, with Smudge in hot pursuit. I chase after her, recalling the time she got stuck in a bush and hoping we don't have a repeat of anything like that. Following the dogs' lead, we turn a corner to find Smudge, but Annie is nowhere in sight, so I call her name.

'Where is she, boy?' I ask Smudge, who runs in circles, unable to locate his best friend. She can't be far as we were literally a few seconds behind them. Five minutes later, though, we still can't find her so, we attach leads to the other dogs and walk on, with a growing feeling of concern. Annie knows this region well, so could almost certainly find her way back to the rescue, but I just hope she isn't lying hurt somewhere.

'Annie.' Euan and I call her name, but there are no barks in response.

'She can't have gone that far in such a short space of time, surely?'

'I'm sure Smudge will lead us to her.'

'Go and find her, Smudge.' I let her friend off the lead once more, and he darts about, sniffing trees and foliage before running on, us trailing behind. The other dogs, as if sensing a problem, begin to bark loudly as well, leaving Annie in no doubt where we are, but she still can't be seen.

'She must be here somewhere.'

'Try not to worry,' Euan tries to reassure me. 'She's probably just headed back to the rescue.'

'I hope you're right, but she has never done that before. She enjoys being out here running free.'

I try to call Judith, before realising that the signal can be a bit erratic at this point in the forest, as is the case right now.

Another ten minutes pass and I'm beginning to feel really concerned when Smudge darts off at full speed, before stopping and barking. We hurry to the scene and can hear a faint bark.

'Annie? Where on earth are you?'

Once more, there is a muffled bark in response. Smudge is dancing around barking loudly.

'It's coming from over there.'

Euan points to a fence, beyond which the remains of an old building can be seen. There's a gap in the fence, and we all head through; a cacophony of barking from the other dogs fills the air, as if sensing there is something wrong and offering their support. Smudge has stopped and is standing over an area of leaves and soil, sniffing around, before racing on. He's standing over a pit of some sort now, barking loudly. Glancing down, I see Annie at the bottom, looking up and barking, her eyes shining and pleading, and I hope that she is unhurt.

'Oh, Annie, are you okay?' I squat down and speak to her and she barks at the sound of my voice.

She appears to be none the worse for her adventure, landing on what looks like a mound of soil at the bottom of a, thankfully, not so deep pit.

'I'll climb down there. I should just be able to lift her up,' says Euan, who is over six feet tall.

'Good boy, Smudge.' I take a dog treat from my pocket and hand it to him. 'You found Annie.'

After Euan deftly passes Annie up onto solid ground, I check her over and we go on our way.

'That's what happens when you run too far ahead.' I pet her and she wags her tail. 'Right, I think that's enough adventure for one day, you gave us a scare,' I tell Annie as I attach her collar to a lead and take the dogs to a stream for a drink and a cool off.

'I dread to think what might have happened if that pit was deep. It should be filled in properly.'

'I think it may have been an old animal trap of some sort,' says Euan. 'I don't suppose too many people walk this way, but you're right, it should be filled in.'

'The place looks as if it's been abandoned for a long time,' I say, glancing at the dilapidated farmhouse.

'Who was it that said never work with animals or children?' says Euan, laughing as we start to head back to the rescue.

'At least there is never a dull moment, I suppose.'

'Too true. Right, I could murder a cold beer when we get back. And when are you going to make more of those scones?' he asks hopefully.

'When would you like some?'

'Maybe soon? Like when we get back.' He flutters his eyelashes and makes me laugh.

'Okay then.'

'That's my girl.' He winks and I think of how easy it would be to actually become Euan's girl. If you didn't mind living with a wonderful, although undoubtedly charmer of a boyfriend, that is.

Back home, Euan grabs a cold beer from the fridge, and we tell Judith and Lars all about the drama with Annie and how Smudge led us to the place where she fell.

'She's too inquisitive for her own good,' says Judith. 'And Smudge is such a good boy, finding her like that. I'll really miss him when he gets rehomed, or should I say if. He just seems too much for most people, with his over-enthusiasm. This might be his forever home now.' She sighs.

'Well, it's not exactly the worst place to live, is it? As dog rescues go, this is definitely the best,' I remind Judith.

'Thanks, Tania, and I like to think it is, thanks to the commitment and hard work of everyone. I would love all the dogs to have a home with a family, though, but I guess not every-thing is possible in life. I know they are well looked after and walked regularly, but animals shouldn't be locked in cages.'

'Most of them do get rehomed eventually. But I see what you mean, Smudge is a bit much for most people, I imagine.'

As promised, I whip up a batch of scones and we enjoy one

with a cold drink outside. Euan eats three, one after the other, and I wonder where on earth he puts it.

'She's a special lady, your aunt, isn't she?' says Euan, when Judith has headed to the kitchen.

'She really is. She has made it her life's work devoting herself to the animals.'

'Do you think that's because she never had any children?'

'Probably. She's a very nurturing person. She always showed me a lot of love and affection growing up. Having children just never happened for her and my uncle Ray, but I know she doesn't live with regrets. She's always put other people and the animals before herself. I think that's why she ought to get out and see a little more of her friends. And let the romance develop with Lars.'

'He thinks the world of her, doesn't he? Anyone can see that.'

'He does. And I know she is very fond of him too. I would feel so much better knowing that she has someone to spend her older years with.'

I had often wondered if she might have returned to England in her later years, maybe sold up and got a little place close to me. Or perhaps even gone and lived close to my parents in Spain.

'I suppose that's what we all want eventually. For now, though, I just want to get out there and explore the world.' He lifts his coffee cup in a cheers.

'You should. We never know what's around the corner, do we?'

'I know that only too well,' he agrees. 'I still can't believe my buddy has gone. I still reach for my phone to text him sometimes.' He sighs.

'Life is definitely unfair, which is all the more reason to appreciate what we have in the here and now.'

'Agreed. And on that note, I'm off to email the lady in

France to see if she still wants me to look after her garden, in exchange for a room. If she does, that will be my next port of call after I leave here.'

'So, you're good at gardening too?' I can't help smiling.

'Garden maintenance. It's a huge, well-established garden. Surely using a lawnmower and pruning the odd bush can't be that difficult, right?' He grins.

Given that she has already met Euan and offered him the room, I think there is little doubt that he will have somewhere to sleep when he heads off to France.

As I finish my drink, my phone bleeps with a text message from Nicos telling me he has had a busy day, and will I be free anytime tomorrow?

I quickly tap out a reply, saying that would be nice and I will ring him in the morning. There is a lot of work to do until a new volunteer arrives. Thankfully, Judith is more and more mobile each day, and actually has to be reminded to slow down at times.

THIRTY-FIVE

The next morning at breakfast, I chat to Lars, who is taking Judith and Yolanda out today for a shopping trip. Having heard about the open trap in the forest, he says he will board it over if I point the area out to him.

'Thanks, Lars, that's very kind of you.'

'Not a problem. There is plenty of leftover timber from the donkey shelter,' he says, and once more, I think of what a considerate man Lars is proving to be.

Judith is literally making great strides now and Yolanda can walk with a stick and is also making remarkable progress. I'm impressed and happy to know two such strong women.

'That was a really kind thing you did, buying the new wood for the shelter,' I tell Lars as we share the washing and drying, whilst Euan is replenishing the donkey food.

'It was my pleasure. What is the point of having money, just sitting there in the bank? My needs are quite simple. And the wood did not really cost a great deal of money,' he reveals.

'Well, it was very generous, and a weight off my aunt's mind, I can tell you. You know how long these insurance claims can take to come through. And thanks for offering to board over the trap.'

'It's fine. I enjoy doing such things. I would hate to think of a child slipping down there and injuring themselves, or a small animal becoming trapped.'

'Well, it is very much appreciated.'

'I feel happy to make a contribution to the place. I have been so happy here these last few months,' he tells me. 'It almost feels like home, although, of course, I will have to return to my real home eventually, I suppose.'

'Do you miss your home?'

'Not really. I miss the country, of course, but maybe not the weather in the winter months. I prefer the temperature a little warmer in my older years.'

Lars originally came here for six weeks and has now been here for three months. It's been a joy to watch his blossoming relationship with Judith since I've been here. I'm so happy for them both.

After the early morning jobs are done, Yolanda is dropped off by Artemis, who looks slightly stressed.

'Goodbye, I will see you soon,' she says, after Artemis has helped her out of the car and she is leaning on her stick.

He manages a smile before he climbs into his car and drives off.

'I didn't realise Artemis was still staying with you?' says Judith.

'He isn't. I just needed him to call over this morning and bring me some money for my shopping trip,' she explains.

'He drove all this way just for that?'

Artemis lives in Agios Nicolas, at least a forty minute drive away.

Yolanda nods. 'Yes. I had to insist. He owes me money. Quite a bit,' she reveals. 'Always he say, it will be in the bank, but no, it never is. Maybe I spoil him because he is my only child. But today I need some cash for shopping. Are we ready?'

'Ready,' says Judith, catching my eye and smiling.

'I'm looking forward to buying some new dresses in the end of summer sales,' says Judith.

'And dancing shoes,' Yolanda adds with a wink. 'It may still be a few more weeks, but I will soon be dancing to the songs on my radio again. Maybe I will even throw a party, remind me that I am not dead yet.' She laughs loudly.

'What are you going to do whilst the women are shopping?' I ask Lars as I walk with him to the driver's side.

'There is a war museum I have always meant to visit, so I will go there, then have coffee somewhere. I can't imagine they will be on their feet shopping for too long. I'll collect them after they have had lunch together.'

'I'm sure they wouldn't mind you joining them for lunch,' I suggest.

'Maybe another time. For now, I would like Judith to spend a little more time with her friend,' he says thoughtfully.

Waving them off, I think how happy Judith looks these days. It took Yolanda having a fall for them to spend more time together, like they once did, reminding them of the value of reconnecting with friends. It seems good things really can come out of a bad situation.

It's a busy day; I check the animal food and order some more to arrive tomorrow, as well as some straw that will be collected by Lars from a farm a few miles away. Euan and I give the donkey area a good clean and, once more, Eric comes and says hello to Euan, even ignoring me a little. The dogs are walked, and a pan of stew is simmering on the stove for later.

Before we know it, it's late afternoon and Judith has

returned with Lars and Yolanda. She shows me two pretty dresses and a pair of sandals she has bought today.

'Ooh they're lovely. Yolanda, did you get your dancing shoes?' I turn to her and ask.

'*Nai*. Do you like?'

She pulls a pair of pretty red shoes with a two-inch heel from her bag.

'They're beautiful. Are you going to throw a party?' I giggle.

'I might do that. Or maybe I will find a dance class.'

'Actually, that's a wonderful idea. You should go online and see if there is anything not too far away,' I say to Judith.

'I cannot dance yet, of course,' says Yolanda. 'But the shoes will remind me that one day I will dance again,' she continues positively.

'Of course you will. Both of you,' I say, smiling at the two women.

Yolanda stays for a cold drink, before Lars takes her back to her house.

'So, what are you up to this evening?' Judith asks as I check on the simmering stew.

'I'm not sure.' It occurs to me then that I haven't heard from Nicos today. 'I might have an early night actually and catch up on some reading. I feel a little tired today.'

Although there is no doubt that if Nicos were to contact me, I am sure I would find the energy.

'I thought you were going to see Nicos,' says Judith, probing my thoughts.

'I did too.' But when I rang him this morning he said he had a work problem to sort out and wouldn't be available to meet up this afternoon. 'In fact, to be truthful, I don't know for certain what is going on between us.'

'How do you mean?' Judith places her glass down and gives me her full attention.

'Well, we seem to have grown closer and I have feelings for

him. Things seem to be working out for him, and I quote, "in every area", yet I can't help feeling a little uncertain about things. Oh, I don't know.' I sigh. 'We've kissed, and I don't expect him to make any sort of commitment to me after only a few weeks, but it's hard at times to know just what he's thinking.'

'Actually, I saw Nicos today,' Judith says. 'Only from a distance. He was sat outside a restaurant.'

'Oh right.'

'Of course, they may have been just friends...' My aunt pauses for a moment. 'But it's only fair to tell you that he was with a woman.'

There is every possibility that the woman was indeed just a friend, yet all the same I feel my heart sink at the news. When I ask my aunt what the woman looked like, she describes the woman I saw arriving at his house last week. It fits the description of his ex-wife.

'He's allowed friends.' I shrug, trying to sound casual. 'And he hasn't made any promises. Anyway. I must get on, I don't want Euan telling me I am slacking.'

I find Euan in the donkey area, having a full-on conversation with Eric about football.

'Fancy a moonlight cruise tonight?' he asks as I approach.

'A moonlight cruise, really?'

'Yeah, but don't get too excited. As romantic as it sounds, it's basically a sail around the harbour with a glass of wine and a few nibbles thrown in.'

'Who said I'd get excited?' I tease. 'Although it does sound nice, actually. I'm just not sure what my plans are later.'

'You mean you are going to wait and see if you get a better offer?' He raises an eyebrow.

Hasn't Nicos been enjoying a day in town, though, with presumably his ex-wife? I can't sit around waiting for him. An evening cruise sounds lovely.

'No, not at all. In fact, yes, let's do it. An evening boat trip sounds really nice.' I smile.

'Great.' He takes his phone from his pocket. 'Assuming they have places left. It leaves the harbour at seven.'

We spend the next couple of hours doing various jobs around the rescue, and soon enough it's six o'clock. After showering and changing, I still haven't heard from Nicos and wonder whether he is still with his ex.

'You look nice,' says Euan, noting my brightly coloured floral dress.

'So do you.' Euan is wearing jeans and a jungle print shirt. 'Oh dear, do you think we are more dressed for a Caribbean beach party?' I laugh. 'Should I go and change?'

'No, let's do it.' He links his arm through mine as we head to Judith's car that she has let us use for the evening. 'We look like proper tourists. Let's pretend we are on a beach holiday.'

Passing Nicos's house, his car is not outside so I decide not to think about him for the time being and just enjoy the evening out with Euan.

After a wander around the harbour, we arrive at the boat that is strung with lights and join the group of people who are ascending the gangplank. We probably look like a couple, wandering the streets, browsing shops, and laughing a lot. Euan really is the easiest of company, and although I have a slight feeling of attraction towards him, he doesn't set my pulse racing the way Nicos does. Chemistry is a curse, I think to myself. It's the thing responsible for our hearts ruling our heads and all common sense going out of the window. No wonder people do crazy things in the name of love.

'Come on.' Euan leads me by the hand to a seat at the rear of the boat. The sun is just beginning to set, and the boat lights are casting a soft glow across the water.

When the boat is full, we set sail across the dark sea, spotting lights from small islands in the distance.

'Are you here on holiday?' We're chatting to a friendly, older couple who are sat nearby, and I tell them all about the dog centre.

'Well, you make a very good-looking couple,' says the lady, ignoring the fact that I told her we were simply friends.

After an hour at sea, enjoying the cooling evening breeze that washes over us as well as a glass of wine and nibbles, we are heading back towards the harbour. The sea is dark now and the sky above a rich indigo dotted with stars. As we approach the harbour, the sound of music can be heard from a bar somewhere.

'I really enjoyed that,' I tell Euan, meaning it. Back on dry land, I check my phone to see if I have any messages, but there are none.

'Fancy a drink?' asks Euan. 'Although, actually, maybe not. I've got to drive us home around those bends.'

'That's true. But don't worry, we can have a couple of drinks back home. I bought a bottle of Metaxa to take to my parents as my mum is a bit partial to Greek brandy. I can always buy another bottle before I visit.'

'Sounds like a plan.' He grins.

Driving home, Euan switches the car radio on and sings along to Greek songs, putting his own words in and making me laugh out loud.

'How was your boat trip?' asks Judith, who is in the kitchen with Lars and about to head up to bed.

'Oh, it was really lovely. We chatted to some nice people on board, you two would really enjoy it.'

'What do you think, Judith?' asks Lars. 'Maybe we should book a trip before the weather changes.'

'I'd like that.' She smiles. 'Anyway, we will say goodnight. See you in the morning.'

After nipping upstairs for the brandy, I take two glasses from a cupboard and we head outside into the balmy evening and stroll to the pool area, away from the dogs. Solar lights illuminate the pool, and we settle down onto the beds in a sitting position.

'Ah, this is nice.' I take my shoes off and wiggle my toes as I take a slurp of the delicious brandy with ice.

'It is.' Euan takes a sip of the brandy. 'Ooh, that's good. I don't think I've tried Greek brandy before.'

We talk about this and that, and an hour later, we've polished off three quarters of the bottle.

'Oh no, I think I'm going to regret this in the morning. I might just sleep here.' I laugh.

'You would definitely regret that in the morning,' says Euan. 'And I don't think Judith would be too impressed.'

'I know. That brandy went down a little bit too well, didn't it?'

I link arms with Euan as we both head to our rooms, me feeling slightly tipsy and pleasantly relaxed.

'Well goodnight, Euan.' I'm outside his room and I go to kiss him on the cheek, when he turns his mouth to mine, and it lands on his lips. It feels pleasant but when he attempts to kiss me properly, I pull back.

'Euan, I need to get to bed. I think I may have had a bit too much to drink.'

'That's a shame,' he whispers. 'Goodnight, Tania.'

As I lie in bed, my head spins as I think about what might have passed between us had I not come to my senses. Euan is a long way from settling down with anyone. He's enjoying his year away from his job, having new experiences and meeting new people. And who can blame him? He might be a perfect person to have a holiday romance with, and I might even have considered it before I met Nicos.

Nicos, who was meeting another woman tonight. I thought

things were going well with him, but the pang of jealousy I felt, the reason I went out with Euan, reminded me how it had been with my ex. I don't want to lose my heart to him, although maybe it's a little late for that. But I can't be certain there is a future with him. And even though I put the mellow feeling down to the brandy, there is no denying that I did quite enjoy the feeling of Euan's lips on mine.

Sleep doesn't come easy, and I toss and turn for a while, wondering what on earth I was thinking. Maybe I ought to head back to England and take up Angie's offer of a room. Or join a nunnery.

THIRTY-SIX

Nicos calls me in the morning as I'm in the kitchen gulping down some coffee in an attempt to liven myself up a little. Brandy is definitely off the menu for the foreseeable future. He asks me if I am free later today anytime as he would like my advice about something, so I agree to call over in the late afternoon.

'How are you this morning?' I ask Judith, whilst I swallow down two paracetamols.

'To be truthful, although the shopping trip was wonderful, I think it's taken it out of me. I feel exhausted today.'

'You should put your feet up then. The three of us can sort the animals out as the numbers we have here at the moment are manageable.'

Judith goes to a drawer in the kitchen and retrieves something wrapped in blue tissue paper that she hands to me.

'I bought this for you yesterday. I thought it would look pretty in your hair.'

I open the paper and turn the pretty mother-of-pearl hairslide over in my hand, the colours changing as it catches the light.

'Oh, thank you, Judith. It's really beautiful.'

'You're welcome. It isn't much, but I thought you would like it.'

'I love it.' I give my aunt a hug.

'Do you think Yolanda will be alright today?' I ask.

'Apparently so, I called her this morning. The woman is a machine,' Judith says, laughing. 'Honestly, you would hardly think she was laid up recently. Or that she is a little older than me. She was on a mission, powering through the city crowds on her walking stick.' She shakes her head and laughs again. 'And we had the most wonderful lunch. I'd forgotten how much fun Yolanda is, she even had the waiters laughing.'

'Oh, Judith, I'm so happy you two had a lovely day. I hope it's the first of many, although you should definitely take it easy for a couple of days,' I advise.

'You're probably right, but I find it so difficult to sit still. Spending time with Yolanda, though, has made me realise that I might not have been the best of neighbours recently. I've been so busy here that I haven't had a lot of time to socialise.'

'No time for regrets, you have picked up the friendship now, haven't you? Even though her accident was unfortunate, it means you two have realised the importance of friends and neighbours. Life tends to give us a little reminder of such things from time to time.'

I think about how I barely knew my neighbours back home, apart from Kerry, as people's lives were so busy.

'Ooh and I must tell you this. There is a shop in town that sells fancy furniture at, frankly, ridiculous prices. I think they would have some competition on their hands if you were to sell your furniture.'

'I could never afford to rent a shop in the city, but I guess I could sell my work online.'

I tell Judith all about Nicos offering the stables as a work-station.

'That sounds perfect! And the couple from the holiday home are arriving tomorrow. Perhaps I could introduce you, especially if they are still interested in revamping their furniture.'

'Could you? That would be great. The shop Nicos took me to for supplies isn't too far from here and they seem to stock everything I could possibly need.'

Outside, Euan and Lars are working away cleaning the dog pens and stocking up the donkey feed. Euan appears to have no sign of a hangover and looks fresh as a daisy when I head outside.

'Morning. How's the head?' He grins as I approach.

'Not too bad, thankfully, thanks to coffee and painkillers.'

'You need water, not coffee. Keep hydrated.'

'I've already drank some, but yes, I will,' I say, thinking that he does have a sensible side.

'I really enjoyed last night,' he tells me as Lars switches off the outdoor tap and winds up a hose.

'So did I.'

'It's a shame the evening ended so early,' he says, with a twinkle in his eye.

'It was late enough for me.'

The sun is hot today, but bearable and there are signs that the *kafsonas* is waning a little. When the work is done, I head over to see Nicos in the late afternoon.

As Nicos greets me, I feel the familiar pull of attraction towards him. When he kisses me on the cheek and I inhale his scent, it has me wanting to wrap my arms around him.

'How are you?' he asks as he gestures to the table on the outside terrace.

'I'm okay. You?'

'Yes, good. I am sorry I didn't see you yesterday, but I had to go to town for a meeting,' he tells me as he pours some water from a jug with ice and lemon into glasses.

'Yes, Judith saw you in Hersonissos yesterday.' I take sip of my water.

'She did? I never saw her.'

'Only from a distance, I believe. Outside a restaurant.'

'Ah, yes. The meeting was with my ex.' He confirms my thoughts.

'And did it go well?' I smile, yet wonder why he has asked me over here. Is it to say that he wants to cool things off between us? Is he hoping to get back with his wife?

'It went very well.' His face breaks into a smile and he reaches across the table and clasps my hands. 'We went to sign some papers in a solicitor's office. I didn't want to involve lawyers, but I decided I can't risk her changing the plans again,' he explains. 'And my son is definitely coming to stay with me this weekend.' His face is beaming, his happiness obvious. 'I would like you to meet him.'

'I would love that.'

'And I have something to show you.'

He takes me upstairs and shows me a small room. It's decorated with a white wardrobe and drawers, with football wallpaper and duvet set.

'Oh, that looks amazing, your son will love that.' I glance around the room. Perfect for a nine-year-old boy.

'I spent the whole day yesterday decorating. Well, after the meeting with my wife. It really was a quick drink,' he tells me and here was me thinking he had spent the whole day with his wife. 'Then early evening I realised I had no food in the house and drove out for something to eat.' So that's why his car wasn't there when I went out with Euan. 'Oh, Tania, I'm so excited to see Lucas. I think I might take him to Star Beach go-karting, or maybe go swimming,' he chatters excitedly.

'That sounds wonderful, Nicos. And I would love to meet him, but maybe for dinner later or something? I think you should spend some time together first.'

'Of course. And I have to thank you for making me realise how important seizing time with my son is. It was bad to hold on to any guilt instead of acting. I see that now,' he says with a broad smile.

I smile back, pleased that he looks so happy.

'So how was your day yesterday?' he asks. 'I called over when I got back from having something to eat. Lars said you had gone out.'

I swallow down a feeling of guilt, although Nicos knows I am friends with Euan.

'Yes, just down to the harbour. Euan was going on a boat trip and asked me if I fancied tagging along.' I shrug, trying to make it sound like it wasn't a big deal.

'That sounds nice. Maybe that's something you and I could do?'

'I would love that.'

'You know I said things were working out for me in my life?' He takes hold of my hand once more. 'I was hoping that includes my relationship with you.' He looks at me with his gorgeous brown eyes that I could almost fall into.

'Oh, Nicos, of course. I was hoping for that too. I thought you weren't sure of your plans.'

'I wasn't. But someone convinced me to go after my dreams.' He smiles. 'I'll get us some wine.'

He walks into the kitchen, and I follow him.

'And here was me worried you were considering getting back with your ex, and all the time you were sorting things out for your son.'

'I told you, me and my ex-wife were over long before the divorce. We were practically living separate lives; she was out with her friends a lot. She met her new love before our marriage was even officially over.'

'I'm so sorry.'

Nicos pours a glass of white wine and hands it to me.

'It's history.' He takes a sip of his wine. 'I think we only stayed together because of Lucas and look how that turned out.'

'Well, I'm glad you have both moved on but are working on both being there for Lucas. I would hate to stand in the way of a reconciliation.'

'There was never any possibility of that, I've told you it's in the past.' He places his wine glass down and pulls me towards him. 'And I prefer to look to the future,' he says, before pulling me in for a long, thrilling kiss.

THIRTY-SEVEN

There are only twenty dogs now that several more have been rehomed, and no more have arrived since. Judith has hinted at maybe only needing two volunteers from now on as the numbers are manageable. Maybe she has thought further about scaling down as she gets older and enjoying more free time.

I've spent the morning in a daydream after yesterday, happy to know that Nicos sees a future with me. We talked until after midnight, Nicos telling me how happy he has been feeling since he moved back here, the forest bringing back many childhood memories.

After our wine, we had gone for a walk beyond the garden, into the clearing where the memory benches are. Nicos told me that it seemed fitting somehow, to be living here, holding the memory of his parents in his heart.

'And it isn't too far for my sister to come and visit,' he said. 'Especially when my son stays. I know she will be thrilled to come over and see her nephew.'

He'd looked so happy, like someone who has suddenly had a cloud lifted from them.

'Please tell me you are not thinking of heading back to England just yet,' he'd breathed.

'I'm in no hurry at all.' I returned his kiss, as he took me by the hand and led me upstairs. And this time I didn't resist.

'It's so good to meet you.'

I'm with Judith, who has arranged a meeting with the owners of the holiday home.

'Oh, and you too. Come on in.' The blonde woman, who looks in her fifties with a wide smile, ushers us inside after introducing herself as Monica. 'And this is Joe.' Her brown-haired husband smiles and shakes me by the hand.

'Judith has been telling us all about your upcycling skills. We'd be happy if you could revamp some of the furniture here, wouldn't we, Joe?'

'We certainly would. It's a lovely house, but a touch old-fashioned. The furniture came with the place, so it stayed. Saved us having to buy a load of new furniture, I suppose, but it could definitely do with a refresh.'

I glance around the large room that is a little overcrowded with pine furniture. One piece, a large dresser, catches my eye. I visualise it sanded down and painted a soft blue or green, to showcase the pretty crockery that already adorns it. The long table could be sanded and varnished and the farmhouse chairs maybe painted in different pastel shades. I suggest all these things to the owners and show them some pictures of the work I have already done.

'That all sounds just wonderful,' says Monica. 'And your work looks very impressive. We are here for two weeks, so maybe you could start on the furniture when we leave?'

'That would be great!'

'That's settled then. I'll leave you a key. We probably should have left a key with someone here anyway, in case of an emergency and to keep half an eye on the place while it is unoccupied.'

'Oh, don't worry, we kind of do that anyway,' says Judith. 'We often walk this way with the dogs and would soon notice if there was anything to report,' she reassures Monica.

'Thank you, that's very good to know, Now, do you fancy a little drink to celebrate?' asks the bubbly Monica, already heading into the kitchen without waiting for an answer. She pops a bottle of Prosecco and fills four glasses. 'Cheers to new friends. I can't wait to see what you do with the furniture.'

We chat about the area, the hot weather and the dog rescue as we finish our drinks.

'It's been really good to meet you, Tania,' says Monica as we leave. 'Why don't you all come for a BBQ tomorrow if you're free? We'd love to meet the locals.' She smiles.

'Thanks, that sounds lovely. I'll check with Nicos to see if he's free.'

'Is that the bloke from the pink house? Ooh he's a hottie, we met him last time we were here, looking over the house. If I was ten years younger.' She sighs.

'Err, you'd still be married to me,' says Joe, rolling his eyes but laughing.

'I know, only joking. You know I only have eyes for you.' She kisses him on the cheek.

I walk away with Judith feeling as light as air. My first commission! I can hardly wait to start it in a couple of weeks when the couple head back to England.

'I'm so happy for you,' says Judith as we walk. 'And who knows, if you set up a website and exhibit a couple of pieces, that fancy shop in Heraklion might buy some pieces from you.'

'That's a really good idea. I might just do that.'

I'm excited to think that I might actually have the opportunity to earn a living over here. Maybe a little advertising is exactly what I need to do to make that happen. I can hardly wait to get started on the project.

'Oh my goodness, what has happened here?' asks Judith as we enter the kitchen.

Euan is on his hands and knees sweeping up shards of crockery from under the table. There is a distinct smell of cooked lamb in the air.

'Err, sorry, but there has been a bit of an incident.'

'What kind of incident? Is everyone alright?' My aunt's hand flies to her throat.

'Oh yeah, everyone's okay, don't worry, but the leg of lamb has copped it. I didn't close the door to Smudge's pen properly, and the lamb was on the kitchen table cooling. Put two and two together.'

'Smudge has had the lamb?'

''Fraid so. Quick as a flash he was, like a ninja dog. He whipped the lamb off the table as I was at the sink. He'd demolished half of it by the time I'd even noticed. And the plate fell onto the floor in the process.'

I'm trying not to laugh, even though I was really looking forward to the lamb for lunch.

'I'm sure there is something in the freezer,' says Judith.

'Sorry,' says a very sheepish-looking Euan. 'I'll double-check that the cage doors are closed next time.'

I head over to see the offending dog, to find Smudge laid out in a food coma.

'Ah, I'm not surprised you feel sleepy.' He barely lifts his head, and just kind of thumps his tail on the ground. 'That's what happens when you're a greedy-guts. You didn't even share with Annie. Well, I won't tell her. Not this time. Just don't do it again.'

He gives a bark in response, before dozing off again.

Nicos arrives just then, and asks me if I would like to go for a walk to the bar.

'You're welcome to join us?' he says, turning to Euan.

'If you're sure, then yeah, why not?' Euan smiles. I think of the moment Euan tried to kiss me and feel ever so slightly awkward us all going for a drink together, but reassure myself that nothing happened between us.

At the bar, my stomach gives a little rumble at the smell of village sausage and halloumi grilling on the BBQ. Euan tells Nicos all about the unfortunate incident with the leg of lamb.

'So I kind of think I owe you lunch. At least a sandwich,' says Euan, heading to the bar.

Sipping cold beers and sausage and halloumi paninis, talk turns to Euan's next port of call.

'Whereabouts in France?' I ask Euan with interest when he talks of where he is heading.

'Lyon. I'll probably hitchhike from Calais, I've done it before.'

'Do you have work lined up?' Nicos asks.

'A bit of gardening, actually, in exchange for a bed.' He tells Nicos about the large country house outside Lyon.

'I will resist the joke about *Lady Chatterley's Lover*.' He grins, and I recall Liz making a similar comment and laugh.

'Strictly business, mate. I prefer my women a bit younger,' he says, staring at me and making me blush bright red, especially when Nicos looks at me too.

'Right, I'd better head back and check that everything is okay.' I drain the last of my beer.

'I'm going for a bit of a trek in the forest. Catch you later,' says Euan, draining his drink and heading off.

'We could have joined him?' says Nicos a few minutes later, when are walking back to the rescue.

'I prefer it being just us two,' I say and he wraps his hand around mine and I feel the usual tingle.

'I think he likes you,' says Nicos as we walk.

'I think Euan likes everyone,' I say, trying to make light of it.

'No, I think he really likes you. I have seen the way he looks at you.'

We stop at a viewing point and look down across a part of the valley that gives a glimpse of the sea in the distance.

'Do I have competition?' He's smiling, but obviously feels compelled to ask the question.

'Definitely not. Euan is a charmer and will soon be flattering another woman on his travels. We're strictly friends. Plus, I think I might be settling here. I have some furniture to finish after all,' I tease.

'I'm pleased to hear it,' he says as he pulls me to him. 'Very pleased.' And then there are no more words, as we kiss and all is right with the world.

EPILOGUE

Two weeks have passed, and I've started work on the furniture for the couple who have the holiday home. Things are going so well between Nicos and his son. Taking my advice, he has been meeting him alone, but today I am going to meet him and I can't help feeling a little nervous.

'I will be back in around an hour,' says Nicos. I have spent the last hour preparing some nibbles and making sure the fridge is stacked with canned drinks and a selection of ice cream in the freezer, as I'm not sure what flavour Lucas likes. We will take him to see the dogs later; Nicos told me his son is a real dog lover.

I'm surprised that I feel a little nervous about meeting Lucas, and find myself frequently glancing at my watch. Soon enough, I hear the sound of a car pulling into the driveway.

A handsome, dark-haired boy who is a miniature version of Nicos steps out of the car, carrying a football that he bounces on the ground as he walks towards me.

'Lucas, this is my friend, Tania,' Nicos introduces me.

'*Kalimera*, Tania,' he says politely.

'*Kalimera. Encantado.* Forgive me if that is not correct. Nice to meet you.'

His face breaks into a smile. 'Nice to meet you too.'

I watch Nicos and his son through the kitchen window, enjoying a kickabout with the football. Nicos is in front of a goal he's bought especially, with his arms out wide, and his son giggles as he takes a shot, and the ball goes into the back of the net.

A short while later they come inside and have some snacks and Lucas enjoys a dish of chocolate ice cream. Lucas alternates between Greek and English, favouring Greek when he talks with his father.

'We will try and speak English when Tania is here,' Nicos tells his son. 'Although maybe she would also like to learn a little Greek.'

'I would like that. *Efcharisto*,' I tell him.

'Would you like to go and see the dogs now?' I ask Lucas when we have cleared away.

'Yes, please. Are they all friendly?' asks Lucas.

'They are. And one in particular is very friendly. Don't be alarmed if he jumps up at you,' I say, thinking of Smudge and his habit of trying to hug people.

'Okay.' He smiles.

As we stroll across the road to the rescue, I tell Lucas a little more about the dogs who are staying there and he is full of questions, one of which I turn to Lars to answer but he seems a little preoccupied.

'I am so sorry, yes, of course. And while you are here, may I have a quick word when you have a moment?'

Nicos shows Lucas the donkey area first, and he races towards them excitedly.

'Can I ride?'

'Actually, I'm not sure.' Nicos looks at me.

'To be honest I'm not sure either,' I say a little uncertainly.

'Obviously, they were used to ferrying passengers around, but they are retired now. I don't know how they would react to having someone sit on them again. Maybe they are traumatised from a life of toil.'

Nicos talks to his son in Greek when Eric saunters over to Lucas and bows his head to be stroked.

'He likes me,' says Lucas excitedly.

'He certainly seems to. Hang on a moment.' I head inside and find a saddle and drape it over Eric, who stands perfectly still.

'Could you give the little guy a ride?' I ask Eric, who harrumphs.

Nicos gently lifts Lucas onto his back and Eric paws the ground for a second with his hoof. We're holding on to Lucas tightly when Eric happily walks off, making a braying sound, much to the delight of Lucas.

'I think he is actually enjoying it,' I say in complete surprise as Eric happily ambles along. 'Maybe he likes children. He rarely gets to see any in the village.'

'Perhaps he does. Maybe he even misses taking people out.'

'I wouldn't bank on it. He's still a little temperamental,' I remind him.

After the donkey ride, and saying hello to the dogs – thankfully Lucas adored Smudge, who indeed did hug him – I tell Nicos I am just popping into the kitchen to speak to Lars.

'Hey, Lars, what's on your mind?' I ask, remembering he wanted to have a word with me earlier.

'I just wanted to run something by you, Tania.' He looks slightly nervous.

'Of course, what is it?'

'I don't know what she will say, but I do know I would like to give your aunt this.' He lifts the lid from a small box and a solitaire glints as it catches the light.

'Lars! You are going to propose to Judith?'

'Yes. Is that okay? I know you are like a daughter to Judith.'

'Of course it's okay, Lars. It's more than okay. I'm so happy for you.' I step forward and give him a hug.

'Happy about what?' Judith asks as she walks into the kitchen.

'Oh, just happy that Lars has decided to stay on here for a while longer. We need some maintenance work doing. Sorry to put that on you, Lars.'

'I am happy to help' Lars winks at me.

As Lars walks me out, he asks if Nicos and I can join them for a meal at Vasilis's restaurant at the harbour later that evening.

'Hopefully it will be a celebration meal. I took your advice and booked a moonlight cruise this evening. I will propose to her then.'

'You old romantic, you.' I nudge him. 'That's a lovely idea. And, of course, we will join you for the celebration meal.'

'That's if she says yes.' He looks doubtful for a second.

'I'm sure she will.'

Thinking about Judith marrying Lars fills me with joy knowing she will have a companion in her older years. Especially someone as nice as Lars.

'What shall we do now?' Nicos asks Lucas as we walk towards the house. 'I was thinking maybe some go-karting at Star Beach. Or maybe you would like to go swimming?'

'The go-karts!' says Lucas excitedly.

Nicos asks if I would like to join them, but I have some fundraising to do online. I was thrilled to receive a message this morning from Kerry in the UK with the news that one of her walks has raised three hundred pounds for the shelter. We had a good chat online and she tells me she is off to Scotland next to walk part of Hadrian's Wall with a group of friends to raise money for a children's hospice.

'Have a good day. Make sure you beat your dad,' I tell Lucas as they head off. I think it will be nice for Nicos to spend some time alone with his son, and look forward to seeing them later for dinner.

'Beat my father?' Lucas frowns for a minute.

'Yes, win.'

'Oh, win. Yes.' He laughs. 'I will.'

I smile to myself, realising his English is not completely fluent.

I spend the afternoon walking the animals with some of the volunteers, then Euan and I sit around the pool.

'I can't believe I'll be moving on this time next week,' says Euan. 'It's going to be hard to say goodbye to this place.'

'You can always come back,' I tell him and he smiles.

'I'm not sure I could take it, watching you fall in love with another man.' He places his hand over his heart.

'Oh behave. I think you know we could never be more than friends.'

'You're probably right.' He grins. 'And I'm sorry I tried to kiss you the other night.'

'So, you remember then?'

'Of course I do. I wasn't that drunk. Still, if things don't work out with Nicos, you know where I am.' He winks. 'Although, actually, you might not. I'm not entirely sure where I will be, after I've spent a month or so in France. But I'll stay in touch, friends for life, hey?'

'Absolutely,' I say, and he hugs me, this time resisting the urge to go in for a kiss.

Judith shows off the beautiful solitaire that evening when they return from the cruise. I have some champagne on ice waiting for them ready to have a toast.

Judith looks flushed with happiness as she shows off her engagement ring and immediately calls Yolanda to tell her the news. I can hear the whoop of delight from the other end of the phone. When she finishes the call, Judith tells us that Yolanda has asked if there will be a party, as she is still waiting for a reason to wear her red dancing shoes.

'Of course. We must have a party,' says Lars. 'Everyone is invited. How about Sunday? A celebration lunch here.'

'Wonderful.' My aunt claps her hands together.

Later, Nicos returns from his day with Lucas, and we drive to Vasilis's restaurant to celebrate the engagement. It's a wonderful evening, filled with laughter and I can't help but feel happy. Judith and Lars are engaged, Nicos is reunited with his son and who knows what the future holds for us as a couple? Even Euan is excited by his next adventure in France.

As Lucas tucks into his food, he tells me all about his driving.

'I beat my father.' He pretends to strike his father and giggles. Then I giggle, and so does Nicos, who is looking happier than I have seen him since I've been here. Suddenly we are all laughing, sat at a table beneath a fig tree in a restaurant and all at once I realise, that there is nowhere in the world I would rather be.

When Lucas returns to his mother the following day, Nicos and I head out for a walk in the forest. He threads his fingers through mine as we stroll along. Presently we stop at a bridge that overlooks a waterfall.

'I was wondering,' says Nicos. 'Now that Lars and Judith are engaged, do you think they might like their own space?'

'What are you saying?' I feel the gentle strum of my heart as I anticipate what might be coming next.

'Well, you told me your room is quite small at the rescue. I am sure the drawers you have refurbished can't be shown off to their best advantage.' He pulls me towards him. 'So, I think you need a much bigger bedroom,' he says, as he nuzzles my neck. 'And as you will be here doing work in the stables...'

'Do you have something in mind?' I feel like I could burst with happiness.

'Move in with me.' He looks into my eyes. 'If you would like to, that is.'

'You're serious?'

'Of course I am.'

I laugh as he literally sweeps me off my feet and twirls me around.

'So, what do you think?' he asks when he puts me down again.

'I think that sounds wonderful, if you're absolutely certain.'

'Are you?' he says, moving closer.

'Yes, I am.'

I realise I have fallen head over heels for Nicos, and as his home is so close to my aunt, it couldn't be more perfect.

'Wonderful. Now find a stick,' he says.

'A stick?'

'Yes. I haven't forgiven you for beating me at crazy golf.' Nicos smiles. 'Let's have a stick race.'

'Pooh.'

'Pardon?' Nicos laughs.

'Pooh-stick racing. As described in *The House at Pooh Corner* by A. A. Milne.'

'Oh, I see.' He laughs.

As we drop the sticks off the bridge, they float along at the same time side by side, before they come to a stop in some tree roots.

'I'd call that a draw,' I say, leaning over the bridge to get a closer look.

'Are you sure?' Nicos frowns. 'I think mine might just be in front there.'

'Definitely not. They are side by side, perfectly in sync,' I say, wrapping my arms around his neck.

'Like us for the rest of our lives. At least I hope so,' says Nicos, before he moves in for a kiss.

As we both stare out across the glorious valley, I feel a contentment I can't recall ever feeling in my entire life. It feels like I was meant to come here this summer. It feels like I've finally come home.

A LETTER FROM SUE

Dear reader,

I want to say a huge thank you for choosing to read *There's Something About Greece*. If you did enjoy it, and want to keep up to date with all my latest releases, just sign up at the following link. Your email address will never be shared and you can unsubscribe at any time.

www.bookouture.com/sue-roberts

I hope you loved *There's Something About Greece* and if you did, I would be very grateful if you could write a review. I'd love to hear what you think, and it makes such a difference helping new readers to discover one of my books for the first time.

I found this book such a joy to write; I particularly loved writing about the forest setting, and of course the adorable animals. I hope the trips to the beach gave it the summer holiday feels too!

I love hearing from my readers – you can get in touch on my Facebook page, through Twitter or Goodreads.

Thanks,

Sue Roberts

KEEP IN TOUCH WITH SUE

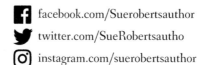

facebook.com/Suerobertsauthor
twitter.com/SueRobertsautho
instagram.com/suerobertsauthor

ACKNOWLEDGMENTS

As always, I would like to thank everyone on the team at Bookouture, especially my editor Natalie Edwards, who believed in the story and helped me every step of the way to make it the best it could be. Thanks also, to the bloggers and readers who help us authors with their enthusiasm for reading. We really do appreciate your thoughts!

I must mention my daughter's two dogs, Annie and Smudge, who feature in this book. They often set off on long walks with their humans, having many adventures, that have inspired some of the scenes in the book. A year ago, the unlikely pairing had a litter of six puppies together. An adorable mix of three black and three golden coloured, all placed in wonderful (hopefully) forever homes.

Thanks to my friend's daughter who gave me a bit of an insight into the daily schedule of an animal shelter, having worked there as a student. Finally, thanks to my family and friends who always encourage me with my writing and drag me out for long walks and coffee stops when I need a break. Sometimes with the dogs, sometimes without. I am grateful to you all.